AN ACT OF DUTY

It was done, no matter how much Cora regretted it. It was done, though she knew that Lord Francis regretted it far more than she.

She was the bride of this man who did not want one—and above all, did not want her.

Her body tensed at the tap on her bedchamber door. The door opened and she saw Francis, looking very gorgeous indeed in a scarlet silk dressing gown.

"Oh, Francis," she said, wondering why she sounded breathless, "did you want something?"

He paused with his hand still on the knob of the door and looked at her with raised eyebrows. "Cora, my dear," he said, "you leave me nearly speechless, as usual." He let go of the knob and came toward her. "Now what could I possibly want on my wedding night?"

Clearly, then, Francis was determined to do his duty. Unfortunately, it was just as clear that the only desire was coming from her. . . .

The
Famous Heroine

Mary Balogh

A SIGNET BOOK

SIGNET
Published by the Penguin Group
Penguin Books USA Inc., 375 Hudson Street,
New York, New York 10014, U.S.A.
Penguin Books Ltd, 27 Wrights Lane,
London W8 5TZ, England
Penguin Books Australia Ltd, Ringwood,
Victoria, Australia
Penguin Books Canada Ltd, 10 Alcorn Avenue,
Toronto, Ontario, Canada M4V 3B2
Penguin Books (N.Z.) Ltd, 182-190 Wairau Road,
Auckland 10, New Zealand

Penguin Books Ltd, Registered Offices:
Harmondsworth, Middlesex, England

First published by Signet, an imprint of Dutton Signet,
a division of Penguin Books USA Inc.

First Printing, February, 1996
10 9 8 7 6 5 4 3 2 1

Chapter 1

The Duchess of Bridgwater, formidably elegant in her purple satin evening gown with matching turban and tall plumes, bedecked and sparkling with the family jewels, looked Miss Cora Downes over with slow and methodical care, beginning at the top of her elaborate coiffure, and ending at her slippers, which were already cramping her toes.

The slippers were cramping her toes because she had unwisely taken the advice of Lady Elizabeth Munro, the duchess's elder daughter, to buy the smaller of two sizes in footwear when in doubt, as gentlemen did not admire large feet. Cora's feet were not extraordinarily large, she had decided, holding them out in front of her, unshod, as she sat on the edge of her bed soon after the advice had been given. And really she did not care much for gentlemen's strange preferences in such matters. Did they crawl around on hands and knees examining a lady's feet before going to any other lengths to discover if she was someone with whom they would not mind dreadfully spending the rest of their days on this earth? But there was no escaping the fact that her feet were somewhat larger than Elizabeth's and decidedly larger than those of Jane, Elizabeth's younger sister. But then Jane was more than usually small and dainty.

And so Cora had bought the slippers in a size smaller than she ought because she had persuaded herself that she was in doubt. She now meekly bore the consequences of her own folly, though she knew she had not really begun to bear them yet. There was a whole ball to live through, a whole evening of dancing—if any gentleman could be coerced into dancing with her, that was. Cora would have squirmed with discomfort at the very real danger that none would if her grace had not been still examining her appearance.

Do not let her use her lorgnette, she instructed some unseen power without moving her lips. *I shall die of mortification.* At the horridly advanced age of one-and-twenty she was decked out in virginal white and blushes and was about to make her debut into the *beau monde*. Jane, who was a mere eighteen years of age, had already made her curtsy to the Queen the year before, though she was still dressed this year in what Cora thought of as "the uniform." When one added to the age difference the fact that Cora was larger than Jane—in *every* way, not just in the matter of feet—the result was depressing.

Elizabeth, who was nineteen, was dressed in pink and had put on, with her gown, a look of ennui that bespoke the seasoned lady of the *ton*. She, of course, was already nicely settled indeed, being betrothed to a marquess of enormous wealth and consequence and alarmingly advanced years— he was three-and-thirty—who happened to be in Vienna this year with the result that the wedding had been postponed indefinitely.

The duchess handed down her judgment at last. She inclined her head once and set her plumes to nodding a dozen times. "You will do, my dear Cora," she said.

That was all she said, but it set Elizabeth to smiling graciously in almost comic imitation of her mama's regal manner and Jane to squealing and squeezing her arm and exclaiming in glee.

"I *told* you you looked beautiful, Cora," she said. Which was a very loose paraphrase indeed of what her mother had said.

Cora tried not to look sheepish and giggled instead. It was strange how laughter, which she had always indulged in with unself-conscious spontaneity, had become giggling as soon as the Duchess of Bridgwater had taken her so determinedly under the ducal wing. Giggling, it seemed, was not a ladylike attribute and must be curbed at all costs. The most a lady could allow herself in company by way of displaying amusement was a well-bred titter. One the few occasions when Cora had practiced tittering, she had ended up with her head beneath a cushion, smothering the bellows of unholy mirth it had given rise to.

"We will be on our way, then," the duchess said, smiling at all three young ladies who had joined her in the drawing room.

She really looked remarkably beautiful when she smiled—and even when she did not, Cora conceded in something like envy. It must be wonderful to have that kind of poise and grace and self-assurance. It was hard to believe that her grace could be the mother of Elizabeth and Jane and of Lord George Munro. It was almost impossible to believe that she was also the mother of the present duke, to whom Cora had been presented for the first time but yesterday. His grace was all elegance and formality and ducal hauteur.

Cora had had the uncomfortable feeling that his grace did not approve of her even though he had bowed over her hand and even raised it to his lips—she had stood rooted to the morning-room floor, stupidly awed by the knowledge that he was a *duke,* a real live duke—and assured her of his pleasure in meeting her. He had even thanked her over the little Henry incident. Little Henry was his nephew, of course, and heir to his grace's heir. But even so it had startled her to find that the Duke of Bridgwater had heard about the little Henry incident. He had even called her a heroine and she had resisted only just in time the urge to look over her shoulder to see to whom he was speaking.

But then, of course, he must have wondered why his mother had brought to town a mere Miss Cora Downes, daughter of a Bristol merchant—a *prosperous* merchant, it was true, and one who had recently purchased a considerable property and renovated a grand old abbey that had been falling to ruins on it—with the intention of taking her about in society with her own daughters, his own sisters. He would have thought it very strange indeed. And so, of course, the explanation of what had happened with little Henry would have been given.

The truth was—at least, it was not *quite* the truth but what was perceived to be the truth—that Cora had saved little Henry from drowning in the shadow of the Pulteney Bridge in Bath and that out of gratitude the duchess, little Henry's grandmama, had taken Cora into her own home to mingle with her daughters and to be elevated to the ranks of gentlewomanhood long enough to be found an eligible gentleman.

The Duchess of Bridgwater was going to find Cora a husband. Not from the ranks of eligible dukes and marquesses and earls, of course, amongst whom she had already plucked a mate for Elizabeth and planned to pluck one for Jane. But nevertheless, a gentleman. A man of fortune and rank and property. A man who had never soiled his hands or enriched his coffers with trade or business. Despite all the wealth of her father, Cora could never have aspired so high if she had not saved little Henry—well sort of saved him, anyway—and so been catapulted into the benevolent good graces of the Duchess of Bridgwater.

Her grace and the girls would not even have been in such a questionably fashionable place as Bath at such an unfashionable time as spring if Lady George had not been suffering through a difficult confinement. But her grace was fond of her daughter-in-law and of her grandchildren and had deprived herself and her daughters of all the pleasures of the first half of the Season in London. Perhaps fortunately for them, the incident of little Henry seemed to have precipitated the arrival into this world of his sister, who was delivered a mere two days later. Mother and child were doing remarkably well and were now being coddled with affectionate indulgence by the proud father.

And so at last, when it was already June, her grace had set off for London with two impatient daughters and a rather alarmed protégée, who wondered how a usually strong-willed young lady like her could find herself in such a predicament. Over the past few years, she had turned down no fewer than three proposals of marriage from remarkably eligible men merely on the grounds that she felt no more than a passing affection for any of them. As if *that* had anything to say to anything, her father had commented each time, rolling his eyes at the ceiling and making clucking noises of frustrated disgust.

Her father was rather tickled over the idea of her marrying a gentleman. So was Edgar, her brother, who had pointed out that she must marry someone and it might as well be a gentleman who might awe her into something like meek ladylike submission. She would make a horrid spinster, he had warned her, all stubborn will and bossiness with no domain over which to exercise her tyranny. She was fond of Edgar. It was a pity that some people had concocted the idea that he had behaved with cowardice in the incident of little Henry. How stupid and how totally untrue. But public opinion was remarkably difficult to manipulate, she had found.

Cora frowned and contorted her face until she could bite the flesh of her left cheek. But she was seating herself in the carriage as she did so and the duchess was seated opposite, watching her.

"You are nervous, dear," she said with gracious condescension. "It is understandable. But you must remember that you are dressed as well as anyone and that you have the manners to equal anyone else's. And the fact that you have my sponsorship will silence any question about your eligibility to be at Lady Markley's ball. Bridgwater has undertaken to present you with some eligible partners. I will do the like, of course. Now do smooth out the frown and the facial contortions, my dear. They are not becoming."

Cora had already smoothed out the frown and had stopped biting her cheek. And a wonderful antidote to her sense of unfairness over what had happened to Edgar with reference to the little Henry incident was remembering why she was in the carriage so grandly dressed—with clothes Papa had been quite adamant about paying for.

She was on her way to a ball. Well, there was nothing so

remarkable about that. She had danced at assemblies at Clifton and Bristol and of course in Bath. She loved the vigor of country dances.

But this was a ball in *London*.

This was a ball exclusively—well, not quite exclusively, considering the fact that she was going to be there—for people of the *ton*.

Cora's stomach chose that inauspicious moment to rouse itself out of its quiet and comfortable lethargy in order to tie itself in knots. And then her dinner decided to protest the fact that it was sitting inside a knotted stomach.

She smiled vacuously at her carriage companions.

"She is a diamond of the first water, Frank," Lord Hawthorne said, sighing and gazing at the lady in question across the expanse of the ballroom. "She refused me a dance last week. Said her card was full. And then granted a set to Denny when he arrived late."

Lady Augusta Haville's bad manners in behaving thus only enhanced her reputation in his eyes, it seemed. Such was the extent of his cousin's humility and confidence in his own charms. Lord Francis Kneller thought as he raised his jeweled quizzing glass to his eye and gazed through it at the lady. But then Bob was young and a trifle gauche and had doubtless blushed and stammered as he stood and bowed before one of the *ton*'s brightest jewels.

There had been only one lady all Season to rival Lady Augusta and she was now gone—to Highmoor Abbey in Yorkshire. As the wife of Carew, damn his eyes. Samantha. Lord Francis's heart took a nosedive to land somewhere in the vicinity of the soles of his dancing shoes, a place where it had resided with disturbing frequency for several weeks past.

He was nursing a broken heart—in the soles of his shoes. He had not even realized quite how deeply in love with Samantha he had been until she had announced quite out of the blue a mere few weeks ago as she was on her way to the park with him in his phaeton that she was going to marry the Marquess of Carew. Carew! Lord Francis had not even known she was acquainted with the man. And yet he him-self had been faithfully courting her and regularly offering for her for more years than he cared to remember.

"Yes," he said absently. "An Incomparable, Bob."

Lady Augusta was of medium stature, was slender, graceful, and elegant. She was gracious and charming—ex-cept when she was rejecting gauche boys and then favoring more suave admirers. She had skin like the finest porcelain and hair like a golden sunset.

She was aware of his scrutiny across the ballroom de-spite the distraction of a largish court of admirers and was indicating in a thoroughly well-bred manner—nothing that would have been remotely apparent to any casual ob-server—that she would not take it at all amiss if he strolled about the floor and stopped to pay his respects and add his name to her dancing card.

"She would dance with *you,* Frank," Lord Hawthorne said with faint and humble envy. "Ah, there are the fellows. Excuse me." And he was off to join a group of other very young gentlemen, who would bolster up one another's es-teem and courage for the rest of the evening—probably in the card room, a more comfortably masculine domain than the ballroom.

Lord Francis lowered his glass and wondered what he was doing in Lady Markley's ballroom. It was the last place he felt like being. But then these days any place on earth was the last place he felt like being. And yet he had realized with some logic and some regret during the past several weeks that there really was no other place to be than any place on earth.

So this place was as good as any.

"An Incomparable," a haughty and rather languid voice said at his shoulder, unconsciously repeating the word he himself had used only a few moments before. "You are thinking of attaching yourself to her court, Kneller?"

Lord Francis turned to greet the Duke of Bridgwater, who was in the way of being a new friend. Though they had been acquainted for years, it was only in the past cou-ple of weeks or so that they had had any dealings together.

Bridgwater was Carew's friend and Lord Francis was
Samantha's—yes, he was, he admitted ruefully, even
though he had wanted to be very much more than just
that— and they had closed ranks, the two of them, he and
Bridgwater, when that fiend Rushford had insulted Samantha and Carew had been forced to challenge him despite a
partially crippled leg and arm. They had both become his
seconds, Bridgwater by Carew's request, Lord Francis by
his own. They had gone to Jackson's boxing saloon to wit-
ness the slaughter and to pick up the pieces of Samantha's
husband—and had remained to bask in the wonder and
glory of Carew's victory.

The clubs of London still had not ceased buzzing with
the story, which might have seemed to be considerably em-
bellished to anyone who had not been there to see it.

Bridgwater had been the one to advise Lord Francis that
it was not the thing to wear his heart on his sleeve in quite
the manner he was doing. Lord Francis had been ready to
challenge Rushford himself even though Samantha had a
husband to look to her protection.

Discovering, as he had done just after the fight, that
Samantha actually loved Carew and had not married him
simply for his vast fortune, had done nothing in particular
to raise Lord Francis's spirits. Neither had his begrudging
admission that Carew was worthy of her.

"I am thinking of it," he said now in answer to the duke's
question. "One likes to keep up one's reputation as a connoisseur of beauty, you know."

"For my part," his grace said, "I would find it unsatisfac-
tory to be merely a part of someone's court. I would prefer
to be the one and only. My pride, I daresay."

"But then there is danger in being a one and only," Lord
Francis pointed out. "The danger of finding oneself netted.
Or caught in parson's mousetrap, to change the image but
not the meaning."

"I have a small favor to ask of you," the duke said, caus-
ing Lord Francis to swing around to look full at him, his
eyebrows raised. He felt a flicker of interest. Life had been
so desperately devoid of interest for weeks now. He must

be impoverished indeed, he thought, if the mere mention of a favor he might do grabbed his whole attention. Perhaps his grace merely wished to know if a lock of his hair was sticking out at the back like a cup handle.

"My mother has arrived in town," his grace said, raising his own glass to his eye and beginning a languid perusal of the occupants of the room through it, "with my two sisters—and a protégée."

The slight pause before the final words and the almost imperceptible pain in the duke's voice as the words were spoken alerted Lord Francis to the fact that the small favor had something to do with the protégée. It would hardly concern Lady Elizabeth Munro. She was betrothed to old What's-His-Name, who was in Vienna, reputedly dazzling the world with his diplomatic genius. And Lady Jane Munro, though young and unattached, was unattached only because Bridgwater had rejected a string of suitors whom he considered unworthy—if gossip had the right of it, as gossip had a habit of not always being. Lord Francis Kneller was the son and brother of a duke, but it was extremely unlikely that he would ever attain the title himself since his brother had already been brilliantly prolific in the production of sons.

No, it could not be Lady Elizabeth and would not be Lady Jane. It would be the protégée.

"I trust they are all in good health?" Lord Francis said politely.

"Ah, yes indeed," his grace said, his glass pausing for a moment and his lips pursing. Yes, she was pretty, Lord Francis thought as he followed the line of the duke's quizzing glass to the young lady on whom it was trained. The quizzing glass resumed its journey. "I would appreciate it, old chap, if you would dance a set with the protégée. Miss Cora Downes." He said the name with something like distaste.

"Glad to," Lord Francis said and wondered what was wrong with Miss Cora Downes. Apart from her name, that was. Her two names did not blend together into anything resembling poetry or even pleasing symphony. "Miss Cora Downes?"

His grace sighed. "It is unlike my mother to act purely out of sentiment," he said. "But that appears to be what has happened in this case. She has taken the girl out of her own proper milieu and has brought her to town to present to the *ton*. It is her intention to find the girl a respectable husband."

Lord Francis coughed delicately behind one lace-covered wrist.

"Oh, not you, old chap," his grace said hastily. "It is just that for all my mother's consequence and influence, I am still afraid Miss Downes will not take. It would be an embarrassment to her grace as well as to the girl herself, I daresay. And therefore to me."

"Her own proper milieu?" Lord Francis's curiosity was piqued. It seemed to him an eternity since he had felt anything as wildly exhilarating as curiosity.

"Her father could probably buy you and me up with the small change in his purse, Kneller," the duke said, "and still have enough left to jingle in his pocket. He is a merchant from Bristol. He has recently bought property and set up as a gentleman. I believe his son has been to all the right schools and has taken up the practice of law. But there is the taint, you know, the lack of birth."

"Ah," Lord Francis said and pictured himself dancing with the girl and having his ears murdered with an uncouth provincial accent. Even that prospect was not utterly displeasing. It would be *amusing*. How long it was since he had been amused! "And my dancing with her will help her to take, Bridgwater?"

"Undoubtedly," his grace said after letting his glass pause on Lady Augusta Haville before he lowered it and observed his surroundings with his naked eye. "Everyone knows that you commune only with the most fashionable and the most lovely ladies, Kneller. Your taste is legendary. You are a connoisseur of beauty, as you yourself just said. You have but to bow to a lady and a host of other men takes particular notice. If you tread a measure with Miss

Downes, other gentlemen will flock to take your place. The girl will dance all night. She will be launched. Mama will be ecstatic. And I will be grateful."

Lord Francis sifted through the flattery and decided that somewhere at the core of it was a sincere compliment. Was the girl so very dreadful, then? She was a merchant's daughter? A merchant with pretensions to gentility? Was she ghastly and vulgar? Why had the very fastidious Duchess of Bridgwater taken her on? He decided to ask the question.

"She is your mother's protégée?" he said, phrasing the sentence politely as a question.

"She saved my nephew's life in Bath," his grace explained. "Jumped into the river when he was drowning and almost drowned herself while fishing him out. A damned heroic thing to do actually. We will be eternally in her debt, and I feel the debt personally as head of the family even though Henry belongs to George. But this seems a foolish way of paying it. Ah."

His glass was to his eye again and directed at the doorway. Lord Francis glanced that way too and saw the Duchess of Bridgwater, her usual regal and beautiful self in purple, Lady Elizabeth Munro as beautiful and as aloof as ever, Lady Jane as small and sweet and innocent as she had looked last year during her first Season, and—and another young lady, who must be the protégée.

She was tall, large—he caught his mind in the act of using the latter word. She was not fat. Nothing like fat. But there was something large about her. *Voluptuous,* he thought, was a more accurate word. If she ever appeared on the stage, she would draw men to the green room like bees to a flower.

It was an unkind thought. She was dressed in virginal white, like Lady Jane—it was rather unfortunate that she stood next to the younger Munro sister—and the gown had been carefully designed to show somewhat less of her bosom than was fashionable. He suspected the restraining hand of the duchess. If the girl's gown had been designed according to strict fashion, cut lower—well, his tempera-

ture threatened to soar a couple of degrees at the very
thought.

He found himself wondering what she must have looked
like when she climbed out of the river in Bath after having
saved Bridgwater's nephew. His temperature *did* rise at
least one degree.

"The protégée?" he asked his grace.

"You see what I mean?" the duke asked, setting aside his
quizzing glass and looking as if he were girding his loins
for unpleasant action. "She looks for all the world as if she
should be in a damned green room."

Their minds sometimes moved along strange parallels,
Lord Francis thought.

"And my mother thinks to find her a respectable husband," the duke said with a sigh. "Come along, Kneller.
You did promise, did you not?"

She was not beautiful. Once the eye could be persuaded
to rise above the level of the woman's neck, one could see
that. Her features were too strong for true delicacy and her
eyes were too wide-spaced and too candid to inspire
lovelorn sighs. Her hair was unfortunately dressed. It was a
rich chestnut color, it was true, and was abundant and shining and clean. But it was far *too* abundant for the curls and
ringlets she wore. One found oneself picturing it worn
down about her waist—with the bosom of her gown cut
lower.

Lord Francis fingered his quizzing glass and raised his
eyebrows.

And then she saw him coming. Her hand shot to her
mouth, her eyes lit up with unholy amusement, and she half
turned her head as if to whisper something to Lady Jane.
Then she noticed Bridgwater, appeared to realize that the
two of them were moving in her direction, and dropped her
hand. She very noticeably blanked her eyes.

But there must have been a speck of dust on the floor in
front of her, Lord Francis thought afterward. There must
have been. Certainly there was nothing else. Nothing that
was visible. So it must have been something invisible over
which she tripped. She did so quite inelegantly—not that

there was an elegant way to trip, Lord Francis might have realized if he had been at liberty to consider the matter—and with a little shriek.

Lord Francis quickened his pace sufficiently to leap forward and save her from quite upending herself on the floor. For one moment before he set her to rights and stepped back in order to regard her with eyebrows that were raised again in polite inquiry, he felt the full impact of that remarkable voluptuous bosom against his chest. And for the same moment it seemed somehow irrelevant that her chemise and gown, his coat and waistcoat and shirt all separated his bare flesh from her bare flesh.

Quite irrelevant indeed. Lord Francis wondered if Prinny was due at tonight's ball. If he was not, one was left to wonder why Lady Markley kept her ballroom so suffocatingly hot.

Miss Cora Downes, to whom the Duke of Bridgwater was proceeding to present him as if nothing untoward had happened even though for a moment he had closed his eyes in pained acknowledgment of the fact that one-half of the gathered guests must have witnessed the uncouth debut of his mother's protégée and the other half would be told of it within the next five minutes—Miss Cora Downes blushed a shade brighter than scarlet and then giggled.

"Oops!" she said, interrupting his grace's opening remarks. "I wonder if it is permitted to go back outside onto the staircase and try it all over again." She spoke rather too loudly and heartily and then giggled once more before suddenly sobering in order to pay attention to Lord Francis's name and to his request that he might lead her into the opening set.

What a deliciously frightful young lady, he thought, feeling genuinely diverted for the first time in two or three eternities.

Chapter 2

◠

She was frankly terrified. And she despised herself for feeling so, since rationally speaking she did not consider herself inferior to anyone. Lady Markley's ballroom was stuffed full of the *ton* in all its jeweled splendor—all the *ton* and Cora Downes. The vast majority of those present were probably mere misters and misseses and misses, she reassured herself as she paused just inside the doorway with her three companions, surely the most conspicuous place of all to stand in any ballroom. She had to resist the urge to look down at herself to make sure she had remembered to put on her gown. The duchess would surely have thought before now of commenting on its absence if indeed she was clad in merely her shift.

Of course, there were undoubtedly several titled people present too. Cora felt a strange bonelessness in her knees—a most unfortunate part of the anatomy in which to feel it. Why be awed by titles? Jane had a title and was a very ordinary, pleasant young lady. And Papa always said that title and birth meant nothing but snobbery. It was wealth and property and the ability to acquire and manage both that really mattered. Cora herself was not really sure that even that was true, but it was a comforting thought to which to cling at the moment.

She tried to look about her at individual people to assure herself that really they were just people—each with two eyes, a nose, and a mouth, so to speak. She saw jewels and

fans and feathers and fobs and quizzing glasses wherever
she looked. Formidable ladies and even more formidable
gentlemen. Many of the latter looked sober and immaculate
—and formidable—in black coats and knee breeches, a
fast-growing fashion that both her father and Edgar ap-
plauded as did all the men of their middle-class world. In
fact, they often had unkind things to say about men who did
not follow it.

And then her eyes lit on a gentleman who was so much
the antithesis of that fashion that he stood out in the crowd
like the proverbial sore thumb. He wore a bright turquoise
satin coat with turquoise-and-silver striped waistcoat and
silver knee breeches. His linen was sparkling white. There
were copious amounts of lace at his wrists and half covering his hands. The knot of his neckcloth was a superior
work of art. Edgar would have declared with some contempt that the man's valet must have sweated for several
hours to create such perfection. The face above the startling
clothes displayed a lazy kind of cynicism as if the man
were bored with his very existence.

Cora thought immediately of a peacock, which was the
first word Edgar would have used, she was sure. Remembering that only titters—and even those solely at appropri-
ate moments—were allowed in her present surroundings,
she clapped a hand to her mouth in order to thrust back the
merriment that was in grave danger of bubbling out of her.
Oh, if only Edgar were here to see—and to comment!

But Jane was here and Jane had a healthy sense of
humor. Cora had half turned to share the glorious joke of
the man's foppish appearance when she froze and humor
died an instantaneous death. The man was moving in her
direction. And at his side was another gentleman, elegant
and handsome in varying shades of dark green. The Duke
of Bridgwater.

Their destination was instantly apparent to Cora. Heavenly days, she thought, her mind robbed of coherence. Oh,
heavenly days.

She had had a problem with clumsiness as a girl. Not as a
child. It had come upon her at about the age of twelve and

had dogged her footsteps—almost literally—for several years after that. Edgar had started to call her a walking disaster and her father's habitual expression when she was about had seemed to be one of resigned glumness, his eyes rolled ceiling- or skyward, as if he were sending up a fervent prayer, "Why me, Lord?"

Miss Graham, her governess, had always been kinder than either of the two men in her life. Miss Graham had always explained to her that she was growing into her body. Her brain had not quite got the message that she was no longer inside her dainty child's body but instead was in this girl's frame, which was developing in alarming ways—Cora's words, not Miss Graham's. Miss Graham had merely explained that the child in her was resisting the developing woman but that finally she would be comfortable with her femininity.

She was still waiting to grow comfortable though she had outgrown the clumsiness. Almost.

On this occasion all she had to do was wait for the Duke of Bridgwater to come up and greet his mother and his sisters and her, Cora—and probably present the turquoise peacock to them. She did not even have to move. She did not know why she did so. Indeed, she did not even realize that she *had* moved until her cramped toes somehow did not advance with the rest of her and she stumbled—and shrieked—in surely the most embarrassing place possible in which to stumble and shriek.

Not that she ever *chose* to be clumsy.

She collided with a brick wall, which fortunately saved her from sprawling out flat on the floor and disgracing herself beyond measure. She righted herself, realized that the brick wall had been a gentleman's chest—the *turquoise* gentleman's chest—and disgraced herself after all.

She giggled.

It was not even honest-to-goodness laughter. It was unmistakably a giggle, occasioned by acute embarrassment. She wondered hopefully if she was exaggerating even ever-so slightly in believing that everyone was watching her. She did not think so.

"Oops!" she heard someone exclaim in her voice—how *many* times had Miss Graham told her that she must learn to wipe that word from her vocabulary? "I wonder if it is permitted to go back outside onto the staircase and try it all over again."

And the same person who spoke giggled—again—at the sadly unwitty joke. And sounded for all the world like a silly twelve-year-old.

It was only then she realized that his grace was speaking—quietly and courteously and quite as if she had not just held up him and his mother and his sisters to public ridicule. He was, she realized, the perfectly well-bred gentleman. He terrified her and had done so ever since Elizabeth and Jane had first started talking about him in Bath with mutual adoration. He was so perfectly handsome and elegant and gentlemanly and—ducal. If he had had DUKE written in black ink across his forehead, he could not be more obviously who he was.

She also realized—too late—that he had presented his companion to her and that she had missed his name. She could only smile with facial muscles that suddenly felt unaccountably stiff as he called her Miss Downes and took her hand in his and bowed over it.

He was taller than she was, she thought irrelevantly—so many gentleman were not. He also did *not*—as so many gentlemen did—have a spot of thinning hair on the crown of his head. His brown hair was of a uniform thickness and was expertly cut so that even when it was windblown it would look just so, she guessed. She also guessed that he spent several hours of each week with his barber—and with a manicurist. She glanced at his perfect hands. It was rather sad that he was so far to the left of true masculinity. *Was* it sad? Perhaps it was not to him. Perhaps he enjoyed looking like a peacock.

She suffered from another affliction in addition to clumsiness—though she had not really suffered from that since girlhood. She suffered from the inability to be always present when it was essential that she be present. She had gone off now into her own distant world, thinking of trivialities like bald spots and peacocks, and as a consequence a few important details of the present moment had passed her by. Like the man's name. And the identity of the person whom her grace was describing as a great heroine to whom they would all be indebted for the rest of their lives.

"Yes, indeed," his grace said with a grave and elegant inclination of his head in Cora's direction.

"Oh, dear," she said, realizing they were talking about her. "All I did was leap into the river without pausing for thought. It was really quite unheroic. And I ruined a brand-new bonnet."

The anonymous gentleman—who would *not* be anonymous if she had only remained present long enough to hear what his grace had named him—pursed his lips and fingered his quizzing glass. It was studded with jewels that looked suspiciously like sapphires, Cora noticed when she glanced down at it. She would wager they were real gems and not merely paste. She wondered if he had a glass to match each of his outfits—and giggled yet again.

"A bonafide heroine indeed," the gentleman said in a voice that sounded as languid and bored as his face had appeared when she first looked into it. "One perhaps might find another lady willing to risk her life for a child, but I declare that nowhere would one find another willing to sacrifice her bonnet in the same cause."

Cora stared at him, fascinated. Was he *serious?* He probably was, she decided.

"Ma'am." He was bowing to the duchess. "With your permission I would request the honor of leading Miss Downes in to the opening set."

Cora brightened instantly. Her great fear, she knew, though she despised herself for feeling it, was of being an utter and total wallflower. But very close behind that fear— and really she did not believe her grace would allow that first one to become reality—was the terror of being asked to dance by a gentleman so very elegant and proper and aristocratic that she would freeze into a block of ice that just happened to have two left feet attached to its base. His grace of Bridgwater himself, for example. She had found herself praying fervently last night—literally praying, with palms pressed together and eyes tightly scrunched shut—that he would not for his mother's sake feel obliged to lead her out. She would *die*.

The anonymous gentleman would not be threatening at all to dance with. Indeed, she would derive great amusement from the opportunity to observe him more closely for all of half an hour. But she almost absented herself too long again in these happy thoughts.

"Certainly, Lord Francis," the duchess was saying, inclining her head graciously and setting her plumes to dancing again. "I am sure Cora would be delighted."

Francis. The name suited him perfectly, being one of those that might belong to either a man or a woman—with a slight variation in the spelling, of course. But *Lord* Francis? He was an aristocrat, then? But quite an unthreatening one, she told herself before panic could well into her nostrils. He was making her a half bow and asking her for the honor of leading her in to the set.

"Thank you, Lord Francis," she said, vaunting her new knowledge. She smiled dazzlingly at him. "It is a set of country dances? How wonderful! I *love* the vigor of a country dance."

She could almost hear Elizabeth's voice as it had spoken just a few days ago, as soon as they knew they were to come to this ball. One must always assume an attitude of ennui at such functions, she had warned. One must never be thought to enthuse. Enthusiasm was something very far removed from true gentility. Her grace had nodded in agreement though she had added with a smile that one need not go as far as to look downright bored. That might be somewhat insulting to both one's hosts and one's partners. Jane had added that one might smile and even look happy as long as one remained demure and did not *bubble*.

And she, Cora, had just said *I* LOVE *the vigor of a country dance* with all the enthusiasm of her lack of gentility.

She thought she saw amusement for the merest moment in Lord Francis's eyes. Ridicule, no doubt. No matter. She was not at all intent on impressing Lord Francis Whoever-He-Was. She really should have listened to his full name.

They were blue eyes, she thought, apropos of nothing. She had always favored blue eyes in men. She had secretly thought that perhaps one of the reasons—though only a very minor one—she had been unable to feel affection for any of the three men who had offered for her was that they had not one blue eye among the three of them. But if that was true, then she was setting about choosing a lifelong mate according to very trivial criteria.

It was perhaps a shame that the first truly blue eyes she had encountered in a gentleman belonged to a peacock. And an aristocratic peacock at that.

A turquoise satin arm with an elegant, lace-bedecked hand at the end of it—on one of the fingers of which was a large square sapphire ring—was poised before Cora and she realized that she was being invited to join a set without further delay. The duke was already talking with another gentleman, who had come along with the obvious intention of dancing with Jane.

Cora set her arm along the turquoise one and repressed the very silly urge to giggle yet again. She had *never* been a giggler. She had no wish to acquire the nasty habit at this advanced stage of her life.

She wished with all the power of her being that she had bought her slippers in a larger size. There was plenty of room for her feet in these particular ones but very little left over for her toes.

She smiled hard, trying not to look gauche.

I LOVE *the vigor of a country dance.* The words rang in Lord Francis's ears as he led Miss Cora Downes onto the floor. She was priceless. He felt marvelously diverted. *And I ruined a brand new bonnet.* When she might have preened herself on her reputation as a heroine, someone who had risked her life in order to save that of a child, she had belittled herself with such an observation.

She was almost, though not quite as tall as he, he noticed. And he prided himself on being considerably above the average in height. She was the possessor of truly glorious curves, which even the loose-fitting, high-waisted style of her fashionable gown could not hide. Of course, muslin was a notorious figure-hugger. She was looking all about her with her eager face and bold eyes, not even attempting to hide her interest and curiosity. She caught his eye and—grinned.

"I am so *glad* you asked me to dance," she said. "I had positive horrors that no one would. And I suppose her grace could not actually *coerce* anyone into it. I daresay his grace asked you to ask me, which was remarkably kind of him considering the fact that I am no relative of his and I am not sure he even approves of me. And it was kind of you too to say yes to him."

Lord Francis supposed that most young ladies must experience such fears. But he had never before heard one candidly confess to them—in a voice slightly louder than was necessary to make herself heard above the hum of conversation and the sound of the orchestra tuning their instruments.

He thought of Samantha and the fact that she must never have felt the fear of being without a partner at a ball. She had always been besieged by admirers and suitors. Tiny, dainty, blond-haired, exquisitely lovely Samantha. Just a few weeks ago he had been dancing with her himself, her most devoted suitor, though she had chosen to believe after betrothing herself to Carew that he had never been serious about her. His heart performed a series of painful somersaults and landed in the soles of his shoes again.

"Perhaps," he said, "I saw you and admired you as soon as you came into the ballroom, Miss Downes, and sought an introduction to you. Have you thought of that?"

She looked squarely at him and he could see that she *was* thinking about it. And then she laughed. It was not a giggle this time, he was happy to find. It was a laugh of unrestrained mirth, drawing to her the rather startled glances of the other couples who were forming their particular set.

"You saw me and admired me," she said. "Oh, that is a good one."

He was not at liberty to consider what the one was or what was good about it. The music had begun and Lady Markley's daughter and her newly betrothed were leading off the first set.

It was indeed a lively country dance, which the ladies performed with grace and precision and Miss Cora Downes performed with—enthusiasm. She danced with energetic vigor just as if there were not a whole eveningful of sets yet to be danced, and with a bright smile on her face.

She danced, Lord Francis decided, as if she should have the ribbon of a maypole in her hand and sunshine on her face and in her loosened chestnut hair and all the fresh beauty of a village green surrounding her.

He watched her with considerable amusement and not a little appreciation—in her own way she was rather magnificent, he decided. And other gentleman watched her too. There was something about her even apart from her height and her curves that would inevitably draw male eyes. Something that was not quite vulgar—not at all vulgar, in fact. But something very different from what one expected to find in a fashionable ballroom in London. Some—well, some raw femininity.

Her grace of Bridgwater might well have problems marrying the girl off, Lord Francis thought. Not just because of her origins—indeed, if it was true that the father was almost indecently wealthy, there would be any number of impecunious gentlemen, and even a few moderately pecunious ones, who would be only too delighted to overlook the fact that he had made his fortune in trade. No, it was the woman's looks and manner that would discourage serious suitors. Any red-blooded male would immediately dream of setting a mattress at Miss Cora Downes's back, whereas precious few of them would indulge in any corresponding dream of leading her to the altar first.

It was unfortunate.

He rather suspected that before the Season was over— unless the considerable awe in which both Bridgwater and his mother were held by the *ton* acted as a restraining force—Miss Cora Downes would be offered more than one carte blanche.

She was breathless and flushed and bright-eyed when the set was over. Her bosom was heaving as she tried to replace the missing air in her lungs.

"Oh, that was wonderful," she said. "Far more fun than any of the assemblies in Bath. There the dancers are mostly elderly, you know, and so the music is slower. Thank you so very much, Lord Francis. You are very kind."

"Thank *you*," he said, taking her arm on his sleeve and leading her back toward the duchess. "It was my honor and my pleasure, Miss Downes."

"May I ask you something?" she said, looking sideways into his eyes. Her own were a dark gray, he saw. He had at first thought them to be black. "What is your *name?* I was woolgathering when his grace presented you to me—or perhaps I was still flustered over the fact that I had tripped over my own feet and would have disgraced myself utterly instead of only partially if you had not stepped smartly forward and grabbed me. I am *always* woolgathering when something important is being said. It drives my papa insane. It drove my governess to despair."

"Kneller," he said, repressing the urge to chuckle. "It is the family name of the dukes of Fairhurst. My elder brother is the current holder of the title."

"Oh," she said with an openmouthed gasp, "you are the brother of a *duke*. I am so glad I did not know it when I danced with you." She laughed.

There was a quality of merriment in her that was almost unladylike and was quite infectious, Lord Francis thought. He would like to draw the cork of any man who offered her carte blanche during what remained of the Season.

Perhaps he would take her under his wing, he thought suddenly. Bridgwater would undoubtedly be relieved and the duchess would surely not be displeased. As for himself, he had perhaps a great deal of a leftover life to kill. He had no wish to spend it pining away to a mere shadow of his former self over a woman who was now in Yorkshire with her new husband, doubtless proceeding with the pleasant business of living happily ever after.

Taking Miss Cora Downes under his wing would amuse him. And perhaps it would protect her from harm. Perhaps too he could steer toward her some likely candidate for matrimony. It might be diverting to become a matchmaker for the few weeks that remained of the Season. It would be a new role for him, one he had never even in his wildest imaginings thought of for himself. It was a feminine role, one his elder sister delighted in. She had been trying to do it to him for so long that it was a testament to her endurance that she had not long ago lost faith in her powers.

It would be an amusing role to assume—if anything in life could ever again be amusing.

He returned Cora Downes to her place, stayed to make himself agreeable to the duchess and Lady Jane—Lady Elizabeth was promenading about the room on the arm of her future sister-in-law—waited until Corsham paused at his side with significant looks and throat-clearing, in the obvious hope of being presented to Miss Downes, performed that office, and had the satisfaction of watching her being led out for a quadrille while her grace and Bridgwater were still marshaling their forces of prospective partners for the merchant's daughter.

Corsham, Lord Francis thought in some satisfaction, was in possession of property and ten thousand a year. His mother was a draper's daughter, his father a second son of a second son. Fortunately he had had a wealthy aunt who had doted on him and left him everything on her demise.

An eminently eligible match for Miss Cora Downes.

"My thanks, old chap," his grace said at his elbow. "I owe you a favor. Fortunately the girl seems not quite vulgar, would you not agree? *Rustic* might be more the word. One can only hope she will improve under my mother's guidance. Though one does hope too that she does not make a habit of tripping over her feet." He grimaced.

Lord Francis chuckled. The sound seemed strange to his own ears. He wondered when he had last laughed.

Chapter 3

~

The Duchess of Bridgwater had already pronounced herself well satisfied. There was no question about her satisfaction with Elizabeth and Jane, of course. Elizabeth had moved almost immediately into the illustrious circle of her future in-laws and had stayed there. Jane had been rediscovered by last year's admirers and had been discovered by several more, who had been properly presented to her by her brother. But then Jane, even apart from her beauty and youth and sweetness, was the daughter of a duke.

No, it was with Cora that her grace was really expressing satisfaction. Apart from the unfortunate fact that she had tripped over her feet at the sight of Lord Francis Kneller's turquoise splendor, and that one heavy lock of her hair had fallen down about her shoulder during the third set, another round of vigorous country dances, and that she had trodden on her own hem at the end of the same set and ripped the stitching out of a stretch of it—apart from those slight mishaps, of which her grace made light, she had behaved quite becomingly. And up to and including the supper dance, she had had a partner for every set except the waltz, which she was not allowed to dance because certain dragons—the patronesses of Almack's, apparently—had not yet given her the nod of approval. Which was all a parcel of nonsense, as far as Cora was concerned, but her grace looked faintly alarmed and very slightly haughty when she mentioned the fact.

It seemed that Cora had taken well.

She took none of the credit to herself. The ladies who spoke with her—there were several—were friends either of her grace or of one of the girls. The gentlemen who danced with her were presented to her by either his grace or Lord Francis Kneller. All of them, she suspected, had had their arms twisted up behind their backs—even if only figuratively speaking—as an incentive to oblige her.

And some of the credit too, she had to admit, was due to the extraordinary story that was circulating. She was a great heroine, it seemed. She had saved the life of Lord George Munro's son—the child was second in line to the Bridgwater title—at considerable risk to her own life. His grace was deeply in her debt. Everyone referred to the story. Everyone looked at her almost in awe—just as if she were someone special.

It was really rather embarrassing. Especially when she recalled how very foolishly stupid she had been to shriek out and plunge into the river the way she had. She had not been heroic at all—only brainless, as Edgar had pointed out afterward while she was mourning over the bedraggled remains of her bonnet. He had taken her and bought her a new one the following morning—before the duchess descended upon her and bore her away to find her a husband from among the ranks of the gentry as a reward for her heroism.

It had been a successful evening. Her grace said so and even Cora felt it. But the trouble was that the part of her that felt it the most acutely was her toes. She dared not take her slippers off to wiggle them or to assess them for damages. She needed no assessment of the eyes. She would be very surprised if there was not a blister on every single toe. She could even feel blisters on toes that were not there. It was very difficult to sit through supper and smile and converse with her partner, Mr. Pandry, and the other people at her table—one of the ladies asked her repeated questions about dear little Henry and his behavior throughout his watery ordeal in the river at Bath—it was difficult to be sociable when all ten of her toes in addition to the ghost ones were screeching for her attention.

To dance after supper was an impossibility. To refuse to dance was an equal impossibility. Half of her mind dealt with the conversation at hand while the other half considered her dilemma. She was ashamed to admit the truth to her grace. A real lady, she rather suspected, would dance even if all ten of her toes were broken and a couple of ankles to boot. A real lady . . . She had never—before the incident of little Henry, that was—even considered the fact that she was not a real lady. She had been very satisfied with who she was. She still was satisfied. She had no wish to start pretending to be anything she was not. She was her papa's daughter. Papa was not, according to strict definition, a gentleman. She loved her papa.

She told the duchess when they had returned to the ballroom that she needed to go to the ladies' withdrawing room and that she might be gone a little while—words uttered with some blushing embarrassment. She declined the offer to be accompanied.

She really did intend to go the ladies' room, but she suddenly remembered from the time she had gone there with her grace earlier to have her hair pinned up again and her hem mended that it was crowded and noisy. If she sat there for any length of time the fact would surely be remarked upon. And she would feel the eyes of the maids stationed there upon her. She turned sharply instead and walked out through the open French doors onto the balcony outside.

It was all but deserted. After the supper break, everyone was ready to dance or to play cards again, she guessed. She discovered a vacant chair behind a large and dense potted plant. She sank gratefully onto it and tried wiggling her toes. The attempt did not help at all. She would not have thought it possible for slippers to cause such pain, but she supposed it made sense that they did so when they were a size too small.

She looked carefully to both sides and even over her shoulder. There was no one in sight. Everyone was in the ballroom. The music had struck up again. She lifted one foot onto the opposite knee, bending her leg outward, and cradled her foot in both hands. For a short while she resisted further temptation. But it was too insistent. She pulled off her slipper and tossed it to the balcony beside her other foot. The freedom, the rush of coolness, even the pain was exquisite. She closed her eyes and sighed.

"Trouble?" a languid, almost bored voice asked.

She snapped to attention, still clutching her foot. And then she breathed out through puffed cheeks in noisy relief when she saw who it was. It was only Lord Francis Kneller. She would have been horribly mortified if it had been any other gentleman. Lord Francis seemed almost like a woman friend. Not that she meant the thought at all unkindly. After an evening of observing him—she had found her eyes following him about the ballroom—and occasionally exchanging a few words with him and dancing with him that once, she had come to believe that he was happy with who he was. As any person should be, she firmly believed.

"Oh, it is just you," she said. Even so she edged down the hem of her gown, which had been up somewhere in the region of her knee. "Sore feet is all. I have slunk out here, where I thought to remain unobserved."

"Just sore?" he asked. "Or blistered?"

"Blistered," she admitted after a short pause. Now she did feel mortified after all. "My feet are too large, you see. I thought to reduce them to greater daintiness with slippers that are too small."

"Not a wise idea," he said and he seated himself on the stone bench that ran beneath the balustrade and took her foot onto his lap. He massaged it with his thumb, avoiding her toes. She was inclined to giggle and pull away at first, but the pressure of his thumb was too firm and too soothing to tickle.

"You are a tall lady," he said. "You would not be able to balance on tiny feet. I believe a certain incident earlier this evening proved that. Besides, you would look funny. Out of proportion."

She chuckled, pain forgotten for a moment. "Vanity is a

dreadful thing," she said. She supposed that he would understand that himself.

"When it causes blisters, yes," he said. "I suppose the other foot is in just as bad a case?"

"Yes," she admitted ruefully.

He set her stockinged foot on the ground and lifted the other onto his lap, easing off the slipper and proceeding to massage the foot as he had the other.

"Not that it is any of my concern, Miss Downes," he said at last, "but where is your chaperon, pray?"

"Oh, what nonsense it is," she said, "this business of chaperons. I had a great deal more freedom before I became a *heroine,* I do assure you."

"Your parents allowed you to roam about unescorted?" he asked, raising his eyebrows. "Dear me."

"My mother is dead," she said. "Edgar—my brother—told me once, a long time ago, that she ventured one look at me after giving birth to me, took fright, and quit this world without further ado. But Papa scolded him for making light of so serious a matter and even thrashed him for it, I do believe, though I was sorry because it was said only as a joke even if it was in poor taste. No, Papa does not allow me to roam unescorted, as you put it. But now that I have become a heroine and a protégée, I may not move a muscle, it seems, without having a female companion accompany it."

"It is for your own protection, I do assure you," he said. "How do you know that I am not about to take great liberties with your person? Indeed, I have already taken liberties. Many ladies I know would faint dead away if they knew I had been fondling your feet for the past ten minutes or so."

Cora threw back her head and laughed. "Oh, I know I am safe with *you,*" she said and then realized that perhaps her words were ill-bred even though she had not meant them unkindly. "You were presented to me by the Duke of Bridgwater himself," she added.

"Does her grace know you are out here?" he asked.

She smiled at him conspiratorially. "I told her I was going to the ladies' withdrawing room," she said. "But it is always so crowded there. It was cooler and quieter out here."

"Stay here." He got to his feet after setting her foot down beside the other. "I shall explain to the duchess that you are ready to go home and see to the ordering around of her carriage if Bridgwater is nowhere in sight. Then I shall come back and escort you to it."

"She will have to know about my blisters," she said. "It seems so ungenteel somehow."

"Even one of the royal princesses would develop blisters if she wore slippers of too small a size and then proceeded to dance for several hours in them with—ah—*vigor*," he said. "I shall return."

And he was gone.

She would be packed up and sent home to Bath, Cora thought. It must be disgraceful to have to leave one's very first *ton* ball early because one had blistered feet. Now her grace was going to have to leave early and Jane and Elizabeth too—and doubtless their dancing cards were full and they were going to have to excuse themselves to all the gentlemen with whom they were to dance. And they would be miserable at having to lose half an evening's entertainment but they would be too well mannered to blame her openly.

If only she had not jumped into that river. There was nothing callous in the thought. Little Henry's survival had not depended upon such theatrical heroics.

Well, she thought, stooping down to pick up her slippers and eyeing them with a grimace, if she was sent home in disgrace, she would not care. She really had not wanted to become the Duchess of Bridgwater's protégée in the first place. But her grace had been importunate and Lord George had been charmingly insistent—and Lady George too, though because of her confinement she had had to relay her pleas through her husband and one lengthy letter—and Papa had thought it a splendid opportunity for her. Even Edgar had told her she would be a fool to reject the chance that was being offered her.

But she had no wish for a genteel husband. Or for a husband at all, in fact. Though that was a bouncer, she admitted in all fairness. Of course she wanted a husband. And of course it would be pleasant to have one who was well set up and genteel in manner. But mostly she wanted a husband for affection and companionship and for—well, for the other. She had no particularly clear picture of what was involved in that other, but she was very convinced that she would like it excessively. Provided she felt an affection for her husband, that was. And she knew that she would like to have children.

Perhaps, she thought, she should merely have had Lord Francis escort her back into the ballroom. She could have sat through the rest of the evening without disturbing anyone else. But it was too late now to think of that. She flexed her slippers in her hands as if she thought to enlarge them a whole size by doing so.

And then Lord Francis appeared again. Cora looked sheepishly beyond his shoulder, but it was just Betty who was standing there, the maid the duchess had brought with them.

"Her grace is making arrangements for Lady Elizabeth and Lady Jane to be chaperoned and fetched home by Lady Fuller," he said. "I shall escort you to the carriage, Miss Downes. I have brought Betty with me so that you will not be forced to the impropriety of moving a muscle without its being accompanied by a chaperon, you see."

Lady Fuller was sister to the Marquess of Hayden, Elizabeth's betrothed. Cora felt better knowing that the evening was not going to be ruined for Elizabeth and Jane.

"Was she very cross?" she asked.

"Her grace?" He raised his eyebrows. "Cross? I do not believe duchesses are ever *cross,* Miss Downes. Actually I believe she was more relieved than anything else. She was coming to the conclusion that you had vanished into the proverbial thin air. No, I would not advise trying to squeeze your toes back into the slippers."

She sighed. "I cannot walk back through the ballroom in my stockinged feet," she said. "Even merchants' daughters know that much about gentility, my lord."

"I would not have brought Betty if that had been my planned route," he said. "Come along. We shall avoid the ballroom altogether."

He took her slippers as she got to her feet, and handed them to Betty. Then he drew her arm through his and led her slowly toward the steps leading down into the garden. Betty followed silently behind. Cora hoped fervently that the few people who were strolling on the balcony would not look downward to notice that she was unshod.

"It is such a shame," she said with a sigh as they descended the steps, "to have to miss the rest of the ball. Just listen to that music. You are very kind, Lord Francis. Would you not prefer to be dancing?"

"When I might be escorting the loveliest lady among the guests to her carriage instead?" he said. "Absolutely not, ma'am."

Cora chuckled. "What a thorough bouncer," she said. "You will go straight to hell for that one, Lord Francis."

"Dear me," he said rather faintly.

They were to walk about the house to the front, it seemed. It also appeared that the house was surrounded on three sides by a cobbled walk.

"This is by far the best part," he said as they reached it, "and the reason I felt it wise to bring Betty along." And he disengaged his arm from hers, turned to her, and scooped her up into his arms.

Cora shrieked.

"It was definitely wise," he said. "Stay close, Betty, if you please."

"You cannot *carry* me," Cora said, feeling considerably flustered and doing with her arms the only thing that seemed possible to do with them—she set them about his shoulders. "I weigh a *ton*."

His voice, when he spoke, betrayed the truth of her words—he was breathless. "The merest feather, Miss Downes," he said, "I do assure you."

He was unexpectedly strong. Even Edgar, who was both tall and husky and who was also very, very masculine—she had seen the way women followed him with their eyes with expressions ranging from wistful to downright predatory—even Edgar had been red-faced and puffing a few weeks ago by the time he had hauled her, dripping, out of the river. And yet Lord Francis Kneller, whom she still could not resist comparing to a peacock, was carrying her along half the length of the back of the house, along its whole width, and then back along the front to her grace's waiting carriage. Cora hoped for the sake of his pride that he would not have to set her down in order to recover breath and muscle power before they reached their destination, but he did not.

There was no reason, she supposed, to believe that a man who dressed so and who spoke and moved with studied elegance and who appeared as a result to be somewhat—well, *effeminate* was not quite the word. It was too ruthless and unkind. She could not think of the word she meant if there were such a word. Anyway, there was no reason to believe that such a man was also a weakling. And yet that was just what she would have expected of Lord Francis Kneller. Nobody, she supposed, fit inside neat little boxes of expectation. Everyone was an individual and must be judged, if at all, on individual merits.

She was well satisfied with the profound insight into life that the evening had brought her. And what if he had been a weakling? Philosophical insights now bubbled up into her consciousness. Would that fact have diminished him as a person? She liked him. He had been kind to her. And at the basest level, he had provided her with amusement.

"Woolgathering again, Miss Downes?" he asked her, his voice still managing to sound languid despite the fact that he was definitely short of breath.

"What?" she said.

But they were at the carriage and he still had the strength left to swing her inside and deposit her on one of the seats instead of doing what would have been easier and simply dropping her so that she could climb the steps herself. He offered his hand to Betty, who bobbed a series of curtsies and allowed him to hand her inside.

"I asked," he said, leaning across the carriage steps and

looking up at Cora, "if I might have the honor of driving you in the park tomorrow afternoon. My guess is that you will not be walking any great distance for the next couple of days at least."

"In the park?" she said. "*Hyde* Park?" It was the dream. It was the pinnacle. Everyone—even the merchant class of Bristol—knew all about Hyde Park in the afternoons during the Season.

"None other," he said. "At precisely five o'clock, ma'am. At precisely the time when there will be so many carriages and horsemen and pedestrians on Rotten Row that only a snail could be content with the speed of movement."

"How splendid!" Cora said, clasping her hands to her bosom. "And you want *me* to drive with you?"

"A simple yes or no would suffice, you know," he said.

She grinned at him and then remembered that ladies did not grin. She was reminded by the arrival of the Duchess of Bridgwater, whom Lord Francis handed into the carriage. The coachman put up the steps and began to close the door. But Cora leaned hastily forward.

"Yes, then," she said. "And thank you. You are very kind."

"This is Elizabeth's doing, at an educated guess," her grace said when they were finally on their way, her voice not unkindly. "Elizabeth holds the strange and rather painful belief that feet must be made to appear as small as possible. I should have remembered that, dear, when I allowed her to accompany you to the shoemaker's. Tomorrow, or as soon as your feet have healed, we must begin all over again. Betty, I believe, wears just the size of these slippers."

Betty brightened considerably.

"Lord Francis said that small feet on a large person would look silly," Cora said.

"And Lord Francis is an authority on feminine beauty and fashion," her grace said. "You would do well to pay him heed, Cora. But I would be willing to wager that he did not imply that you are *large*. Did he perhaps use the word *tall?* He is far too well-bred to have used the former."

She was not in disgrace after all, Cora thought. She sank back against the squabs and relaxed. It really was fun to be part of the *ton* for a short while. Tonight she had danced with numerous gentlemen and even with a duke's son—it did not matter that he dressed like a peacock. The blisters had been won in an almost worthwhile cause. She had enjoyed herself greatly. And tomorrow she was to drive in Hyde Park at five o'clock in the afternoon.

She closed her eyes and thought of the letter she would write to Papa and Edgar tomorrow morning.

Lord Francis Kneller was in the depths of gloom. He toyed with his breakfast, pushing the kidneys into a neat triangle at one side of his plate and lining up the three sausages like soldiers at the other. One soldier was taller than the other two—he moved it to the middle for better symmetry. He could not decide at quite what angle to set his toast on the plate for best aesthetic effect.

His heart was squashed flat against the soles of his riding boots.

He had been feeling almost cheerful when he had got up after only a few hours of sleep following the Markley ball. All through his morning ride in the park he had felt almost cheerful. He had kept thinking about the rather odd Miss Cora Downes, and somehow every thought had brought amusement—and occasionally an actual chuckle—with it.

He had been somewhat exhilarated at his plan to bring her into fashion, perhaps even to find her the husband the Duchess of Bridgwater had brought her to London to find. He had thought that perhaps at last he would have something *amusing* on which to fix his mind and his energies. It might not be easy to bring Cora Downes into fashion—though none of her partners last evening had looked as if he had had to be coerced into dancing with her. There had been some lascivious glances, of course, especially when she had been dancing most vigorously.

By the time he had reached home and stabled his horse

and walked back to his rooms for breakfast, he had still felt
almost cheerful. There was always the qualification of the
almost, of course. Always deep within, sometimes beyond
the medium of conscious thought, was the awareness that
today, no matter how much he was out and about in Society, he would not see Samantha.

He had been *almost* cheerful. This afternoon he would
take Miss Downes up in his phaeton and would drive her in
the park and see what amusement might be derived from
doing so.

And then he had sat down to breakfast and his newspaper
and his letters. And instead of reading the paper first and
then tackling the post, he had thumbed through the latter
and discovered a letter from Gabe—his close friend, the
Earl of Thornhill. And because Gabe was his friend, and
because he lived in Yorkshire on the estate adjoining Highmoor, the Marquess of Carew's seat, Lord Francis had
opened and read the letter before anything else.

The crops were all planted and growing. The sheep had
all lambed, most of them successfully, and the cows had all
calved. Everything, in fact, appeared to be going well with
Gabe's life even though he pretended to complain about a
projected visit to Harrogate with his wife and children in
order to shop. Lord Francis knew that Gabe doted on his
wife and family and would take them to Peking to shop if
he thought it would give them pleasure. Though not at the
present time, of course. Lady Thornhill was increasing—
Lord Francis had known about that before—and Gabe was
strict about the amount of traveling he would allow her to
do at such times.

"And our neighbors, Frank," Gabe had written just when
Lord Francis had been feeling elated and mortally depressed at the conviction that they were not going to be
mentioned at all. "Nothing will do but Jennifer must call
upon them almost every day when they are not calling upon
us, and since I will not allow her far out of my sight when
she is in such a delicate way, I call upon them almost every
day too—except when they are with us. All is domestic
bliss there. We have been delighted and a little surprised to

find it, though in truth I am the only one surprised. Jennifer declares that Samantha would not have married for anything less than love (you know what incurable romantics women are and ought to know that Jennifer is perhaps the most incurable of all). But if you had any doubts, Frank, and I know you were a particular friend of Samantha's, then you may put them to rest. She did not marry Carew for his title and wealth. My wife was purple with indignation when I was unwise enough to suggest to her that such might be the case. And one more *on-dit,* Frank, before I take up the theme of the beginning of this letter and beg you to come and spend part of the summer with us—the children claim that summer will not be complete without the presence of Uncle Frank, who swam and climbed trees and played cricket with them last year. One more *on-dit*— Jennifer whispered to me and I am whispering to you, in the strictest confidence, of course, that our Marchioness of Carew is to present her marquess with an heir or—heaven forbid—a daughter sometime within the next nine months."

Lord Francis read the rest of the letter with eyes to which his mind was not attached.

So she was with child. It was hardly surprising when she had been married for longer than a month. Of course she was with child. It did not matter to him. He had lost her as soon as she betrothed herself to Carew. He had lost her utterly on her wedding day.

Now he lost her just a little more again.

Chapter 4

~

I do believe she is about to become a nine-days wonder," the Duke of Bridgwater said to his mother after all her afternoon visitors—except him—had left. Although he lived alone in a large town house, his mother always chose to open her own house, left her as part of her legacy in her husband's will, whenever she came to town for longer than a week at a time. She was so accustomed to being mistress of her own house, she always said by way of explanation, that she would doubtless be an obnoxious, domineering mother if she lived with her son.

"It is very gratifying indeed, Alistair," the duchess replied. "One realized that Elizabeth's status as Hayden's betrothed would draw visitors and one hoped that Jane's eligibility would do likewise—do you not agree that she is in remarkable good looks this year? But one could only be anxious about Cora. I find her delightful though I recognize that there is something about her that is not quite the thing. But one could not help but wonder if her origins would be too much of an impediment in town."

His grace withdrew an enameled snuffbox from a pocket, flicked it open with a practiced thumb, and proceeded to set a pinch of his favorite blend on the back of one hand.

"Instead of which," he said, "she very near outshone Jane this afternoon. It is to be wondered, by the way, if Jane will find someone to her liking during what is left of the Season this year. It became tedious last year sending away all those suitors who came to me with their offers merely because she had assured me each time that she could not possibly, possibly marry so-and-so. I believe I acquired notoriety as an ogre of a brother."

"Jane is still very young," his mother said, "and very full of ideals. She still believes that somewhere out there is the person who was created with the sole purpose of being her mate. I believe, Alistair, that she is not alone among my children in harboring such a belief."

The duke sniffed a portion of the snuff up each nostril and paused for it to take effect. In doing so, he avoided responding to his mother's comment.

"It appears," he said when he was able, "that one does not even need to stress the fact that Miss Downes will undoubtedly be the recipient of a very large dowry indeed when she marries. At least, I have not stressed any such fact yet. Have you?"

"Not at all," his mother said. "People have chosen to take to her for a far more noble reason. She is the heroine of the hour. It is very gratifying."

"I have often wondered." His grace regarded his mother with lazy eyes, which perhaps held a modicum of humor. "*Would* Henry have drowned without Miss Downes's heroic act?"

The duchess looked shocked. "Of course he would have drowned," she said. "Cora saved his life at considerable risk to her own."

"Can Henry not swim?" his grace asked. He knew the answer. He had taught the child himself the previous summer.

"Alistair!" her grace exclaimed. "A five-year-old who takes a tumble fully clothed into a cold river is scarcely likely to remember the skills taught him almost a year ago."

"I suppose not." His grace returned his snuffbox to his pocket. "And so a number of visitors called this afternoon for the express purpose of conversing with the heroine and congratulating her. There were even one or two eligibles among them. Did they come out of curiosity alone, do you think? Can any of them be brought to the point?"

"I believe Mr. Corsham is a possibility," the duchess said. "He danced with her last evening and you say he inquired about her after I had fetched her home. He is just the sort of young man who would be eager to marry a fortune, Alistair. He has the one his aunt left him, but he is still very much a younger son."

"I shall be sure to have a word with him at White's," his grace said, "and steer the conversation toward the enormous wealth of Mr. Downes, in addition to his recent emergence as a man of property."

"Mr. Pandry might be brought around as well," the duchess said. "Sir Robert Webster might not. He would not wish to risk the reputation of a baronet's title by taking a bride of inferior rank. Lord Francis Kneller was remarkably kind to her last evening, and he is to take her driving in the park later. Did you know? He is out of the question as a suitor, of course, but his notice can do her nothing but good in the eyes of the *ton*."

"Yes," his grace agreed. "It is well known that Kneller takes notice only of those ladies who are worth noticing. He was obliging me last evening and clearly decided to take my plea seriously enough to extend the invitation for today. I shall encourage him to continue to take notice of her. He needs employment. He has recently suffered a severe disappointment."

"Miss Newman?" his mother asked. "I heard of her recent marriage to your friend the Marquess of Carew. I was surprised, I must confess. I thought Lord Francis to be the favorite among her suitors, and heaven knows he paid determined court to her for long enough."

"But Carew bore off the prize," his grace said, "and Kneller needs diversion while he looks about him for another Incomparable to whose court to attach himself—his words, not mine, I do assure you, Mama. He can do Miss Downes nothing but good. Perhaps he can teach her to be a little less—exuberant."

The duchess laughed. "I find her delightful, Alistair," she said. "But you are right, of course. She needs polish. I actu-

ally saw her throw back her head last evening and laugh. I
was caught between horror and amusement."

"If it had been Lizzie or Jane," her son said, his eyebrows raised, "there would have been no question of
amusement, Mama."

"Oh, no, indeed," she agreed fervently. "I do hope that
between us, you and I—and perhaps Lord Francis, if he
will be so obliging—will be able to smooth out some rough
edges. Cora deserves a respectable husband after what she
did for dear Henry, Alistair."

"We will try what we can do, Mama," he said. "But I
hope for your sake she will not blame us at some future
date for lifting her out of her own class and making her unhappy."

Cora could not remember a time when she had enjoyed
herself more. All her anxieties of last night and this morning and the early part of this afternoon had been for naught.
Not only was it not raining, but the sun shone down from a
cloudless sky and the day was hot, though only pleasantly
so by five o'clock in the afternoon. In addition to these
happy circumstances was the fact that Lord Francis Kneller
had not forgotten his appointment to take her driving in
Hyde Park. He arrived punctually at half past four.

She was wearing her favorite of her new day clothes—a
bright yellow muslin dress with blue sash and blue cornflowers embroidered about the scalloped hem, and a straw
hat whose brim was trimmed with artificial cornflowers and
which sported a wide yellow ribbon stretched over the brim
of the hat and tied beneath her chin. She carried a blue
parasol. She wore a pair of her old shoes, a regrettable fact,
but better than wearing no shoes at all—which seemed the
only alternative for today at least.

Cora was feeling very smart indeed. Her papa had given
her a vast sum of money to bring with her to London, with
the strict instructions that a certain specified amount of it
was to be spent on fashionable clothes. And Edgar had
made her a gift of another large sum with which to buy her-

self baubles and gewgaws, as he had phrased it. She had been happily obedient to the wishes of both.

Another fact was contributing to her happiness. She had had a dreadful thought sometime during the night, when she had woken to think back to the ball and to flex her stinging toes gingerly against the bandages a maid had swathed them in. And the thought had haunted her all day. What if Lord Francis Kneller's appearance last evening was uncharacteristic of him? What if he was not after all a rather foppish gentleman? What if he appeared today to take her driving, looking as forbiddingly masculine and aristocratic as the Duke of Bridgwater had looked in her grace's drawing room? She would die. He was *Lord* Francis Kneller, after all. His father had been a duke. His brother was a duke. Her tongue would tie itself into one giant untyable knot and she would doubtless simper and stammer and blush her way through the ordeal of a drive in the park with him.

Not that a duke's son or even a duke was inherently superior to Papa and Edgar and the other men of their class with whom she was acquainted. But it was one thing for the head to know that. It was another for the body and the emotions to act in accordance with the belief.

She had longed for and dreaded the arrival of Lord Francis Kneller. She had bitten both cheeks to shreds.

Yet again all her fears had been for nothing. He was standing in the hall of her grace's house when she came downstairs at the summons of a footman, and she felt herself exhale in relief. His coat was not quite pink or quite a mulberry color. It was halfway between the two. She remembered Edgar's saying that some of the fops of the *ton* liked to appear as if they had been poured into their coats. Cora was reminded of those words as she looked at Lord Francis. And his pantaloons too. They were of fine gray leather and molded his form so tightly that she might have blushed if he had been anyone else. Certainly she was aware of splendid calf muscles—she had had the proof of their strength last evening when he had carried her all the way to the carriage. His Hessian boots were so glossy that she was convinced that if she bent over them she would be able to make sure that the bow of her hat was tied at just the right angle beneath her chin. And his neckcloth was as elaborately tied as the one he had worn last night. He carried his hat and whip in one hand.

His appearance, elegant and gorgeous, quite reassured her and made her joy complete. But the crowning glory was the high-perch phaeton into which he lifted her when he had escorted her outside. It was a splendid confection of a vehicle, all show and lack of practicality. It was painted a bright blue and yellow. How fortunate, she thought, that she had dressed to match it. Two almost identical chestnuts were harnessed to it.

"This," she said later, as they were turning into the park, "is surely the most exciting afternoon of my life." And then she turned her head in order to smile apologetically at him. "I am not to enthuse, am I? Lady Elizabeth has constantly to remind me of that. But no matter since it is only to you. I shall behave myself when we are among the crowds, I promise." She opened her parasol since she had just become aware that they were very close to being among the crowds, and gave it a vigorous twirl above her head.

"Just so," Lord Francis said, looking at her. "But why young ladies feel obliged to squash the natural exuberance of their spirits in order to appear *tonnish* escapes my understanding at the present moment."

"I believe it appears gauche," Cora said. "Or *rustic*. That is what Elizabeth says anyway. Oh, my!" Such a crash of vehicles and riders and walkers it had been impossible to imagine though she had been told about it. No one could possibly be out for the sole purpose of a drive or a ride. Or even a walk.

"It would be far more sensible," she said to Lord Francis, "for everyone to leave their carriages and horses at the gate and merely stroll here. It is obvious that everyone has come here to talk."

"Ah," he said, "but how would we impress one another, Miss Downes, if we could not be outdoing one another in the splendor of our carriages and the superiority of our cattle? We can observe one another's clothes and persons at any ball or concert. What would the day have to offer of novelty?"

"How absurd," she said.

"Quite so," he said agreeably. "Absurdity is amusing, Miss Downes. Endlessly entertaining."

She wondered if he ever dressed out of any sense of the absurd and decided that he probably did not. But there was no more time for private reflection or even for conversation tête-à-tête. They were among the throng and they were not being ignored.

Whatever he might be, Lord Francis was no outcast with the *ton*, Cora discovered now even if she had not noticed it the evening before. Gentlemen hailed him and very often stopped to exchange civilities. Ladies, both old and young, had their carriages stopped in order to converse with him. Old and young tittered at his practiced and smoothly flattering gallantries. Some, particularly the older ladies, gave as good as they received. Cora guessed that ladies felt it safe to flirt with someone like Lord Francis.

But it soon became obvious to her that she herself was not invisible. Several people merely nodded pleasantly to her when Lord Francis presented them to her and then continued their remarks to him. But far more people seemed to have approached him with the intention of making her acquaintance and commending her on the jolly good show of her heroism in the little Henry incident. Two of the gentlemen she had danced with last evening—Mr. Corsham and Mr. Pandry—rode up beside her and engaged her in conversation while Lord Francis chatted with other people. Mr. Corsham remarked with a smirk that now he knew the identity of the gentleman with whom she had told him earlier she was engaged to drive, he would likely slap a glove in the face of Lord Francis the next time he saw him alone. Mr. Pandry asked her if she was to attend a certain ball next week and hoped she would reserve a set for him.

It was all very flattering. So were the particular attentions of two or three gentlemen to whom Lord Francis presented her as the heroine they must have heard of by now

and daughter of the Mr. Downes who had recently purchased and rebuilt Mobley Abbey near Bristol. Cora had
not even realized that Lord Francis knew those facts himself.

She was enjoying herself immensely.

But as usually happened, her mind wandered from the
here and now after some time. There were just too many
people at whom to smile and nod, too many names to remember, and too many faces to which to have to attach
those names in the future. She withdrew a little into herself,
became more of a spectator than a participant.

It was very clear that a number of people had come to the
park neither to take the air nor to converse. Some had come
merely to be seen and admired. The lady in pink, for example, who was walking her dogs, four tiny poodles, each on
the end of a different-colored silk leash. An insignificant
little maid moved along slightly behind her mistress. The
pink plumes in the lady's pink bonnet must be at least four
feet high, Cora thought. Her mind was occasionally prone
to exaggerate. And she carried herself with great dignity, a
proud, half contemptuous smile on her lips. The dogs were
for picturesque effect, Cora decided. But poor little
things—it had not been the wisest idea in the world to bring
them into such a crush. They were in considerable danger
of being trodden upon.

And then there was the gentleman in green and buff, who
was riding a magnificent black horse, which was far too
spirited for the crowded circumstances. He was a very
proud and haughty gentleman too, Cora thought. He had a
decidedly prominent nose but no chin at all. He had a quite
fascinating profile.

They fancied each other, Cora suddenly realized. The
lady was lifting her chin and her bosom and was tugging on
the leashes entirely for the chinless gentleman's benefit,
and he was prancing on his black horse for hers.

How very, very amusing. If only Lord Francis were not
engaged in conversation with an elderly lady and gentleman who had finished congratulating her and were tackling

the weather with him, she would be able to point out the scene to him. He would be entertained by it, she was sure.

But as the two approached each other, Cora became aware of something else. The trotting poodles and the prancing black were soon going to be trying to occupy the exact same spot of land. It did not take a vivid imagination to guess which animals were going to have the worst of it. There were going to be a couple of squashed poodles at the very least.

"Oh," she said in great agitation just as Lord Francis and the elderly couple took their leave of each other and he turned to her. "Oh, dear. Oh, dear."

There was neither time to explain the situation to him nor to shout out a warning, though she did the latter anyway. But at the same moment she hurled herself over the side of Lord Francis's high-perch phaeton.

During what had remained of the morning after his ride and his nonbreakfast, Lord Francis had sat in White's, reading the papers and conversing with various acquaintances. Actually he had maneuvered the latter activity so that he spoke with the gentlemen he wished to speak with. It had not been difficult to steer the conversation to last evening's ball and the new arrivals—any new faces were to be remarked upon this late in the Season. And it had not been difficult to focus upon Miss Downes and her heroic deed. It had been, as Walter Parker remarked, "a demned fine show."

And it had not been difficult to drop the subtlest of hints about the father and Mobley Abbey and the splendid job he appeared to have done in restoring it to modern grandeur. It went without saying that the man must be enormously wealthy. It also went without saying that the daughter's dowry would in all probability be more than substantial.

Now Lord Francis had the satisfaction of seeing his hints begin to bear fruit. A number of the gentlemen he had spoken with this morning happened to be riding in the park this afternoon—he had, of course, mentioned the fact that he was to drive Miss Downes there at the fashionable hour—

and deemed it a courtesy to stop to pay their respects to him and their gallantries to his companion.

Being a matchmaker, he was discovering, was providing definite amusement. And God knew, he was desperately in need of amusement.

She was looking really quite handsome this afternoon in yellow and pale blue. The vivid colors suited her far better than last night's virginal white. And her smiles, her sparkling eyes, and her general exuberance were a little less conspicuous in the outdoors. Not that he had any particular objection to them anywhere.

But he sensed her tiring after a while. She was a little quieter, a little more withdrawn. He supposed all this must be somewhat bewildering to a young lady who had not been brought up to it. He would maneuver his phaeton out of the crowds after this particular conversation, he thought—she had not participated in it beyond nodding and smiling in acknowledgment of the usual congratulations on her heroic deed. He would drive her through a quieter part of the park and then take her home. The afternoon had done well for her. He had hopes that with very little more effort today's admirers would turn into tomorrow's partners and escorts and the day after tomorrow's suitors—well, one or two of them anyway. Even one would be enough—only one of them could marry her, after all.

He would keep an eye out, of course, to make sure that no mere fortune hunter bore her off. Not that it was his responsibility to see to any such thing. There were the duchess and Bridgwater to look to her interests, not to mention her father and brother. Lord Francis had no doubt that the father at least was a shrewd judge of a man's character and motives.

He turned to her, his mouth opening to suggest that they move on. But several things happened in such close succession that he was never sure afterward if his mouth had been left hanging open to the breeze or if it had snapped shut. Her gaze was fixed on a point a little to one side, away from him, her whole manner was agitated, she muttered, "Oh, dear. Oh, dear," and with a shriek, she hurled herself over the side of his high-perch phaeton. To her certain death it seemed. Only perhaps a fraction of a second passed before he went after her, abandoning his horses to their own devices, but in that split second he saw several things. He saw Lady Kellington walking her poodles and issuing come-hither glances to Lord Lanting, who was preening himself before her on his giant black and proceeding to come hither. He knew that the dogs were too accustomed to this sort of scene to be in any danger from the horse's hooves and that the horse was too well trained to trample them anyway.

He also saw that Miss Cora Downes, if she survived the descent from his phaeton, would be in considerable danger from those hooves.

He jumped.

Those close enough to observe what followed—and there were many—could not have found more thrilling entertainment even at Astley's, Lord Francis thought ruefully later, when he was at liberty to think. Lady Kellington's poodles yapped with sudden panic at the descent of a shrieking whirlwind into their ranks and tried to break loose in as many directions as there were dogs. The lady clung on to their leashes and screamed. Lord Lanting's black whinnied and reared. His lordship roared but displayed superb horsemanship in not being ignominiously tossed into the crowd. Cora Downes shrieked—or rather, she continued to shriek—and grabbed for poodles before the horse could plant all four feet back on earth, or on whatever happened to be between them and earth. Somehow she succeeded in gathering two of them under one arm and one under the other. Almost at the same moment Lord Francis himself, muttering what he hoped later had not been either obscenities or blasphemies, launched himself at her, grabbed her about the waist, spun her away from those dangerously flailing hooves, and landed heavily on the grass with her and an indeterminate number of poodles beneath him and colored leashes twined all about him.

Lord Francis's first sane thought since he had sat perched up in his phaeton was of the spectacle they were offering to the avidly curious eyes of the *ton*. To do him justice, it was of Cora he thought first. Before he rolled off her and released the furiously barking dogs, he checked hastily to make sure that her dress was decently down about her legs. It was.

But moving off was not simply a matter of rolling to one side. They were both entangled in leashes, and the dog that had remained free was now rushing in wild circles about its fallen comrades, making the tangle worse.

"The devil," Lord Francis muttered, struggling free with a superhuman effort.

Miss Cora Downes was laughing. "Ouch!" she said. "Are there supposed to be two suns up there? Are the dogs all safe?" Her face, he saw, was flushed. Her eyes were dazed—or rather her *eye*. Her hat had swiveled about her head so that it covered one side of her face. One of her short, puffed sleeves had almost entirely parted company with the rest of her dress. Her bosom, decently covered, fortunately, was heaving.

"Lie still," he commanded her, sitting up and preparing to take inventory of his own various parts and garments. She must be suffering from a concussion.

But suddenly reality rushed in with considerable noise and motion. The poodles were all free, though they were hopelessly tangled together, and barking. Lady Kellington was on her knees in the midst of them, trying to hug them all at once while they tried all at once to lick her face. Lord Lanting was on his feet just behind her, a firm hand on the bridle of his horse, which was still snorting and rolling its eyes. A whole army of other people was gathered about.

"My darlings, my darlings," Lady Kellington was crooning. "You are all safe. You might all have been killed."

"I say, Lucy," Lord Lanting said. "I say, I am most awfully sorry, old girl. I do not know what got into Jet. He don't usually behave like that."

Lord Francis could have given him an idea or two on what had got into the black—she was currently lying face up on the grass, gazing at two suns through one eye.

But she was not to remain neglected for long. Lady

Kellington gently pushed away her poodles, having assured herself that they were all not only alive, but unharmed, and turned to grasp one of Cora's hands in both of her own.

"Oh, my dear," she said. "My dear, you have saved the lives of my darlings. How will I ever be able to thank you?" And she raised Cora's hand to her face in order to wash it with her tears.

"Oh, I say," Lord Lanting added, his eyes turning in Cora's direction, "a splendid act of courage, m'dear."

"You might have killed yourself," Lady Kellington said through her tears.

The crowd acted like a Greek chorus. There were mutterings and murmurings and a few quite distinct voices. All of them were singing the same tune. All of them were chanting the praises of Miss Cora Downes, who had saved the lives of Lady Kellington's poodles at considerable risk to her own life.

The leather of his new pantaloons was scuffed beyond repair, Lord Francis noticed with deep regret. So was one of his boots. One side and one sleeve of his coat were covered with dust. His white shirt cuff was stained green from the grass. So, he noticed with a grimace when he turned his arm, was the elbow of his coat. His hat was nowhere in sight.

"By Gad," someone said, "she is Miss Downes. The Duchess of Bridgwater's protégée. She was at Lady Markley's last evening."

"The one who saved Bridgwater's nephew by jumping into the river in Bath after him." Someone else had taken up the chorus.

"The heroine!" It was almost a communal whisper of awe.

Chapter 5

❦

It was a little mortifying to emerge from a daze to find
oneself lying prostrate on the grass verge in Rotten Row
in Hyde Park, gazing up at a blue sky that was rimmed
about like a fluted picture frame by the concerned faces of
half the *ton*. It was even more mortifying to realize that one
reason for the distortion of one's vision was the fact that
one's new hat, which one had thought looked very fetching
earlier in the afternoon, was now being worn sideways.

Cora dared not look down to observe the state of her
dress.

She realized then what was being said. They were calling
her a heroine—again. Because she had saved a poodle or
two from extinction beneath a horse's hoof.

She laughed.

"If you please," someone said firmly as the picture frame
moved in closer to the center of the sky, "it would be wiser
to give her air. She is winded, I do believe, and perhaps
suffering from a concussion as well."

Lord Francis Kneller's voice. She felt a rush of gladness
when she recalled that it was with him she had been driving. She would have felt horribly embarrassed if it had been
any other gentleman. Of course, she was feeling horribly
embarrassed anyway. She laughed again.

Someone was weeping all over her hand. The lady in
pink—the owner of the poodles. The poodles! Were they
all safe? But they must be if she was being hailed as a hero-

ine. *Had* she been heroic this time? She rather thought she had.

And then Lord Francis was bending over her. His hair looked adorably rumpled. His coat was dusty. His elbow was grass-stained. Oh, dear, he would be dreadfully upset over that. The coat really was a gorgeous shade of pink.

"Miss Downes," he said, "are you all right?"

"Oh, perfectly," she said and sat up, lifting her arms at the same moment to straighten her hat and try to inject a little decorum into the scene. Her father, had he been present, would have been tossing his eyes skyward. Edgar would have been calling her a clumsy booby or something lowering to that effect. Sky and picture frame did a complete spin before slowing down. "Oops," she added.

There were murmurings of concern from the picture frame.

Lord Francis helped her to her feet and even brushed some grass from her dress. There was a swell of sound, almost like a cheer, from the gathered *ton*—presumably in congratulation over the fact that she was upright.

"No, no," Lord Francis was saying, "I shall convey Miss Downes home myself. If someone would just hold my horses' heads for a moment."

She leaned heavily against his arm—it was such a nicely solid arm—while the world about her made up its mind whether to stop completely or swing around again. She was not quite sure afterward how she got back up into the high seat of his phaeton. She rather believed that he climbed up there with her in his arms, though how that could have been accomplished was beyond her comprehension. Certain it was that he drove away—magically a clear path, lined with spectators, opened for him—with her fitted tightly against his side, one of his arms about her to prevent her from toppling either forward or sideways, something she might well have done.

Something was bothering her—apart from the painful throbbing at the back of her head. She had not summoned up the courage to feel back there yet, but she suspected that she must have a goose egg sitting on the back of her skull. She frowned.

"You saved me," she said. "It was wonderfully courageous of you. You might have got hurt."

He looked down at her—somehow her head, hat and all, was nestled on his shoulder. "Miss Downes," he said dryly, "you render me speechless."

But that was not what had been really bothering her. She frowned again. "Lord Francis," she said, "were the dogs *really* in danger?"

Edgar would not have waited to be asked—he had not done so after the incident of little Henry. But then Edgar assumed all the annoying privileges of an older brother. Lord Francis Kneller was far more polite.

He did not answer for a while. During that while Cora realized how shockingly improper it was to be riding in the streets of London like this. She felt very thankful yet again that it was only Lord Francis. His arm and his shoulder really did feel remarkably comforting.

"The dogs certainly did panic," he said at last. "As did the horse. Someone or some creature might definitely have come to harm. I can only wish that I had been the one to land on the bottom so that it would have been my head that was banged. I wonder how I am to explain to her grace that you came to harm while under my protection."

"Oh," she said, trying to sit up and changing her mind hastily, "but you saved me from much worse harm, as I shall be sure to explain. There would have been no danger, would there, if I had not jumped down. The dogs would not have panicked and neither would the horse." It was a horrid admission to make even to herself. Honesty compelled her to admit it to him as well.

Surprisingly he chuckled. "It is a debatable point," he said. "But it would be as well to keep that fact between the two of us, Miss Downes. Your image as a heroine has swelled to twice its size this afternoon. That can do you no harm at all on the marriage mart."

"Oh," she said, mortified. "Does it push up my value?"

He chuckled again. He sounded genuinely amused, she

was relieved to find. He was not unduly annoyed with her, then.

"Let us just say," he said, "that it will do you no harm to be seen as heroic. And there is no doubt at all that your actions with regard to Bridgwater's nephew truly were."

Cora grimaced. "You should talk with my brother about that," she said.

He looked down at her again. His way of guiding his horses with just one hand was remarkably impressive, she thought.

"They were not?" he asked her.

"Edgar says that the child would have swum to the bank without my assistance," she said. "He says that I almost drowned him."

Lord Francis's voice sounded amused when he spoke, but he did not laugh again. "That was remarkably unhandsome of him," he said.

"Well," she said, "he *is* my brother, you know. Do you have brothers or sisters, Lord Francis?" Then she remembered that he had a brother who was a duke.

"One brother and two sisters," he said. "Two of them older than me. I know what that can be like. But let us not disallow your image as a heroine, Miss Downes. The *beau monde* is enormously cheered by it. We are a jaded lot, you know. We must constantly seek novelty and entertainment. A female heroine is irresistible."

"So we must tell lies?" she asked him doubtfully.

"Not at all," he said. "We need say nothing. There were a dozen witnesses to this afternoon's heroic act, Miss Downes, and a hundred more who will convince themselves that they were witnesses. They will describe what they have seen, and each new teller will embellish the story told by the one before. You will find that single-handedly you have saved four innocent and lovable poodles from certain death—not to mention having saved Lady Kellington from an irreparably broken heart."

"Oh," she said. But her thoughts were diverted. "Why does the road keep rushing up toward me when I can feel that you are holding me securely in place?"

"Close your eyes," he said, his arm tightening about her.

She did not even realize until she was inside the hall of the Duchess of Bridgwater's town house that she had allowed him to carry her there. This was becoming something of a habit—an unfortunate one for him. She wondered what soap or cologne he used. It smelled good. It was subtle. Almost manly. Well, she thought, to be fair she must admit that on anyone else she would not have thought of qualifying that judgment. And she really did not care that Lord Francis Kneller favored bright, foppish colors and elegant manners. She liked him just as he was.

Edgar would have scolded her without stopping for endangering other lives as well as her own and for acting so brainlessly. He would have done so even knowing that she had banged her head and was not feeling quite the thing.

"She has had a slight accident," Lord Francis was explaining to her grace. "I believe it is altogether possible that she has a lump on the back of her head that will need attention. If you will allow me, ma'am, I will carry her up to her bed."

"Soames." Her grace's voice was one of calm command. "You will send for Sir Calvin Pennard and ask him to attend me without delay, if you please."

Sir Calvin, Cora guessed, must be the duchess's physician.

"Follow me, Lord Francis," her grace said, still in the same tone of voice. "I hope there is a good explanation for what happened."

"I do believe you will hear explanations in every drawing room and ballroom in town for the next several days, ma'am," he said. "Miss Downes was injured in the performance of an act of extraordinary courage."

Cora looked once into his face and held her peace. She really was feeling very dizzy indeed. And she remembered now that her toes were still rather sore too.

Miss Cora Downes was confined to her room for two days following the incident in the park. Sir Calvin Pennard, the Duchess of Bridgwater's physician, had insisted upon it, mainly for the sake of her head, but partly too for the sake of her feet.

She was allowed no visitors during those two days. Her grace and Elizabeth and Jane kept her company. The only exceptions to the prohibition were the Duke of Bridgwater, who made his bow to her one afternoon, inquired after her health, and congratulated her on her act of bravery, and Lord Francis Kneller, who paid a courtesy call and was invited to Miss Downes's boudoir, where her grace's maid played chaperon.

"I feel so *silly*," Cora said, stretching out her hands to Lord Francis and forcing him to cross the room to her when he had intended merely to stand inside the door for a few minutes. It was true that she was fully dressed and that her hair was up, though in a looser, more luxuriant style than he had seen before, but she was reclining on a daybed and he found himself having to suppress improper thoughts. "I am *never* ill and *never* bedridden. How kind of you to call. And how tiresome you must find me."

He squeezed her hands, released them, and seated himself on a stool beside her. She spoke with utter candor and no noticeable intent to draw a disclaimer or a compliment from him.

"On the contrary," he said anyway. "I am honored that you have admitted me when so many have been turned away after presenting their cards, Miss Downes."

"Everyone is *so* kind," she said. "Especially when I was so foolish. I have even been sent *flowers*. Look at them. My room looks like a *garden*."

She spoke with an enthusiasm and an emphasis on certain key words that were not at all ladylike. Most ladies of his acquaintance would behave with wilting grace under circumstances like these. Cora Downes was clearly fretting from the inactivity.

"You are," he said, "a heroine, ma'am. Every gentleman in town wishes to make his bow to you. Every lady wishes to kiss your cheek."

"How absurd." She laughed, throwing back her head and showing her very white teeth and making no attempt whatsoever to reduce her amusement to a mere simper. "Lady Kellington has called twice and sent a servant three other times to inquire after me."

"Lady Kellington," he said, "is rumored to love her poodles more than she has ever loved any person, including her late husband and her four children."

"That is because dogs are invariably affectionate to their owners," she surprised him by saying. He had expected a reaction of shocked disbelief or of riotous amusement. "Sometimes when I want to wound Edgar—it is usually when he has been scolding me for something or other—I tell him that I love Papa's dogs more than I love him. He tells me that is because the dogs do not have enough brain power to recognize my shortcomings."

"Older brothers and sisters," Lord Francis said, wonderfully diverted, "are a pestilential breed."

"Yes, they are," she said. "But I miss Edgar. And Papa. I suggested to her grace this morning that she send me home as soon as I am deemed well enough to travel. I have been nothing but trouble and embarrassment to her. But she says I must stay until she finds me a husband. I think it will be an impossibility. No man who is a *gentleman* will want to marry *me*."

Lord Francis wondered if all young ladies who were not quite ladies discussed such matters freely with near strangers. But he would wager not. Miss Cora Downes was one of a kind, he suspected.

"I believe you will be surprised, then," he said. "Perhaps you should be warned, Miss Downes, that you are very much in fashion."

She fixed him with an intent stare. "In fashion?"

"Indeed yes," he said. It was quite true. He had expected it, especially as it was late in the Season and everyone was starved for novelty. But it had happened even more forcefully than he had anticipated. "Drawing room and ballroom and club conversations have centered about little else but you and your heroic deeds in the past two days. And it is a veritable mountain of cards that are piled on the table downstairs. I believe that when you finally go out, Miss

Downes, or even just downstairs, you will find yourself besieged."

She paled. "I *hate* being conspicuous," she said.

Which, in light of her behavior in the park a few afternoons before, was a rather comical thing to say. He did not laugh.

"I believe," he said, "that her grace's wishes for you may well be fulfilled quite soon. And your own too. I assume you do want a husband?"

"Oh, yes," she said. "But not one who wants me only because he thinks I am a heroine, or because Papa is wealthy. Not one who will remind me every day for the rest of my life that he has elevated me on the social scale. Only one who will like me and perhaps love me as well. And one I can feel affection for. And respect. And not an old man. Not one above—oh, thirty at the most. And not an old poker face. I would like someone who knows how to laugh, someone with some sense of the absurd. Life is frequently absurd, you know. Why are you chuckling? What have I said?"

"Nothing," he assured her. But he was enjoying himself. He had woken this morning feeling mortally depressed again and had realized that he had been waltzing with Samantha in his dreams and she had been smiling at him and telling him that she was with child. Only as he woke up had he realized that it was not his child. Oh, yes, life was frequently absurd. Much as he had admired Samantha for the last several years, he would never have expected to feel like a sick and lovelorn boy at her marrying someone else. "I imagine, Miss Downes, that you will have your choice of several candidates. You must make a check list and interview each one."

"You are making fun of me." She looked sharply at him and then went off into peals of laughter again. "Now what I should do is marry *you*." She held up a staying hand even as he felt a slight stirring of alarm, and laughed merrily once more. "But I will not. You are *Lord* Francis Kneller and your brother is a duke. You are far too high on the social scale for my comfort. Besides—" She blushed, bit her lip, and smiled.

He waited with raised eyebrows for the completion of the sentence, but it did not come.

"I am devastated by your rejection, ma'am," he said. He got to his feet. It was time he took his leave. "I shall go elsewhere to nurse my broken heart."

"Oh, must you leave?" She looked suddenly wistful, but she smiled again. "Yes, I suppose you must. It was very kind of you to come and to take me driving the other afternoon—I did not have a chance to thank you at the time. And to dance with me that first evening. You are a very kind gentleman. I believe you must be a close friend of the Duke of Bridgwater and are obliging him. But you have made me happy too. Good afternoon, my lord." She offered her hand.

"It has been my pleasure," he said, bowing over it and even lifting it to his lips.

He liked her, he thought as he was descending the stairs a minute later and taking his hat and cane from her grace's butler. She interested him and amused him. He really must see to it that she was well married. There would be no lack of suitors. Already several would-be husbands were sounding him out on the subject of Miss Cora Downes and her prospects—and he was not even a relative or guardian. He had learned from Bridgwater at White's this morning that there were others. Both the duke and his mother had been approached by several interested parties.

She could be betrothed and married within the month if she chose to be. He would miss her—a strange thought when he had known her but a few days. But she was the only person he had found since the marriage of the Marquess and Marchioness of Carew who could take his mind off his own personal depression and even make him laugh.

It was strange, he thought as he wandered along the street—he had not brought a carriage with him. Different as the two women were—he would be hard put to it to discover one point of likeness between Samantha and Cora Downes—there was a certain similarity in his relationship with them. He and Samantha had teased each other a great deal. He had teased her earlier this year about being in her seventh Season. He had told her that if she was unmarried at the end of it, she must don caps and retire into spinsterhood. She had teased him about his appearance. He had dressed partly to amuse Samantha, though not entirely, he had to admit. He hated to swing to soberness in gentlemen's dress and fought the trend. He dressed to please himself.

Perhaps the reason Samantha had never taken his courtship or even his marriage offers seriously was that she did not take *him* seriously. A man who always teased and joked could be seen as a man without depths of feeling or character, he supposed. He could remember how alarmed Samantha had been at his first angry reaction to her telling him about her betrothal. And so he had retracted his words, assuring her with a smile that he had been merely trying to make her feel bad—and had succeeded.

Cora Downes did not take him seriously either. Why else would she have announced so boldly that she should marry *him?* Would she have said that to any other man in this world? And what was that "Besides—" that would keep her from marrying him? Besides he was a shallow man who could never be taken seriously?

It was as well, of course, that Cora Downes felt that way. He wanted no more than a teasing relationship with her and she wanted no more with him—her ambitions were very modest. She had no aspirations to the aristocracy in her search for a husband.

But it was a disturbing insight into himself he had just had, for all that. Was he so cleverly masked that no one could see beyond the mask? Maybe that was as well too. Bridgwater had certainly known his feelings for Samantha—had even warned him not to wear them on his sleeve. But he doubted anyone else had known, and he doubted that even Bridgwater realized that he was still pining. It would not do at all for anyone to know how constantly he had loved a woman who had spurned him and recently married a man she had not even met six months ago.

The very thought of anyone knowing made him shudder.

It was all unbelievably true, what Lord Francis had warned her about. She was in fashion, as he had phrased it. In her language that soon came to mean that she was very much on display.

Everyone wished to gawk at her. It was not a polite word to use of the *ton,* but Cora was learning something about the *ton.* Its members were very much like ordinary people except that they couched their behavior in somewhat greater elegance. Everyone gawked. And everyone wished to pay their respects to her and to congratulate her.

The story of the Hyde Park incident had crystallized by the time she made her appearance again. Lord Lanting, it appeared, had lost control of his mount, a fierce, unmanageable beast, which could—and would—squash a dozen poodles or half a dozen maidens underhoof without a qualm. Had not the animal been at Waterloo and learned its ferocity there? Lord Lanting had done his valiant best, poor man, but he had lost control.

Lady Kellington's poodles had been for it. There was no doubt in anyone's mind that there would not have been a single survivor if events had been left to take their natural course. Lady Kellington herself had already foreseen their imminent demise and had been in the hysterical stage of a first-class fit of the vapors. The scene had been set for a spectacular disaster.

Enter Miss Cora Downes, heroine of the Bath incident involving that poor dear infant, Lord George Munro's son, the Duke of Bridgwater's nephew. Miss Cora Downes, with no thought for her own life and safety, had launched herself from the high perch of Lord Francis Kneller's phaeton— she might easily have broken both ankles, not to mention her neck in the process—and had thrown herself between the beast's flashing hooves and the innocent, shivering dogs and plucked them to safety in the nick of time.

Miss Cora Downes had survived the ordeal. But only just. Sir Clayton Pennard, the Duchess of Bridgwater's personal physician, had pronounced the young lady in grave danger. Only his skill and the devoted care of her grace and the indomitable will of the heroine herself had effected her miraculously speedy recovery.

A few times Cora tried to remind her admirers that it was Lord Francis who had really saved her life and that of a few of the dogs—just as she had tried to remind other people in Bath that it was her brother who had saved both her and little Henry. But Lord Francis, apart from being the owner of the phaeton, had no part in this story.

The duchess's town house was besieged with callers, just as Lord Francis had predicted. Cora would have felt even more embarrassed about it than she did if Elizabeth had not been off, out with her future in-laws a great deal of the time, and Jane had not had steady calls from the Earl of Greenwald, her favored suitor. Lady Kellington whisked Cora off two days in a row, for a picnic the first day and to dinner and the theater on the second. At her first ball after the incident, Cora might have filled her card up twice over and even more, so eager were gentlemen to dance with her. Fortunately, by the time the Duke of Bridgwater arrived and made his bow to his mother, there were no sets left to grant him, though he did ask her. Less fortunately, there were none to grant Lord Francis either. He grinned and winked at her when she told him so.

"That is such a lovely shade of lemon," she said kindly, referring to his coat. Her suspicions of an earlier occasion seemed to be correct. The handle of the quizzing glass he wore on a ribbon this evening was studded with topazes. He wore a topaz ring on one finger of his right hand.

"My dear Miss Downes," he said, fingering his glass and pursing his lips, "as usual you render me speechless. Now I may not compliment you on your gown without inducing you to say *'Touché'* in response."

Her grace pronounced the evening a marked success, and indeed Cora agreed. She had not missed any sets apart from the two waltzes—though late in the evening she had been brought the exciting news that she had been approved and might waltz to her heart's content at all future balls. And at the end of the evening, even though she was weary and footsore, there was not a single blister to be nursed.

Her grace was even more gratified the next morning when Mr. Bentley called privately on her and asked her to whom he must make application for the heroine's hand. Her grace replied that perhaps he should speak first with Miss Downes herself since she was of age. Cora, in the presence of her grace, refused Mr. Bentley—she had never been more surprised in her life—which the duchess said afterward was the right and proper thing to do since she certainly did not need to accept the very first offer she received. There might seem to be some desperation in such overeagerness. But it was extremely satisfying to know that Cora's matrimonial prospects were very bright indeed. Mr. Bentley was the third son of a baronet.

Cora was pleased. Certainly she had had no chance to be bored since she had emerged from her room with a lumpless head and rejuvenated toes—and larger slippers. And certainly too her dream of seeing London and participating in some of its most dazzling social events had come true. She had danced and danced at her second ball and enjoyed every moment of it. Some of the gentlemen she had met—even apart from Mr. Bentley—seemed interested in her as a person and were not at all daunted by the fact that her father was a merchant and her brother a lawyer.

She was very pleased indeed. She wrote and told her papa so.

And yet part of her was unaccountably lonely. She kept remembering telling Lord Francis Kneller what kind of husband she would like. She had never put it into words before, but she had spoken the truth to him. And she kept remembering telling him as a joke—which, of course, he had taken in good part—that she ought to marry him. And she kept thinking what a shame it was that he was quite disqualified as a prospective suitor. For the reason she had given him and for the reason she had only just stopped herself in time from giving.

How could one tell a gentleman—even such a kindly and good-natured gentleman as Lord Francis—that one could not marry him because he was not a masculine man? The very thought that she had almost said it aloud could turn her hot and cold at the same time.

She did not mind that fact about him. She really had admired his lemon satin coat. And she admired him for not being hypocritical, for dressing the way he wished to dress.

Now if only she could find all his other qualities in an eligible gentleman. Especially his ability to laugh.

She missed him, she thought when she had been back out in Society for a few days and had spoken with him only that once at the ball. But how absurd it was to think of missing someone one had met only three times before that.

It was her papa and Edgar she really missed, she decided. And her life with them—where she belonged.

But how ungrateful she was to think thus!

Chapter 6

⁓

B y the end of the morning Cora had decided that she was not going to marry a gentleman.

The duchess was writing letters in her private sitting room. Lady Elizabeth had taken the carriage to Lord Fuller's on Grosvenor Square to assist Lady Fuller in the final plans for her ball—one of the last the Season would have to offer. Lady Jane had made a secret assignation to meet the Earl of Greenwald quite accidentally either in the park during a morning walk or at the library, depending on the weather. It really was not an *assignation*, Jane assured Cora, flushing with guilt. It was more that he had said that he *might* ride in the park if the weather was fine and she had commented on the strange coincidence that she might walk there—if the weather was fine. Presumably they had made similar commitments to the library if the weather was *not* fine.

And so Cora had agreed to accompany Jane. Indeed, it was essential to the plan that she do so. Jane could not possibly go alone to the park, even if a maid trailed along behind her as she would do anyway if the two of them went.

Cora never particularly enjoyed walking alone with Jane although she was excessively fond of her. Jane was small and dainty and pretty and always behaved with perfect decorum—except perhaps when she made almost-assignations with earls who had not yet made any formal offers for her.

"Mama would lecture me for a month without pause if she thought I had arranged to meet his lordship in the park," Jane herself confessed. "Alistair would not need to lecture. He would merely have to look at me in a certain way and I would wither up and die. But of course I have made no such arrangement. If he happens to be riding in the park and I happen to be walking there and we happen to meet and stop to exchange civilities, that cannot be deemed an arranged meeting, can it?"

Cora was not quite sure what all the fuss was about. But she did know that Jane fancied herself in love and as a result had departed ever so slightly from strict propriety. The fact cheered Cora a little. But she still disliked walking out alone with Jane. She felt so very large and clumsy beside her. She always had to reduce her stride to about half its usual span and she always had to resist the urge to droop her shoulders in order to look shorter and less conspicuous. Miss Graham had told her she must never do that. Apart from the intrinsic virtue of good posture was the fact that a tall person who hunched over only succeeded in making herself appear taller and more conspicuous.

And so they walked in the park side by side, their maid a little distance behind them, and Cora soon forgot about the awkwardness of her person in her enjoyment of the morning. The sun was shining and the air promised heat later on. But this morning it was only comfortably warm with a stiff breeze to fan the face and make one imagine that one was almost in the country.

It was the perfect morning for a quiet walk. Of course, sooner or later the Earl of Greenwald would ride by and pause for a chat, but apart from that there were peace and a cozy chat with Jane to be enjoyed. The park was always pleasantly empty and quiet during the mornings.

And then Mr. Parker rode toward them—for one moment Jane thought he was the earl and had almost visible heart palpitations. Mr. Parker paused when he came up to them, inclined his head and touched his hat, reminded them that it was a fine day, and then invited himself to dismount and walk a little way with them since indeed it was such a fine day.

And then Mr. Pandry and Mr. Johnson appeared, walking briskly together, also in the opposite direction from that taken by the ladies. They too paused with the usual gallantries, decided that it was far too fine a day to hurry anywhere, and turned to stroll with the ladies and Mr. Parker.

Before their walk was half an hour old, they had gathered no fewer than eight fellow strollers and enjoyers of the weather—all male and all congratulating themselves with jocular good humor on their good fortune in being able to take a turn about the park with the heroine—and with Lady Jane Munro, of course.

All of them had either danced with her or applied to dance with her the evening before, Cora noted. Several of them had called upon her grace since she had emerged from her sick chamber. A few of them had sent bouquets or posies. One of them had kissed her hand last evening after she had danced a minuet with him. A few of them were handsome. Most of them were taller than she, and even one who was not was on an exact level with her when he wore riding boots. All of them were gentlemen. One of them was heir to a baronet—he had informed her of that last evening. Three of them had been presented to her by the duchess, four by the duke, and one by Lord Francis Kneller.

This, Cora supposed, giving her parasol a twirl, was what success felt like. She knew beyond a doubt that all these gentlemen were interested in her, even though all of them were scrupulous about dividing their attentions between her and Jane. For one thing, none of them were titled gentlemen. They had been presented to her because they were possible matches for her. None of them would be allowed within a mile of Jane as a suitor. But even apart from that practical fact, Cora knew with her woman's intuition that their interest was all in her.

Eight gentlemen—*gentlemen!*—strolled in the park when they might be off elsewhere about their more congenial masculine pursuits. Eight gentlemen hung on her every word, laughed at her every sally into wit, jostled with one

another to be closest to her—though all were well-bred
enough to keep a proper distance, of course. Eight gentlemen were giving serious consideration to making her their
wife—subject to her acceptance. It was a good feeling.

It was success.

And it would be hasty success. The Season was almost
over. There was no time for a leisurely courtship. She
would receive a few more marriage offers before she returned to Bristol, she knew. Mr. Bentley already had offered—and had been refused. She had panicked when it
came to the point though she had no possible objection to
him beyond the fact that he must be at least three inches
shorter than she was—it might be four, but she could
hardly ask him to stand back to back with her while someone measured merely to satisfy her curiosity.

She could be a married lady—with the key word being
lady—before Christmas. Papa would be proud of her.
Edgar would nod his approval. Her children would be assured a place in society. She would be able to sponsor
Edgar's children. Not that they would need sponsorship—if
he ever married and had them, that was. Edgar had been to
good schools and he was successful and wealthy in his own
right apart from being Papa's heir, and he was very gentlemanly. Besides, times were beginning to change, as Papa
always said.

Cora had been woolgathering. At the same time she had
had her arm linked with Jane's and had been occasionally
patting her hand. Eight gentlemen and no sign of the very
one they had come here to run into accidentally on purpose.
But she felt Jane brighten suddenly, and sure enough, the
Earl of Greenwald himself was cantering along the green,
looking very dashing in clothes only Weston could have
made. Even Cora was beginning to recognize the excel-
lence of his tailoring.

The earl looked somewhat taken aback when he spotted
the two ladies in the midst of a throng of gentlemen. One of
those ladies—Jane—was busily conversing with one of the
gentlemen. Cora raised a hand and waved to him, smiling

gaily. Only then did Jane look up and appear surprised and prettily confused to see his lordship.

His lordship joined the parade.

Her grace's maid paced determinedly behind, though what she would have done if the gentlemen had all decided to pounce en masse on her two charges was not at all clear, especially to her own mind.

And then something happened to cause mass diversion and mass entertainment. A series of shrieks turned everyone's attention ahead along the way. But the immediate fear that someone was in distress was put to flight when it was seen that the screamer was a small hatless child who was chasing after his missing hat. The hat itself, a splendid confection in blue and white with ribbon streamers—all of which matched his outfit—was bowling merrily along in the breeze, pausing only long enough on the grass for the child to have it within a fingertip of his grasp before dancing gaily off again. A buxom woman—apparently the child's nurse—was puffing along behind him, alternately urging him to catch the hat when he was close to it, and pleading with him to let it go when it blew away again.

The scene afforded great merriment in Cora's group and inspired the gentlemen to elevated heights of wit.

Mr. Johnson whistled piercingly. "At it, lad!" he yelled.

The outfit and the hat were clearly new, Cora thought. She could imagine how very proud the boy must have felt this morning to don them and be taken into the park to display them for all to see. And now the hat with its gay streamers was in danger of being lost forever.

"Oh," she said, handing her parasol without thought to the nearest gentleman and grasping the sides of her skirt. "Oh, the poor child." And she was off and running.

The hat was bowling toward her group. But not quite in a straight line. If they stood still it would sail by yards away from them. The poor child would never catch it. And so Cora went streaking off to intercept the hat and left her admirers gawking after her and realizing too late that they had lost the chance to display superior gallantry in her eyes.

The trouble with wind, Cora thought, was that it never

blew quite steadily. One could never predict with certain accuracy where it would blow a certain object by a certain moment. She made several grabs for the hat when it came close and each time it hopped when she lunged or came to a halt when she hesitated or changed direction when she had it for sure. But it was close. She would have it in just a moment.

This was *fun*, she thought, beginning to laugh and beginning to realize what a spectacle she must be making of herself for those who were watching. Coordination had never been her strong point.

She was laughing helplessly and with imminent triumph as her hand descended finally for the kill—only to find that the hat lifted itself straight upward and the top of her bonnet almost collided with a pair of muscular legs clad in black leather pantaloons and boots designed to accentuate their muscularity.

"Dear me," Lord Francis Kneller said, "fun and games, Miss Downes?" He was holding the hat between a thumb and forefinger.

She laughed at him. "You wretch!" she said. "It was mine. I had run it to earth."

He raised his eyebrows and she realized several things. He was standing beside his horse, which had lowered its head to munch at the grass. On the other side of his horse was another with a silent rider on its back—the Duke of Bridgwater. From some distance away there was a chorus of gentlemen's cheers. And from a very short distance behind there were the pantings of a winded child.

"My hat," he cried with a gasp. "Give me my hat."

"Dear me." Lord Francis raised it higher. "What do you say, sir?"

"Give me it," the child insisted, glaring.

"Not," Lord Francis said, sounding infinitely bored, "until I hear the magic word, my young sir."

"You must call me *your grace*," the child said with haughty command.

The Duke of Bridgwater coughed delicately. Lord Francis's arm stayed where it was. Cora's jaw dropped and she stared at the little boy.

"Oh, your grace, your grace." The nurse had come puffing into earshot. "You must not run off like that. It is only a hat. Make your bow and thank the lady and gentlemen."

"He has my hat," the child said, pointing.

The nurse looked helpless.

The Duke of Bridgwater's voice sounded even more bored than Lord Francis's had just done. "Even dukes say thank you for favors rendered, my lad," he said. "Take it from someone who knows. Miss Downes has done you a service even without being aware of your illustrious identity. Lord Francis Kneller has retrieved your hat and will be only too delighted to return it to you. It would not fit his own head after all, would it? Let us hear it now."

"Who are you?" The child frowned up at him.

"A fellow duke," his grace said with a sigh. "Who happens to be much larger and far better mannered than you are, lad. And who happens too to possess a far heavier hand, which at this moment is itching to be put to use. What do you have to say?"

"Thank you, ma'am," the child said, looking at Cora and inclining his head to her. "Thank you, my lord." He bowed to Lord Francis, who tossed him the hat, which he caught.

His nurse behind him was bobbing curtsies indiscriminately in all directions. She took the child's hand and hurried him away.

Cora looked into Lord Francis's face and exploded into laughter, though she would rather not have done so with the duke close by. It had been such a ridiculous incident.

"Finchley's brat," his grace said by way of explanation. "The *late* Finchley, that is. He was not much of an improvement on his son, it pains me to say."

Lord Francis was pursing his lips and Cora realized that her bonnet must have blown back on her head and that doubtless her hair beneath it resembled a tangled bush. Sometimes she wished her hair did not grow quite so thickly, but she could not bring herself to have it cut even though short hair was all the crack. Papa thought short hair on women was scandalous.

Cora lifted her arms and did some hasty repairs.

"Another heroic deed, Miss Downes?" Lord Francis asked her. His riding coat was a glorious shade of puce.

"Chasing after a child's hat?" she said. "Hardly."

But his grace was clearing his throat again. "Miss Downes," he asked, "is that by any chance my *sister* in the center of the group of cheering gentlemen?"

To be quite fair, they were no longer cheering, though several of them were grinning and one of them was laughing out loud. And another of them cried "Bravo!" as she looked toward them.

"Oh, dear, yes," Cora said. "We were walking here, your grace, for the air and the peace and these gentlemen walked or rode by and were obliging enough to accompany us for a short distance."

His grace had a quizzing glass to his eye and was looking in some distaste at Jane and the nine gentlemen.

Lord Francis chuckled. "And your maid looks as if she is wondering how she may divide herself in two and chaperon both of you in order to keep all decent and proper," he said. "Do take my arm, Miss Downes. We will solve her problem by having you rejoin Lady Jane."

The duke stayed where he was, holding the reins of Lord Francis's horse as the two of them walked away.

"How glad I am that *you* arrived," Cora said gaily. "Without you—and his grace—I do believe the infant duke would have chewed me up and spat me out. I had sentimental images of a poor child who was about to lose his new hat and would cry all day and all night over its loss and never be able to afford one to replace it until next year at the very earliest."

"Doubtless," he said, "with so many witnesses, Miss Downes, you will find that this heroic act will be added to the other two in order to swell your fame."

She laughed. "Oh, what nonsense," she said. "If I had been a true lady, I would have fluttered my eyelashes at one of the gentlemen and he would have raced after the hat for me."

"And the incident would have lacked all sense of drama," he said. "You are to be at Lady Fuller's ball tomorrow evening?"

"Yes, indeed," she said. "Lady Elizabeth is betrothed to her brother, you know. Will you be there too, Lord Francis? Will you come early enough to engage a set with me this time? I was sorry last evening to find that there were none left for you."

"I have noticed a tendency in you to take words from my mouth, Miss Downes," he said. "Will you do me the honor of reserving a set for me tomorrow evening."

"Yes." She smiled dazzlingly at him. "Can you waltz? I have been *approved*, though I think it all a parcel of nonsense, and now may waltz myself."

"Then I will request that you write my name in your card next to the first waltz," he said.

They were almost up to the others, a fact that she found regretful. She would prefer a quiet stroll with Lord Francis. But a nasty thought struck her. "Oh, dear," she said, "I asked you to dance with me, did I not? That is something a lady *never* does. I gave you no choice but to be gallant, did I? And I dare not ask now if you really *wish* to dance with me because of course you would be gallant again and say that of course you do. I *do* apologize."

"Miss Downes," he said, "you do seem to have perfected the art of rendering me speechless."

"Well," she said, "no matter. It is only you and you do not mind if I occasionally ask you to dance with me, do you?"

He looked sidelong at her but did not reply. She found herself surrounded by laughing, admiring gentlemen, who congratulated her on her prompt action with regard to the young Duke of Finchley's hat.

"Well done, Miss Downes," Mr. Parker said.

"Jolly good show," Mr. Pandry agreed, returning her parasol to her.

"Miss Downes is tired," Lord Francis said, sounding

bored again and faintly haughty. "She has wisely decided to return home with Lady Jane. Good morning, gentlemen." He made them all a slight bow.

The Earl of Greenwald was the first to leave after glancing across to the Duke of Bridgwater, who was still sitting on his motionless horse some distance away, observing the scene. The others wandered away too, one by one or two by two.

"Ladies?" Lord Francis bowed to both Jane and Cora before glancing at their maid—who was looking remarkably relieved. He turned and walked back to the duke and his horse without looking behind him.

"Cora." Jane grasped her arm and hurried her back in the direction from which they had come. "Do you think Alistair believed there was an assignation?"

"Goodness," Cora said, "I hope not. Why would any woman in her right mind make assignations to meet so many gentlemen at the same time and in the same place?" She laughed. "Unless it were because there is safety in numbers. Do you like puce, Jane?"

"Lord Francis always looks elegant," Jane said. "Do you believe Alistair *knew*?"

"I doubt it." Cora patted her hand reassuringly.

They lapsed into silence, each thinking her own thoughts about the eventfulness of their morning walk.

Cora's thoughts were quite decisive and rather disturbing. She was not going to marry a gentleman, she realized. Gentlemen were silly. Remarkably so. Mr. Bentley had proposed marriage to her when he scarcely knew her merely because she was in fashion and wealthier than he was—or such was her educated guess. All eight gentlemen this morning had been silly, preening themselves before her in the hope of winning her favor. *Her*—Cora Downes! All of them had thought the distress of a little child comical— though, as it had turned out, he had deserved a little distress in his life. None of them would have given a thought to rescuing the wretched hat themselves. And yet all of them pretended deep admiration for her mad and undignified dash after it.

And these were supposed to be her prospective *husbands?* She would lose patience with any one of them within a week—within a *day.* She would rather marry any of the men she had rejected at home. At least all of them were worthy men. She would rather marry someone of her own kind. Someone with a little sense between his two ears. What nonsense all this business of heroism was. She should have told her grace so before all this started. But of course the prospect of coming to London—and while the Season was still in progress—had been irresistible.

If there had been any doubt left in her mind about her decision not to marry a gentleman, it was put to rout as soon as she thought of Lord Francis. She had been so very glad to see him. She would have given anything to have walked off with him and forgotten about all her foolish suitors. And she was already warmed to exuberance at the thought of dancing with him again tomorrow—*waltzing* with him. And yet she was not thinking of Lord Francis in terms of marriage. How absurd! She felt a deep friendship for him, almost an affection—well, perhaps *quite* an affection.

If she could have felt so much more gladness to meet and walk with a friend, then, when eight prospective husbands had been waiting to receive her back into their admiring midst, how could she possibly take them seriously?

She would a hundred times rather spend a morning or afternoon with Edgar than with any of them. She would a thousand times rather spend them with Lord Francis. Lord Francis could make her relax and laugh. She could say anything she wished to say to him without fear of shocking him. Lord Francis liked her, she believed. She preferred to be liked than to be admired. Especially when she suspected—when she *knew*—that the admiration was all feigned. How could anyone possibly admire *her?* She looked down at Jane's bonnet and felt her own largeness again.

No, she was not going to marry a gentleman. She was going to go home to Bristol when she decently could and keep house for Papa until her ideal man came along. If he ever did. If he did not, well, then, she would remain a spinster for the rest of her life. There were worse fates—she could be a wife to one of this morning's eight gentlemen.

She hoped Lord Francis waltzed well. She would wager he did. He did everything else so elegantly. She had only ever waltzed with a dancing master. She looked forward with such eagerness to twirling about a London ballroom in the arms of a gentleman with whom she could relax and perform the steps without tripping all over his feet—or her own.

She hummed a waltz tune and Jane smiled at her.

"I have promised the first waltz tomorrow evening to Lord Greenwald," she said. "Is he not the most handsome gentleman you have ever seen in your life, Cora?"

Cora was feeling quite cheerful enough to concede the point, though she believed that to any impartial observer Edgar would have the edge.

"Much obliged, Kneller," the Duke of Bridgwater said as they resumed their morning ride. "My mother made a huge mistake, I believe."

"You believe so?" Lord Francis looked at him.

"You must confess," his grace said, "that there was something perilously close to—vulgarity about that scene, Kneller."

Lord Francis chuckled. "I might have chosen the word *farce*," he said. "I am beginning to think that farcical situations find out Miss Downes wherever she goes in public. But she is not vulgar, Bridgwater. I must quarrel with you there."

His grace sighed. "No, I did not call her so," he said. "Strangely, one cannot help but like the girl. But I must admit to some uneasiness when I recall that Jane's chief companion here is a woman who vaults down from high-perch phaetons in the middle of Rotten Row in order to rescue a few miserable curs from a danger that was doubtless more apparent than real. And one who attracts admirers like bees to flowers and then leaves my sister in the midst of them while she dashes away, all bare ankles—and even one

knee, I swear, Kneller—in order to catch a runaway hat."
He sighed again, sounding considerably aggrieved.

Lord Francis could only continue to chuckle. "She
showed them a thing or two, though, Bridgwater," he said.
"Apart from the ankle and knee, I mean—I missed the
knee, unfortunately. The ankles were well worth looking at,
though. Come, you must admit that she is refreshing. I derive enormous amusement from her. And the admirers
should please you. It was for the purpose of finding her a
husband that her grace brought her here, was it not?"

"*A* husband," the duke said. "Singular, Kneller. I am beginning to lose sleep over the chit. She refused Bentley,
you know."

"Good," Lord Francis said without hesitation. "The man
has not enough humor with which to paint his little fingernail. He would not be amused by her at all. She can do better."

His grace sighed yet again. "I hope Greenwald comes to
the point this year," he said. "He had to leave in a hurry last
year—sick aunt or some such thing. I believe Jane has a
tendre for him. How thankful I am to have only two sisters.
Perhaps I will be able to concentrate on my own life once
they are both settled."

"Ah," Lord Francis said. "You are thinking about setting
up your nursery, Bridgwater?"

His grace frowned. "I had in mind other, ah, pleasures to
precede that particular one," he said, "though I suppose that
is inevitable too. One tires a little of mistresses, do you not
find?"

"I swore off them a year or more ago," Lord Francis said,
feeling his mood slip.

"And there is something to be said for nurseries, I suppose," his grace said. "I never thought to see Carew so
happy. Lady Carew is in a delicate way, so he informs me."

"Yes," Lord Francis said.

The duke looked at him sharply. "Oh, sorry old chap," he
said. "I was not thinking."

Lord Francis raised his eyebrows. "No harm done at all,"
he said with a wave of one hand. "Ancient history."

"Glad to hear it," the duke said. "You are going to Brighton for the summer? You have not attached yourself to Lady Augusta's court, I see. Maybe there will be some new beauties there."

But Lord Francis was too busy fighting a familiar drooping of the spirits to give the matter serious thought. He concentrated on images that would perhaps restore his humor. The image of Cora Downes, for example, her skirts hitched almost to her knees, dashing across the grass, flushed and windblown and laughing, in pursuit of a ridiculous little child's hat. Or the imagined picture of her waltzing with all her usual exuberance—in his arms.

Yes. He smiled. There was something about Cora Downes that would lift the lowest of spirits. Farce did follow her about. And a certain innocent charm. And of course she was deliciously lovely despite the bold face and tall stature. Perhaps because of them. And certainly because of the generous endowment of curves in all the right places.

"I have made no definite plans for the summer," he said.

Chapter 7

L ord Francis knew as soon as he arrived at Lady
  Fuller's ball that the Prince of Wales was expected.
  Not that one ever *expected* Prinny to honor any social
invitation even if it had been duly accepted. He went where
he wished to go, and no one, including the prince himself,
ever knew quite where he wanted to go until the last possible moment. But at least if he had accepted an invitation,
preparations were duly made.

It was clear that the Regent had accepted his invitation to
Lady Fuller's ball.

How did he know? Lord Francis asked himself rhetori-
cally. It was easy to know. Every window and French door
in the ballroom was tightly shut even though it was a warm
night outside. Already, although the dancing had not even
begun and all the guests had not arrived, the air was heavy
with the scents of flowers and perfumes. Soon, once the
dancing was in progress, it would be unbearable.

The Prince of Wales was terrified of drafts. Coveted invitations to Carlton House and the Pavilion at Brighton
were also dreaded invitations. It was a physical ordeal to be
a guest of Prinny or to be a guest at a function he had decided he might favor—if he was in the mood.

Lord Francis looked about him, acknowledged a few
friends and acquaintances with a nod or a discreet raising of
the hand, and located the Duchess of Bridgwater and her
party. Her grace, her usual elegant self in dark green, was

looking rather pleased with herself. As a chaperon she had good reason to be pleased. At least the largest gathering in the whole room was clustered about the two young ladies in her charge. Those about Cora Downes were almost exclusively gentlemen.

Lord Francis fingered his quizzing glass and then raised it to his eye.

"Yes, all is as it should be," the Duke of Bridgwater said from beside him a few moments later. "He has come up to scratch."

"Pandry?" Lord Francis frowned. The man was shorter than she was by a good two inches and he was already, at the age of five- or six-and-twenty, showing signs of portliness to come. Not to mention incipient baldness. All of which were no rational disqualifications for him as her husband. But Lord Francis hoped she would have better taste.

"Greenwald," his grace said. "He called on me this morning and we came to a very amicable settlement. It seems the same can be said for his visit to Jane this afternoon. She is—glowing, would you not agree, Kneller?"

Lord Francis changed the direction of his glass. Yes, indeed. Lady Jane Munro was talking with Greenwald's mother while the earl stood beside them, looking a comic mixture of smugness and sheepishness. Lady Jane herself was glowing, as Bridgwater had just said.

"My congratulations," Lord Francis said. "Two sisters and both well settled."

"Johnson called too this morning," the duke said. "For Miss Downes, of course. I had to direct him to my mother since I have no authority to negotiate on her behalf. It could well be a memorable day for my mother."

"Johnson?" Lord Francis's brows snapped together again. Johnson had a pea for a brain. And he was at least *three* inches shorter than she was.

"He has a very respectable property in Berkshire," the duke said, "and a tidy income. She will have done very well for herself if she has netted him. I had better pay my respects and kiss the bride-to-be yet again. Would you care to join me, Kneller?"

Lord Francis kissed the hand of Lady Jane a few moments later, shook the hand of Greenwald, and made his bow to the duchess. The betrothal had not been officially announced yet, but no secret was being made of it. The cluster of people about the couple was clear proof of that.

Cora Downes was in the center of a group of gentlemen—her usual court. His use of that word gave Lord Francis a mental jolt. Only the Incomparables of the *ton*'s beauties ever acquired courts that gathered about them wherever they went. Lady Augusta Haville was the queen of the Incomparables at this stage of the Season. Earlier she had been a mere shadow of a rival to Samantha Newman. He and Gabriel, Earl of Thornhill, had always teased Samantha about her court. And Gabe had teased *him* about his membership in that court—its most devoted member.

And now Cora Downes, the most unlikely candidate of all, had acquired her own court, all within two weeks. And in the midst of it she looked quite as comfortable and quite as animated as Samantha had ever looked.

The thought that he was after all attaching himself to someone else's court this year amused him as he wove his way to her side and smiled at her. Not that he was really a member, of course. Courting Miss Cora Downes was the very farthest thing from his mind. But he felt a certain protective instinct toward her, and some of the members of this court were not eligible suitors at all. There was one notorious fortune hunter among them, one inveterate gambler, and any number of fools. Of course, by now all his concerns might be academic. By now she might have betrothed herself to Johnson.

She tapped him on the arm with her fan and smiled brightly at him. "Pink," she said. "It is my very favorite shade of pink."

It was his favorite evening coat. Samantha had always teased him mercilessly about it as had Gabe when he stayed at Chalcote just after Christmas—because Samantha had been there too, visiting her cousin, Gabe's wife. But Miss Downes, he believed, though she smiled, was not teasing. It

seemed almost as if she were—being kind to him? He had
no chance to ponder the strange thought.

"Have you *heard?*" she asked him, leaning toward him
as if she thought thereby to give them some privacy. Her
cheeks had flushed and her eyes had grown anxious. "The
Prince of *Wales* may be coming here this evening."

"He does not always honor such commitments," he said
"I would not get my hopes up too high if I were you, Miss
Downes."

"My *hopes?*" Her voice was almost a squeak. "I shall die
if he comes, Lord Francis. I shall just *die.*"

But he was given no chance to deal with her fears himself. There was a chorus of protest and reassurance from
her court, though for a while she kept her eyes fixed on
him. How could a great *heroine*—who had saved the life of
a child by plunging into an icy river and the lives of four
poodles by diving beneath the flashing hooves of a fierce
horse—how could a heroine be afraid of meeting Prinny?
The group made much mirth out of the idea.

Lord Francis merely took her hand and patted it in avun-
cular fashion and asked her between the mirth and her de-
parture with Mr. Dalman for the opening set of country
dances if she had remembered to reserve the first waltz for
him.

Her white gown, which was almost obligatory evening
wear during her first Season in town, did not suit her, Lord
Francis thought, watching her broodingly while he tapped
his finger on the handle of his quizzing glass. She was far
too vivid a creature for white. And the evening coiffure, all
curls and ringlets piled high, did not suit either. It made her
look too girlish, an impression that was incompatible with
her height and her figure. He had preferred the looser style
she had worn in her boudoir. He rather believed he would
like it best unconfined down her back, but that was not a
practical idea. Neither was it a wise idea in a room that was
already quite stifling hot.

If she were an actress, he thought, or an opera singer—
she could easily be an opera singer with that bosom—she
would crowd a green room to overflowing every night,

even without the attendant heroism. And he rather thought he might be one of the men crowding it.

It was a thought that was not worthy of him at all. And certainly not fair to her. There had been not the slightest hint of loose behavior in her since he had known her. He was ashamed of himself. Damnation but he *liked* her. He had no wish to be also lusting after her. He had been without a woman for too long, he thought ruefully. It had seemed somehow disloyal to his broken heart to go seeking out a willing bedfellow for mere sexual satisfaction.

"Not dancing, old chap?" his grace asked. "Are you for the card room?"

"No, I think not," Lord Francis said. "I am engaged for the first waltz." She was twirling down the set with Dalman with such enthusiasm that if he should happen to release her hand by some chance, she would go spinning off into space—doubtless with a shriek. His lips twitched. He could almost wish it would happen. Farce had not touched upon her tonight yet.

The duke cleared his throat. "It would not do at all, you know," he said. "Fairhurst would have your head."

His brother? Lord Francis turned sharply and looked, startled, at his recently acquired friend. "*What* would not do?" he asked.

"She is a merchant's daughter," his grace said, picking at an invisible speck of lint on his sleeve. "And you are a duke's son and brother. Not that it is any of my concern, Kneller, but I have heard a few murmurings. And I *was* the one who asked you to take notice of the girl and help bring her into fashion."

Lord Francis was not normally given to extremes of emotion. Perhaps that was why he was having such difficulty coping with an unexpectedly broken heart. But he felt a sudden blazing of anger.

"A few murmurings," he said, his voice as icy as his heart was fiery. "My brother would have my head. It seems to me, Bridgwater, that you do your fair share of being your brother's keeper. Except that you are not my brother or even any kin of mine."

The duke took a snuffbox from a pocket, snapped the lid open, seemed to decide that the taking of snuff in a ballroom was not quite the thing, closed the lid, and put the box away again.

Bridgwater had advised him not to wear his heart on his sleeve over Samantha, Lord Francis remembered, still steaming. And now he was advising him against lusting after a merchant's daughter. God damn it all to hell! Bridgwater had been a mere passing acquaintance until a few weeks ago, before his friend, that damned Carew, decided to play Romeo to Samantha's Juliet.

For two pins he would pop Bridgwater a good one right here. Serve him right too.

"You are quite right, my good fellow," his grace said and left without another word or glance.

And damn him to hell and back again, Lord Francis thought. He did not even have the decency to know when a quarrel was being picked with him. The cowardly scoundrel had walked away.

She was weaving in and out of a line of gentlemen in her set, her eyes sparkling, her lips smiling, her feet moving with surprisingly light grace. Those murmurers were damned wrong. So was Bridgwater if he believed them. Never more wrong in their lives. Devil take it, he knew what he must look for in a bride when the time came. The time had not come and perhaps never would. The only woman he had ever loved was married to someone else and was in a delicate way.

His heart weighed down the soles of his dancing shoes again.

"Oh," Cora said, "how *hot* it is in here. I shall *expire* from lack of air." But despite her discomfort she smiled. She could not remember being happier in her life, which was surely an absurd thought when all she was doing was dancing with Lord Francis Kneller. Waltzing with him. As she had suspected, he waltzed superbly.

"Do you wish to stop and rest?" he asked her. He had

watched her all through the dance but he had spoken little and had not smiled a great deal.

"No," she said. "Oh, please no. This is so *very* wonderful. I have never been happier in my life."

"Have you not?"

He smiled then, gently with his eyes, and she felt a rush of intense feeling for him. A protective, warm, maternal affection. She almost wished that someone would comment—with a sneer—on his pink evening coat, which she really did think rather splendid. She would give that person such a length of her tongue that he would slink away as if whipped and bruised.

"I am so happy that my first waltz is with *you*," she said, smiling warmly at him. "It is such an intimate dance, is it not? I would be mortally embarrassed with anyone else and would be treading all over his feet. I can relax with you. I know you are skilled enough to keep your feet from beneath mine."

"You do yourself an injustice," he said. "You are an excellent dancer, Miss Downes."

She felt herself glow at the compliment. Lord Francis was so very graceful himself. "Thank you," she said.

He was looking at her again in that quiet, unsmiling way. She smiled at him.

"What is wrong?" she asked.

"Nothing," he said. "I rather believe something might be very right, in fact. Are congratulations in order, by any chance?"

She looked at him blankly for a moment and then threw back her head and laughed aloud before she remembered where she was. "You are referring to Mr. Johnson," she said. "Oh, I ought not to laugh, Lord Francis. He came calling this afternoon and stammered his way through a very earnest speech. I do assure you I did not laugh at him. Indeed, I was much obliged to him. I let him down quite gently. I did not hurt him, you know. He is not in love with me, only with what I have become for this fleeting moment, poor man."

"And you are not in love with him?" he said.

"Oh, goodness, no," she said. "Or with any of them, I am sad to say. Sad for her grace's sake, that is. She was kind enough to bring me here to find a husband for me and it must seem to her that she has achieved undreamed-of success. Several more of them are going to offer within the next week or so, you see. But I cannot take any of them seriously. I realized that yesterday morning when they were all so silly in the park and all made fun of that poor child and his hat—though he was not a poor child as it turned out, was he? Was he not a horrid little brat? Anyway, I realized as soon as I ran into you—I almost did so literally, did I not?—that I could not care for any of *them*. I would as soon stroll in the park with just you than with twenty of them put together. So that is telling me something, is it not?" She grinned at him, remembered their surroundings, and reduced the grin to a smile.

"Yes, indeed," he said.

She waited for him to make his own comments on the absurdity of the events in the park the day before, but he said nothing. The heat was affecting him, she guessed. And really it was quite overpowering. She looked away from him in order to drink in the splendor of her surroundings. In a few weeks she was going to be back home again, where she belonged and where she wanted to be. But she knew too that she would always remember these weeks and the wonder of the fact that for a short time she had been accepted by the *ton* and even fêted by the *ton*. And she would always remember Lord Francis Kneller and his pink and lemon and turquoise coats—and his kindness.

She was about to turn her head to smile at him again when she suddenly froze. A group of gentlemen had appeared in the ballroom doorway. Lord and Lady Fuller were hurrying across the room toward them. The music stopped abruptly. There was a buzz of well-bred excitement.

And then the gentlemen parted so that another could step into the doorway and pause to observe the scene. An enormously large gentleman. A gentleman larger than any other Cora had ever seen in her life, she would swear.

"Oh, dear. Oh, dear," she muttered and wondered what had happened to all the air in the room—and where she had misplaced her knees.

"There is nothing to fear," Lord Francis had drawn her arm firmly through his and held it now against his side. "He is only a man, Miss Downes."

Which was about the stupidest thing anyone had ever said to her in her life. She could hear the sound of teeth clattering and drowning out all other sounds. Only a man! He was the Prince of *Wales*.

And then she wished she had not verbalized his name in her mind.

All the dancers had retreated to the edge of the ballroom and waited in anticipation of His Highness's finishing with greeting his hosts and proceeding deeper into the room.

Cora tugged on Lord Francis's arm. "I have to leave," she told him. "I have to go." But she knew even as she said it that in order to leave she was going to have to skirt about that huge mound of royalty standing in the doorway. "Oh, dear. Oh, dear. Let us hide. Find somewhere to hide."

She thought she saw amusement in his eyes for a moment and felt horribly betrayed—her only friend was turning against her. But it was gentle concern, she saw when she looked closer.

"He is going to promenade about the room," he said, "and stop to exchange civilities with the chosen few. There are several hundred here who are only too eager for that honor, Miss Downes. We will skulk in the background here and merely bow and curtsy when everyone else does. I can assure you that the royal eyes will not even alight on you. But you will be able to go home afterward to boast that you have been within arm's length of the Prince Regent himself."

His voice was calm, matter of fact, almost bored—but a little too kindly to be entirely so. He spoke that way only to reassure her, she knew. She was reassured though her heart thumped and she felt as if she had just run five miles uphill against a stiff wind. Why did someone not pump air into the room?

A great dense mass of persons began to move slowly clockwise about the ballroom. The Prince of Wales was hidden somewhere among them, Cora tried not to tell herself. A wave of bowing gentlemen and deeply curtsying ladies preceded their progress, though every few moments all came to a halt as the hidden prince presumably favored some poor soul with his notice.

Cora cowered back against the wall as they drew closer and tried to worm her way slightly behind Lord Francis while clinging to his arm at the same time. She distorted her face and nibbled furiously at one cheek. If only she could suddenly discover a door at her back. If only she were four feet tall instead of being far closer to six.

And how foolish she was being. She was Cora Downes. If everyone in this room were to line up in order of rank, she would be at the very back of the line. Dead last. She was a nobody. A nothing. The realization was enormously reassuring. She relaxed marginally, though the thought did touch the edge of her consciousness that it would not take a great deal to cause her to vomit. The thought was pushed aside with haste.

"Oh, dear. Oh, dear," she muttered as the cavalcade drew closer. The Duke of Bridgwater was part of it. In fact, he appeared to have the royal ear. The royal ear and the enormous person to which it was attached hove into sight. A slight tightening on her arm reminded her to sink into a curtsy. Horror of horrors, she had almost been left standing upright five feet above all the persons who surrounded her. As it was, she crouched low and looked down hopefully for trapdoors.

One more moment and they would pass.

"Ah," the haughty and languid voice of the Duke of Bridgwater said quite distinctly. "Here she is, sir."

"Where, Bridgwater?" the man mountain asked, and Cora emerged from her curtsy to find a million eyes riveted to her person—at least that many.

"Curtsy again," Lord Francis muttered to her as a path opened magically in front of them and he led her forward.

She curtsied as he led and almost had her arm yanked

from its socket. Fortunately Lord Francis seemed far more in control of his faculties than she and allowed her to dip down where she was before taking her forward to stand before the Illustrious Presence.

She would die. There was nothing left in life to do now but die. Preferably now or sooner. Before the agony could be prolonged.

Everyone was still looking at her. Everyone was also smiling at her. From some distance away there was the faint smattering of applause. She felt the hysterical urge to giggle.

"My dear Miss Downes." Her *hand* was in the Prince of Wales's *two hands*. He was drawing her to her feet. She had curtsied again. She had lost the support of Lord Francis's arm. She looked about her wildly, but he was there at her side. "I beg leave to offer you my own personal thanks as well as those of the nation for your act of extreme bravery in saving the life of the Duke of Bridgwater's nephew."

"Oh, it was really nothing at all, Your Majesty," someone said. "I-I mean, your gr—. Oh dear, I do not know what I mean."

There was a burst of laughter from everyone within earshot and the prince himself shook alarmingly with it.

"Your modesty becomes you, my dear," he said. "His Majesty and I need more subjects like you. Enjoy the ball."

And the procession moved on. The dipping and bowing proceeded to Cora's left.

The people about her were nodding and smiling and murmuring their own congratulations—though whether for her supposed heroism or for the honor that had just been accorded her Cora neither knew nor cared. She grabbed for Lord Francis's arm

"I am going to faint," she told him. "Or vomit."

"Come." He led her back behind the crowds, who were still standing and watching the royal progress and craning their necks to see whom else he would favor with his personal notice. Cora was gasping. She was in deep distress.

And then blessedly there *was* a door and he was opening

it just wide enough to usher her through and follow himself before closing it behind them.

Fresh air. And darkness. And privacy.

Cora drew a deep breath and then really did faint.

Chapter 8

❦

Fortunately she had warned him. And fortunately too it was the first of her predictions of what was about to happen to her, rather than the second, which came true. He caught her sagging body in his arms, looked hastily about in the darkness, to which his eyes had not yet accustomed themselves, spotted a wrought-iron seat not far away on the balcony, and carried her toward it.

Carrying Cora Downes about in his arms was becoming a habit, he thought. An uncomfortable habit, for more than one reason.

He set her down on the seat and took the empty place beside her. He set one hand at the back of her head and eased it downward almost to her knees. He should, he thought belatedly, have spoken with someone before stepping out of doors, and sent a message to the Duchess of Bridgwater. It was not at all the thing to be out here alone like this with a single young lady.

If that damned Prinny had not decided to put in an appearance, of course, all the French doors would have been wide open all evening and lamps lit on the balcony. There would have been guests strolling out here and his being with Miss Downes would have been almost proper.

But then if Prinny had not come, she would not have fainted. The waltz would have been at an end by now and she would have been dancing with her next partner. He would have been on his way elsewhere. Oh, yes, indeed he would.

"Oh, dear," she said, addressing her knees, "did I faint?"

"Take some deep slow breaths," he advised her. "The air is cooler out here. You will feel better in a moment."

"How very foolish of me," she said after following his directions. "Thank heaven it was only you who saw me have a fit of the vapors. I *never* have fits of the vapors, you know. But then I have never been in the presence of royalty before."

He felt uncomfortable again. As he had while they had waltzed. She had misinterpreted his attentions to her. She was falling in love with him—had perhaps already fallen. Almost every time she spoke to him she expressed a preference for him. But only tonight, after Bridgwater's words, had he noted the fact. He did not believe she was setting her cap at him. She was far too open and candid for that. Yet she was not even trying to hide her feelings. She must assume that he shared them.

Bridgwater had been right. He had been amusing himself bringing the woman into fashion, introducing her to eligible gentlemen, playing matchmaker, and all the while he had been giving the impression that he was taken with her himself. He had given her the same impression.

What a coil! He had been so preoccupied by his feelings for Samantha that it had not struck him anyone could possibly think him interested in any other woman. And yet he had been at pains to hide his broken heart.

"You acquitted yourself very well," he said. "The aftermath will be our little secret, Miss Downes."

She sat up and looked at him. He could not tell in the darkness if she had recovered her color, but he set a steadying arm about her shoulders just in case.

"He actually spoke to me." She set her palms against her cheeks. "He actually took my hand in his. And *I spoke to him.* What did I say? Did I make an utter cake of myself?"

"Not at all," he said.

"Yes, I did." Her eyes, fixed on his, widened in horror. "I called him 'Your Majesty.' And then I remembered that only the king is called that, but I could not remember what I should call him—and *I told him so*. Ohh!" She wailed out her distress and hid her face on his shoulder.

He wished she would not. She had a physical presence it was difficult to be unaware of when she was close. He wished he had not set his arm about her shoulders. It appeared she had recovered from her faint even if not from her mortification.

"He was charmed," he said.

She started to laugh then, her head still against his shoulder. At first it was silent laughter and he thought in some alarm that she was shaking with grief. But soon she was chuckling softly and then laughing helplessly.

Even when one had entirely missed a joke, Lord Francis had learned in the course of his life, it was sometimes impossible to remain serious in the presence of someone else's mirth. He found himself chuckling along with her.

"I was bobbing like a cork in the ocean," she said. "And I swear there were no bones at all in my knees. It is amazing I did not fall flat at his feet." She succeeded in delivering this speech only after several pauses for merriment en route.

"He would have been even further charmed if you had," Lord Francis said. "He likes nothing more than to see people prostrated by his majestic presence."

They both found this little conversational exchange irresistibly hilarious.

"He is e-enormous," she said. "If I *had* fallen and he had trodden on me, I would be as flat as a piece of paper. You would be able to write a letter on me."

"Yes," he agreed. "There is a great deal of visible majesty there, is there not?"

She set her arm about his neck, presumably to steady herself, while they bellowed with unholy—and quite unkind—glee.

"Oh," she said. "Oh, my chest hurts. Would we be charged with treason if we could be heard saying such disrespectful things?"

"We would have our heads chopped off in the Tower," he said. "With a giant ax by a hooded headman."

They found the prospect of such a gory fate enormously tickling. They clung to each other, snorting and wheezing, absorbed by silliness—as Lord Francis reflected afterward when it was too late to go back and behave with more dignity and more decorum. He could not remember any other occasion when he had so abandoned himself to uncontrolled foolishness.

The Prince of Wales had not come to Lady Fuller's ball to dance. He had come to receive the homage of the *ton* and play the part of grand, majestic gentleman. Having received the one and acted out the other, he took his leave, and the ball resumed. But before the excitement had quite died down and before the music had struck up once more, there was something imperative to be done. Lady Fuller had the message taken to several footmen, and her guests, seeing their intent, followed them gratefully to the French doors and prepared to spill out onto the balcony for fresh air and blessed coolness before the serious business of enjoying themselves began again.

That, at least, was the scene as Lord Francis recreated it for himself in his imagination much later. He was not inside the ballroom to observe for himself, of course.

He was outside.

Sitting on a wrought-iron seat like an actor on stage, invisible to the audience until the curtains were swept back and all eyes focused on him. Or, in his case, until the doors were thrown open and the light of hundreds of candles streamed outward to illuminate him to the interested gaze of several dozen members of the *beau monde,* among whom was the Duke of Bridgwater.

Sitting on a wrought-iron seat, apparently in close embrace with Miss Cora Downes. With nary a chaperon in sight.

"Oops," Cora Downes said, startled out of her laughter and dropping her arm from about his neck with what could only be interpreted as guilty haste. "Oh, dear."

Lord Francis behaved even more foolishly. He lugged his arm awkwardly from about her, smiled idiotically at no one in particular, and muttered to no one in particular, "I escorted Miss Downes outside for some air and privacy."

Well! He recovered both his famous ennui and the handle of his quizzing glass a moment later and got to his feet with his usual elegance to bow over Miss Downes's hand and inform her that he would escort her to her grace's side.

But it was very much too late, he feared.

"Hayden is returning from Vienna in September," Elizabeth announced calmly at the breakfast table just as if the fact did not concern her personally. "Lady Fuller received a letter from him yesterday. He hopes to celebrate our nuptials before Christmas."

Jane sighed and looked back at the announcement in the *Morning Post* for surely the two dozenth time since they had sat down. "I do hope so, Lizzie," she said. "I cannot marry before you, but Charles would marry by special license if he had his way. He is that impatient."

"Special licenses are vulgar," Elizabeth said. "And so is calling your betrothed by his given name, Jane. I would not dream of addressing Hayden by his even after our marriage."

"But then Charles and I *love* each other, Lizzie," Jane said gently.

Which was a decided hit, Cora thought. She sighed inwardly. She wished that one day she would be able to say that too. *But then So-and-so and I love each other. So-and-so would marry by special license if he had his way. He is that impatient.*

She was envious of Jane. Not jealous—the Earl of Greenwald was a gentle young man, a type she could never fall in love with herself even if he was in her own social milieu. But she wished she could fall in love too. She was beginning to despair of ever doing so. There had been those three worthies at home. There had been Mr. Bentley and Mr. Johnson here and she knew without conceit that there would be others. She could feel nothing except gratitude and a little irritability for any of them. But she was one-and-twenty already. She was on the shelf.

She sighed again and smiled.

The duchess was smiling too—at her daughters. She must be well pleased. Both of them settled and so well settled, Elizabeth with a marquess and Jane with an earl. Neither was married yet, of course, but then a betrothal was as binding as a marriage especially when settlements had been carefully drawn up and signed by each of the prospective grooms and the Duke of Bridgwater.

How pleased Papa would be to draw up such a settlement for her, Cora thought. Perhaps she would never be able to give him that pleasure.

The duchess was looking at her. "Have you finished your breakfast, Cora?" she asked. "I would like a word with you in my sitting room if you have."

Not another marriage offer already, Cora thought in dismay. She always found it so painful to say no even when she knew that it was only Papa's wealth that had provoked the proposal—though one of her suitors in Bristol had been a very wealthy man in his own right, she must admit.

"Yes, your grace," she said, getting to her feet.

But it was a scold she was being taken aside for. Very gently expressed, but a scold nonetheless. They had been very late home last night—or this morning rather—and they had all been very tired. Jane had been marvelously happy over her betrothal, and all of them had been abuzz with the brief appearance of the Regent and his kind condescension in speaking with Cora and congratulating her on her bravery in saving little Henry's life.

Her grace had left any unpleasantness for this morning, Cora guessed now.

"It is of course quite understandable that you would be overcome with awe at being singled out by the prince," her grace said when Cora had made her explanations. "I can see that you would want to escape for a while to collect yourself. But you really should have sent for me, my dear. Or Lord Francis should have done so. I find it strange that he would have behaved so thoughtlessly."

"It was really not his fault," Cora said, hastening to his defense. "I told him I was going to faint or *vomit*. He acted promptly. It would have been unspeakably embarrassing if I had done either in public. Especially with the Prince of Wales *still there*."

The duchess smiled for a moment. But only for a moment.

"Cora," she said, looking closely at her charge. "You have not developed a *tendre* for Lord Francis, my dear? He is the brother of the Duke of Fairhurst, and while you are very ladylike and your father owns Mobley Abbey and you are an acknowledged heroine, we must still be realistic. It would be unwise—"

But Cora interrupted her with a merry laugh. "Have a *tendre* for Lord Francis?" she said. "Oh, no, your grace. That would be remarkably foolish." Did not her grace *know?* "I like him excessively but there can be no possible thought of anything else."

The duchess looked at her in silence for a moment and then nodded. "And what about him?" she asked. "He could never think of you in terms of matrimony, Cora, brutal as I might seem in putting it to you thus baldly. I have never known him to behave improperly—quite the contrary, in fact. But you are extraordinarily attractive even if your face is not classically pretty. I do hope—"

But Cora's eyes had widened. Her grace did *not* know. How droll. "Lord Francis is quite unaffected by my charms, I do assure you, ma'am," she said—though of course she had no charms for him to be affected by even if he were so inclined, despite what her grace had just said out of her kindness. "And he has been nothing but a perfect gentleman to me."

"And yet," the duchess said gently, "you were seen to be in close embrace with him out on a dark and deserted balcony, Cora."

Cora giggled despite herself. "We were laughing," she said. "I had been badly frightened and then I had fainted. I reacted by making a joke of it all and Lord Francis found it funny too. We were merely laughing and holding each other up."

It sounded remarkably foolish in the retelling. But shared

laughter was a wonderful thing. She and Papa and Edgar sometimes did it, all three of them together. Not often, it was true, because Papa was a sober businessman and Edgar was a dignified lawyer. But when they were alone together and got started on some topic that amused them all, they could work it and tease it and exaggerate it until they were all holding their sides and wiping the tears from their eyes.

It had never happened with anyone else—anyone outside her own family. Until last night with Lord Francis. She felt an enormous affection for him. She would never see him again after the next week or so. How she wished he were her brother too. He and Edgar both. She pictured herself tripping along a street in Bristol or Bath between the two of them, an arm linked through each of one of theirs. Edgar and Lord Francis would like each other, she believed. Though perhaps not. Men like Edgar did not always approve of men like Lord Francis. The thought saddened her.

"I believe you, dear," the duchess said. "But perhaps it should be remembered that decorum dictates that one should carefully avoid even the appearance of impropriety. When a man and a woman are discovered alone together and in each other's arms, it is unlikely that most people will conclude they are merely sharing a joke."

"Yes, ma'am," Cora could appreciate the truth of that. "Have I disgraced you? I am so very sorry. And sorry too if I have compromised Lord Francis. Though I do believe that most people will not misconstrue his behavior." Surely most people must know.

Her grace smiled. "Gentlemen are not compromised, dear," she said. "Only ladies. This can be smoothed over, I am quite sure. After all, everyone was very sensible of the fact that you had just been singled out for congratulations by the Prince Regent himself. And even apart from that you are riding high in the esteem of the *ton* at present. But you must be careful, Cora. The *ton* is a fickle body."

"Yes, ma'am," Cora said.

"You are to go to the library with Jane this morning?" her grace said with a smile. "I do believe there is to be an accidental meeting there with Greenwald. Run along then, dear. And do stay by her side, will you not? You will not chase after windblown hats and leave her alone?"

Cora flushed. It seemed that her grace saw and knew far more than was apparent to either her daughters or her protégée.

"No, ma'am," she said and fled the room.

She had been indiscreet. She would never understand the world of gentility, she thought. But then it did not matter. She would not be in that world for much longer. Soon she would be back in her own, where the rules and expectations were not quite so strict and where people did not spy on one another in such gleeful expectation of catching one another in some misdemeanor. But for the sake of the Duchess of Bridgwater, who had been kind to her, she would be careful of her behavior for as long as they remained in town.

She was longing to see Lord Francis again, though. She wanted to tell him what people thought and what her grace had said. He would appreciate the joke no end. They would have a good laugh over it.

Oh, dear, she thought, she was going to miss him dreadfully when she left town and returned home.

Lord Francis Kneller called upon the Duke of Bridgwater when the latter was still at breakfast. He was shown into the breakfast parlor and invited to partake of the contents of the dishes displayed on a sideboard. He grimaced slightly and seated himself empty-handed at the table.

His grace set aside the *Morning Post,* which was opened to the page of announcements, looked shrewdly at his guest, and nodded to his butler, who quietly left the room.

"Well," Lord Francis said, picking up the napkin the butler had set beside his empty place and tapping the silver holder with one fingernail, "give me your candid opinion, Bridge." It was the first time he had used the shortened form of the duke's title that his closer friends used. But he did so unconsciously. "Do I owe her an offer?"

"Good Lord," his grace said, his fork suspended midway between his plate and his mouth.

"You are not her father or her brother or in any way her guardian," Lord Francis said. "And I believe she is of age anyway. But you have chosen to take on some responsibility for her. Well, then, do I owe her an offer?"

The duke set his fork down, the food impaled on its tines untasted. "It had not occurred to me that you would even consider making one," he said. "You have *not* given the matter serious consideration, have you?"

"I had her alone," Lord Francis said. "In a dark place where there was no one else to lend even the semblance of propriety. I had my arms about her. She had hers about me. We were seen by a shudderingly large number of the *ton*, yourself included. I certainly cannot blame anyone for concluding that we were embracing, especially in light of the first asinine words I uttered."

"Were you *not* embracing?" his grace asked faintly.

"We were *laughing*," Lord Francis said. "But that seems woefully irrelevant at the moment. I believe I owe her the protection of my name."

"Good Lord," the duke said. "I was coming to see you after breakfast, Kneller. To instruct you in no uncertain terms that I would not have my mother's protégée offered carte blanche. I assumed that was your intention, perhaps even already your expressed intention. She is after all extremely—well, beddable. But my business this morning was to tell you that it just would not do, that you would have to go through me before effecting it."

Lord Francis scraped back his chair with his knees as he stood abruptly. He felt a return of last evening's fury. "Carte blanche?" he said. "Me to Miss Downes? Are you out of your mind, Bridgwater? She is a lady."

"Ah," his grace said quietly, "but she is not, is she?"

Lord Francis had never seen red. But he knew now what was meant by the expression. "I could call you out for that," he said through his teeth.

The duke looked at him, raised his eyebrows, and laid his napkin unhurriedly on the table. He set a finger and thumb on either side of the bridge of his nose. "Sit down, Kneller," he said. "Let us not become farcical."

"There is nothing farcical about suggesting that Miss Downes is the sort of woman to whom one might offer carte blanche," Lord Francis said. But he sat down again when the duke merely closed his eyes and rested his elbow on the table.

"Good Lord," his grace said, "you are in love with her, Kneller."

"Nonsense," Lord Kneller said. "Stuff and nonsense. But she has character and charm and courage, Bridge, and does not deserve to be discussed between us as someone who might or might not agree to be my mistress. The very thought!"

"I would certainly meet *you* before I would allow such a thing," his grace said. "Her father allowed her to come here under my mother's sponsorship and protection. Under *my* protection, in other words. You cannot marry her, Kneller. It would be a disaster for both of you."

"Yes," Lord Francis agreed after thinking about it for a moment. Though he had thought of nothing else all night. He had tried to imagine the interview he would have with his brother after making the announcement and had succeeded all too well. Besides, she would never be comfortable in his world. Look what had happened last evening when old Prinny had put in an appearance. "But what will happen to her if I do *not* offer? Was she irrevocably compromised?"

"By no means," his grace said with a sigh. "I will spend my day wandering from drawing room to drawing room. I shall call on my mother first and make sure that she does the same. We will both be amused by the terror with which our sweet, innocent heroine greeted her moment of fame with Prinny. And amused too by the way she took to her heels afterward and clung to you in fear and trembling when you went after her to console her and bring her back. No one will dare contradict me, and no one will even think of disbelieving my mother when she is at her most gracious."

"And the story would be almost entirely true," Lord Francis said. "Except that we were *laughing*. Relief on her part that it was all over, I suppose, and genuine amusement on my part. She has a way of amusing me." He spoke rather sadly. He would not be able to allow himself to be amused by her ever again.

"Yes, well it will be done," his grace said, reaching for his snuffbox even though he had not quite finished his breakfast. "And no more nonsense about offering for her, Kneller."

Lord Francis got to his feet again, pushed his chair under the table, and grasped the back of it. "I am much obliged to you, Bridge," he said, "for her sake. If there is any scandal, it is entirely my fault. She is far more innocent than her years would lead one to expect. I believe she had no notion at the time that there was anything worse in the situation than a measure of embarrassment. If there is no way of smoothing all over, you will make sure that I know?"

"Indeed," his grace said, his snuff-bedecked hand poised before his face. "But if that happens, Kneller, we will send her quietly home. Scandal would not follow her there into her own world, you know."

Lord Francis drummed the fingers of one hand against the chair for a moment before nodding curtly and taking his leave.

He felt considerably better, he thought as he hurried away down the street on foot. He had been very much afraid that Bridgwater would have a marriage contract all drawn up to wave beneath his nose as soon as they met. Not that Bridgwater had any authority to draw up any such document, of course. But even so . . .

Perhaps he had escaped. Perhaps she had escaped.

But one thing was sure. He was not going to be seen within half a mile of Miss Cora Downes for what remained of the Season.

The thought was strangely depressing.

For the first time in several weeks Lord Francis quite deliberately conjured up a mental image of Samantha Newman, now Samantha Wade, Marchioness of Carew. Quite deliberately he tortured himself with images of her walking hand in hand with Carew about Highmoor Park in Yorkshire. Quite deliberately he reminded himself that she was increasing.

Quite deliberately he forced himself into an agony of loneliness and self-pity.

His heart no longer felt as if it were in the soles of his boots. It felt as if it were six feet beneath the ground.

Damnation but life was an unpleasant business these days.

Chapter 9

∽

There was, of course, no scandal. Cora had not expected there would be. How foolish! All that had happened was that she had been seen laughing helplessly in Lord Francis Kneller's arms—Lord Francis of all people. It had been embarrassing to be so caught, but nothing else. No one with any sense would have suspected anything else. And apparently no one did.

For the next week she was besieged by admirers, both old and new. She had two marriage offers and declined them both. None of her gentlemen admirers referred to the incident at the Fuller ball—at least not to *that* incident. A few were dazzled by the fact that the Prince of Wales had actually spoken with her.

A few of her lady acquaintances made oblique reference to *the* incident, it was true. One of them told her she was fortunate indeed to have Lord Francis Kneller as part of her court. Apparently he added something called *tone* to it. With Lord Francis as a member of one's court, it seemed, one was assured of attracting many more members. If that was true, Cora thought, then he had been extraordinarily successful. Of course he was not really paying court to her, but perhaps he had intended to bring her to the attention of other gentlemen. She must remember to ask him about it the next time she saw him. They would have a laugh over it.

The Honorable Miss Pamela Fletcher—who had not

taken well at all this year, largely because of a nasty disposition, in Cora's estimation—was a little less kind.

"Lord Francis Kneller has attached himself to Miss Downes's court," she explained kindly to one young lady," because he is so accustomed to being part of *someone's* court, poor gentleman." She sighed.

No one then present cared to feed her the lines that would enable her to enlarge on the observation. But neither did anyone start talking furiously about the weather or any other innocuous subject. Everyone looked mildly embarrassed, except for Cora, who looked mildly interested. And so Miss Fletcher continued uninvited.

"Lord Francis was a part of Samantha Newman's court for *years,* you know," she said, speaking to Cora, though it was obvious she thought Cora did not know. "He was devoted to her. It was rumored that he was heartbroken when she married the Marquess of Carew earlier this Season. But who could blame her?" She looked about the group with a smile, inviting agreement. "The marquess is lamentably lacking in good looks and he is a *cripple,* though one does not like to use such a vulgar word aloud, but he is said to be worth more than fifty thousand a year. I might have been tempted to marry him myself if he had asked." She tittered merrily.

Miss Fletcher, Cora concluded, was seriously deficient in brain power. If Lord Francis had been a member of a lady's court for *years,* was not that indication enough that he had had no real romantic interest in her? Lord Francis heartbroken because his lady love had married another man for his fortune? What nonsense. She stored up this little tidbit of gossip to share with him too. She was going to tease him about Samantha Whatever-her-name-was, now the Marchioness of Wherever.

But the trouble was, even though the week following Lady Fuller's ball was an extremely busy one, and even though there were more gentlemen than enough to dance with Cora and drive with her and walk with her and converse with her, there was never the only one with whom she could *enjoy* doing those things. During the whole week she did not exchange a single word with Lord Francis Kneller. She saw him only twice—once at the theater when she was there with a party made up by the Earl of Greenwald, and once when she was shopping on Oxford Street. On neither occasion were they close enough to each other to exchange more than a distant and cheerful wave.

It was most provoking and most dreary. She had decided she wanted nothing to do with suitors, yet she dealt with nothing but suitors all day and every day. She wanted only a friend for the final two weeks she was to spend in London—a friend with whom she could relax and chat and laugh. She saw nothing of the only real friend she had in London—though that seemed an absurd and disloyal thought when she had Jane and even Elizabeth to be her friends.

She had known she was going to miss Lord Francis when she returned to Bristol. But she had not expected to have to start missing him so soon. Of course, he owed her nothing. He had been far kinder than could have been expected of a gentleman of his rank. He had tired of taking notice of her. He did not even think of her as a friend. How could she even have thought he might? The realization was a little humiliating.

There was just a week left in London. Apart from the usual daily rounds of entertainments, there was one in particular to which she looked forward. She was to go to Vauxhall Gardens one evening, again as part of the Earl of Greenwald's party. She had not been there before and was excited at the prospect of seeing the famous pleasure gardens at night, when they were reputed to be magical with their lamp-laden trees and shady walks and pavilion and music and food and fireworks.

It would be one last thrilling memory to store away before she went home again. How she longed to be at home! How she longed to boast to Papa and Edgar about all she had seen and done. How she longed to tell them about meeting the prince. She had mentioned in her letter only that he had attended the Fuller ball, at which she had been a guest. She had hugged to herself the main detail—*that he had spoken to her personally*—to tell them face-to-face. She wanted to watch their expressions when they heard it.

Oh, yes, she longed to be home. But first there were Vauxhall and a final week of merrymaking.

He did not know quite what he was doing still in London. There was no real reason to stay and the Season was all but at an end. Several people had already left. But where would he go? He had an estate of his own in Wiltshire, left him by his mother, but he always felt restless, even lonely there unless he took a house party with him. He did not feel like organizing a house party. He could go to his brother's for a few weeks—there was always a standing invitation for him there, and the children would be delirious with joy. Or he could go to either of his sisters'. Both of them would go into instant action trotting out before him all the local eligible hopefuls. No, he was not in the mood for family, especially the matchmaking members of the family—and even his sister-in-law was not entirely blameless in that department. He could go to Brighton, where the entertainments of the Season would continue almost unabated in new surroundings. But he did not feel like more of the same. He could go to Chalcote in Yorkshire to visit Gabe and Lady Thornhill . . .

No, he could not. Highmoor adjoined Chalcote and they visited back and forth almost every day, Gabe had written. He could never go back to Chalcote—not for a long, long time, anyway, until he could be sure of doing so without making an ass of himself. He certainly did not want to see her with a growing womb. The very thought invited something near panic.

And so he stayed on in London simply because there was nowhere else he fancied going. Besides, for a few days he was not certain that scandal had been averted in that unfortunate affair at Lady Fuller's ball. He could not understand what had got into him on that occasion. He could not recall laughing helplessly over nothing since he was a boy, and he certainly could not recall ever clinging to a female while he did so. And they had been seen. It was alarmingly humiliating. He was not at all sure that Bridgwater and his mother, even with all their consequence and influence, would be able to persuade the *ton* that what had been witnessed by so many had not been a passionate embrace.

He stayed so that he might offer for the woman if worse came to worst. It was another alarming thought. Fairhurst would have his head, Bridgwater had said. It was perfectly true—but his head would be had by chewing more than by chopping. Even a younger son of a Duke of Fairhurst was expected to be rather high in the instep. Even Samantha would have been somewhat frowned upon as his bride.

Samantha—he wished he could stop thinking about her. He was weary of doing so. He was tired of nursing a broken heart.

There was no scandal. Either the *ton* was far more sensible than it usually was—surely no one would seriously believe that he had been either courting or dallying with Miss Downes—or it was so dazzled by the honor Prinny had just paid her inside the ballroom that it readily forgave her minor indiscretion in celebrating her victory with an exuberant hug with her partner of the moment. Or Bridge and his mother had accomplished a very good day's work in deadening the growing gossip.

Lord Francis did his part by staying in case he was needed, but by keeping his distance from the dangerous person of Miss Cora Downes. It meant ducking out of ballrooms whenever he saw her in them and scooting down streets when he spotted her, so that they would not meet face-to-face, and doing an about-face with his horse in Hyde Park one afternoon, leaving the park only a few moments after entering it because she was there driving with Pandry. It meant being watchful and devious.

It meant being a little depressed.

He was missing her bright chatter and gay laughter. He was missing the expectation of farce in her company. There had been something farcical even in the fact that rollicking laughter had almost precipitated them into scandal and a forced union. He had to admit to himself at the end of one week that the high points of the week had been the two occasions when he had been unable to duck out of her sight and had been forced to lift a hand in acknowledgment of her. Both times she had smiled brightly and waved gaily.

Just as if she really cared. He remembered his discomfort at the ball and his growing conviction that she had allowed her feelings for him to grow too warm. He hoped she was not in love with him. But he had to confess on both occasions that she did not look quite like a woman who was pining over an elusive lover.

He danced with Lady Augusta Haville once during the week—the first time he had done so even though he had been thinking about it for some time and she had been signaling her willingness for an even longer time. The morning after, he received an unexpected invitation from Lady Augusta's mama to make one of an evening party to Vauxhall. Why not? he thought with a shrug, the invitation still in his hand after he had already decided to refuse. Why not? He had been to Vauxhall only once this year. It was always worth a visit. And if there was any lingering gossip about Miss Downes and him, then he would put it finally to rest by appearing in public with Lady Augusta and her party.

He penned an acceptance.

Vauxhall was indeed magical. As soon as they entered it from the river entrance, Cora knew that it would be this place above all others she had seen in London that would remain in her memory and in her dreams. It had been a hot day and the evening was still warm, with just enough of a breeze to set the lamps to swaying in the branches of the trees, sending their colored circles of light dancing over the paths beneath.

An orchestra played in the pavilion and a few couples were already dancing in the space before it. Vauxhall was the place for lovers, Jane had said earlier, blushing and making sure that she was out of earshot of her mother—and even of Elizabeth. There were broad paths for strolling and there were a few narrower, darker paths along which a couple might lose themselves for a few minutes if they were clever enough to arrange it and discreet enough not to be gone long enough to be missed.

Perhaps, Jane had said, her hands clasped to her bosom and her eyes closed, so that Cora knew that really she was thinking aloud—perhaps at Vauxhall she would be kissed for the first time. Jane and the Earl of Greenwald, Cora guessed, were hotly in love and were finding irksome the fact that their wedding must wait until after her elder sister's.

It must feel good, Cora had thought, to be hotly in love. She thought so even more when they arrived at Vauxhall. Although they sat down first in their reserved box to eat supper, she longed to dance and to walk along the shady paths. She wished there were someone a little more romantic than Mr. Corsham with whom to do both—she wished there were someone with whom *she* would wish to steal a kiss. But she intended to enjoy herself anyway.

Her spirits were dampened somewhat when she spotted Lord Francis Kneller in another box not far distant from her own. He had not seen her yet. He was with a party that included the very lovely Lady Augusta Haville and several other ladies and gentlemen, all of whom, Cora realized, had titles. Just a few weeks ago she would have been terrified of all of them just on that count alone.

He was seated next to Lady Augusta and was deep in conversation with her. He looked his usual elegant, just slightly to-the-left-of-masculinity self. His coat was lavender, his waistcoat silver.

In fact Cora's spirits were a little more than dampened. She felt downright depressed, if the truth were to be told. She was not jealous—Lord Francis would not flirt with Lady Augusta any more than he would flirt with her or any other lady. But she was envious. She wanted him to be seated next to her, looking at her, deep in conversation with her. Oh, dear, she thought, she *was* jealous. She wanted him for *her* friend. She did not want to share him.

Share? She almost laughed aloud even though Mr. Corsham was in the middle of a very serious description of a pair of grays he had almost bid upon at Tattersall's this very week. There was no question of sharing Lord Francis. He was not interested in her any longer. He had not spoken to her in a week. He might have come to Lord Greenwald's box at the theater during the intermission to pay his respects to her. He might have hurried down Oxford Street to greet her. But he had kept his distance both times. Now tonight he had not even noticed her though she had already stolen at least twenty glances at him.

Supper was over finally and she danced, first with Mr. Corsham and then with a viscount who was the unfortunate possessor of two left feet and the inability to feel rhythm. Then she walked with Mr. Corsham and two other couples, including Jane and her earl. The duchess and the earl's mama stayed in the box.

It was all so very beautiful, Cora thought as they strolled. She tried to imagine that she was walking with someone very special. Though it did not really matter that she was not. The place and the evening were lovely in their own right. Peaceful. Soothing. She tipped her head back and tried to see the sky and the stars beyond the lamps and the swaying branches of the trees.

Lord Francis had also walked along this way. He had had Lady Augusta on his arm and another couple had gone with them. They had not yet returned. Perhaps, Cora thought, they would meet farther along the path. Perhaps they would stop and converse. Though she did not really want to do that. She knew now that he had been deliberately avoiding her during the past week. She would not force him into a meeting. And she would not be able to talk or laugh with him, anyway, when he had Lady Augusta on his arm and she was on Mr. Corsham's.

No, she hoped they would not meet.

Jane and the earl had slipped to the back of the group. Soon enough, Cora noticed, they disappeared altogether. She smiled to herself. They would as quietly reappear after a few minutes, she was sure. They were ever discreet, those two. The other couple had got a little way ahead.

And then there was a distraction, just at the moment when Cora thought she saw Lord Francis and his group approaching from a distance. A rather poorly dressed woman—anyone who could pay the admission fee could get into Vauxhall and perhaps there were ways of getting in without even having to pay—said something to Mr. Corsham and caught at his sleeve. He spoke gruffly to her and tried to shrug off her hold, but she clung tenaciously and launched into a tale of woe that would doubtless have caught Cora's interest and sympathy if she had been at leisure to listen. But she was not.

A young child darted out of the trees to her left and wailed at her, clinging to her evening gown as he did so. He was a thin, ragged, barefooted little urchin. Cora bent to listen to him, all frowning concern.

"Me bruvver," he said with a gasp. "He's stuck up a tree, missus. He's too scared to come down. An' we'll be whipped for sure if we gets caught in 'ere." Having delivered this pathetic speech without pause, he resumed the wailing, and the clinging turned to tugging.

Cora spared one fraction of a moment—no longer—to glance in Mr. Corsham's direction. But he was still engaged in trying to detach the woman from his arm and apparently had not noticed the child. Yet somewhere to Cora's left, among the dark trees, a child was caught in a tree and might fall out of it at any moment, and both boys would be in trouble if caught. Without a doubt they had sneaked into the pleasure gardens, hoping to observe all the splendor of the proceedings from the branches of a tree. Poor little mites.

Without even a word to Mr. Corsham, Cora grasped the child's thin hand and sallied off with him into the darkness. It did not even enter her mind that it was a strange coincidence for both her escort and her to be accosted with woeful stories almost at the same moment.

"Do not be afraid," she instructed the little boy in her most reassuringly maternal voice. "We will have your brother down from his tree in no time at all. I am an expert tree climber. The secret is never to look down—*never*. And as for being whipped, I shall see that no harm comes to either of you. Doubtless it was naughty of you to sneak in without paying, but everyone knows that boys will be boys."

The child trotted and panted at her side.

"Now," Cora said when they were deep along surely the narrowest, darkest path in Vauxhall, "where is he? I do not hear him crying. He must be a brave lad." Or one so petrified by terror that he could not even utter a sound.

" 'Ere, missus," the child said, speaking quietly and tonelessly and coming to an abrupt halt.

Cora stopped too and peered upward. And felt an arm come about her waist from behind and another about her neck. And smelled the disgusting odor of onions and garlic and rotten teeth and sweat. A hand found its way over her mouth while she stood in mute surprise.

"Quiet, my luverly lydy," a hoarse male voice advised her, "an' nobody will come to no 'arm. Tyke 'er bracelet, Jemmie, an' be quick about it. Oi'll get this."

Jemmie, the pathetic little urchin with the brother up a tree, set about trying to relieve Cora not only of her bracelet—an extremely expensive gift Edgar had given her for her last birthday—but also of her wrist. The male of the disgustingly bad breath and body odor raised the hand of the arm that was about her waist and grabbed the pearls that Papa had given her mother on their fifth wedding anniversary, only months before her death.

Cora bit his hand, stamped on his foot, and backhanded the boy simultaneously. It was an extremely unclean hand, and it was against her principles to strike a child. But she was very angry indeed. She had come into this dark thicket to risk her own safety and one of her favorite gowns in climbing a tree to rescue a petrified infant—and as a reward she was being manhandled and robbed.

It was marginally satisfying to hear the man yelp and the boy screech.

If she could only turn, she thought, she would be able to deliver her finest blow, the one Edgar had instructed her to deliver if ever she found herself in a tight corner—this corner felt about as tight as a corner could get. Edgar had actu-

ally blushed when teaching her, but he had been quite
adamant about it.

The trouble was she could not turn.

But suddenly the child seemed to be levitated straight up
into the air and then went flying through it to land sprawling several feet away—fortunately he released his hold on
both Cora's wrist and her bracelet before he began the
flight. At the same moment the unwashed man released his
hold on her person and her property, roaring as he did so.

Cora whirled about, making the instantaneous decision to
use her *right* knee as her right leg was perhaps a little
stronger than the left. But she had no chance to use either.
She was forced to stand and watch like a helpless female as
someone else grappled with the robber—someone who
looked suspiciously in the darkness as if he might be wearing a lavender evening coat.

The boy fled quietly into the night.

Cora clasped both hands over her mouth. He would be
slaughtered. Oh, the dear gallant man. He knew nothing
about thugs and ruffians as did she, who had lived in Bristol for most of her childhood and had frequently been taken
to the docks by her father.

He was going to be killed at the very least.

She waited for an opening to come to his assistance. It
came quite soon, when the ruffian came staggering backward. Fortunately, he must have tripped over a tree root.
Cora steadied him with both hands from behind for a moment and then allowed him to continue his fall. She kicked
him in the side with her slippered foot when he was down,
doing marvelous damage to her recently healed toes.

"There," she said crossly, setting her hands firmly on her
hips and glaring down at him, "take that!"

Obviously the thief knew when he had met his match. He
pressed the heel of one hand against his jaw, grimacing and
working it from side to side, and then scrambled in un-
gainly haste to his feet and disappeared into the darkness
after his young accomplice.

"Well," Cora said, peering after him, "we certainly taught *him* a lesson."

But then she whirled about, in sudden mortal fear lest before his flight her assailant had murdered Lord Francis Kneller.

Chapter 10

⌒

He had seen her as soon as she arrived at Vauxhall, one of a party of ten, which included Greenwald and Lady Jane Munro and the mothers of the newly betrothed couple. They had taken a box quite close to the one he occupied with Lady Augusta and her party.

It would have been the easiest thing in the world to have caught her eye and smiled and nodded. Indeed, several times he had felt her eyes on him. He could have strolled across to the other box to pay his respects. He need have stayed only a few moments. Instead, he had pretended not to notice her. He had ignored her altogether.

It had been a gauche and inexplicable thing to do. He could not understand why he had done it. It was not as if he had quarreled with the woman. Far from it. The last time they had been together they had laughed so hard that they had had to hold each other up. And it was not as if she had ever meant anything to him. Good Lord, he had not avoided even Samantha after she had announced her betrothal. He had been a guest at her wedding. It had been foolish to behave as he had tonight.

But the trouble was that with every minute that passed, it had become more difficult suddenly to notice that she was there at Vauxhall, in full view, a mere few yards from the box he occupied. He had even looked away from her when she danced. He had been very relieved when someone suggested a walk.

He would put matters right when they returned, he had decided. He would hand Lady Augusta back into the box and stroll across to Greenwald's, pretending that he had just noticed them. Not that it would sound very convincing. Even the Duchess of Bridgwater and Lady Jane must be wondering why he had suddenly become so blind. Cora Downes must be feeling quite upset with him. Lord, he hoped she did not fancy herself in love with him.

But it had seemed that he would not have to wait until the return to the pavilion. He had walked the length of the main path with Lady Augusta and another couple, deftly turning aside the former's hints that they explore one of the darker side paths. They had been strolling back again, enjoying the warmth of the evening, admiring the lanterns and the dancing colored lights they created on the path, nodding at acquaintances who passed them.

And then in the distance he had seen the unmistakable tall figure of Cora Downes approaching on Corsham's arm. For some reason he could not fathom, Lord Francis had felt jittery and breathless at the prospect of meeting her. He had considered after all drawing Lady Augusta off the path. He had not done so because he knew that the woman wanted to be kissed, and that after she was kissed she would as like as not expect him to call upon her papa tomorrow morning to discuss marriage settlements. He had become adept over the years at avoiding such situations.

Perhaps, he had thought fleetingly—but he had dismissed the thought as absurd—that was why he had attached himself to Samantha Newman's court for so long. Samantha had never been in search of a husband. And though he had loved her and offered for her several times, he had never really expected her to have him. There had been deep shock in discovering that she *would* have someone else and in haste too. Shock and humiliation. And heartbreak.

What would he do? he had wondered now. Nod pleasantly to Cora Downes and walk on by? Stop to converse with her and Corsham? Normally he did not have to think consciously about such matters. Normally he acted from instinct. What would instinct have him do, then? Stop and talk, of course. It would be the polite thing to do.

But before he had been able to do it—before he had been anywhere close to doing it—he had seen Miss Downes and Corsham fall prey to one of the oldest tricks in the book of thieves. A woman had approached Corsham from his side of the path and caught at his arm. Doubtless she would be spinning him a tale of poverty and starving children. As soon as his attention was engaged, a pathetic little urchin had approached Miss Downes from her side of the path and clutched at her gown. His tale would be even more heartrending and of course it would be falling on the most fertile ears in London. She had disappeared with the child almost immediately. Corsham and the other couple with them had not even seen her go.

There would be one more in the trees, of course. A man, in all probability, someone strong enough to relieve her of her jewels and valuables. And perhaps too—though not likely in the presence of the lad and with the woman not far away—of her virtue and even her life.

"Pardon me," Lord Francis had said hastily to Lady Augusta, who had had her head turned back over her shoulder while she addressed some remark to the couple who were strolling with them. "Someone to whom I must pay my respects." And he had gone hurrying down the path in unseemly haste and crashing into the trees after Miss Downes and the boy—Corsham had still been demanding that the woman unhand him.

Lord Francis had lost a few moments trying to force a path among dark trees before he realized that a few steps to his left there was a ready-made path, albeit a narrow one. But he had been quite right. Even in the darkness he had been able to see that there were now three figures ahead of him, a man and a boy dealing with a struggling woman. Both the man and the boy had let out sounds of pain just before Lord Francis launched himself at them, mindless with fury.

The boy had been easy to deal with. Lord Francis had merely lifted him from the ground with one hand on the collar of his ragged coat, and flung him. At the same moment he had got his arm about the man's neck, just as the man had his about Miss Downes's. The element of surprise had been on Lord Francis's side. The man had released his prey with a roar of mingled surprise and rage, and had spun about.

Lord Francis had not spent several mornings of each week for several years past at Jackson's boxing saloon for nothing. He was fit and he was competent, even skilled, with his fists. Jackson had always told him that he could be one of his star pupils if only he had a little more desire. Desire tonight was no problem at all. A few preparatory punches gave him the opening he needed and he landed a right upper cut to the man's chin with a satisfying crunching of bone and snapping of teeth. The villain reeled and in the natural course of things would have crashed to the ground within another second or two.

Nothing ever followed its natural course when Cora Downes was involved, of course. Somehow she had got herself behind the tottering rogue and reached out her hands to steady him. For one moment Lord Francis thought she was holding the man up so that he could deliver another blow. For the same moment he was terrified that she would be taken down with the man and squashed beneath him. But she stepped deftly aside, let him fall, and then kicked him in the side.

"There," she said fiercely, planting both hands on her hips, "take that!"

She probably hurt her foot more than she hurt the thief's side, Lord Francis thought. The man scrambled to his feet almost immediately and made off into the darkness. It was probably as well to let him go rather than try to confine him and take him into custody. Lord Francis made no move to pursue him. Miss Downes stood looking after him.

"Well," she said, "we certainly taught *him* a lesson."

Bless her heart, Lord Francis thought, relief beginning to replace his rage, she had restored the sanity of farce to a potentially nasty situation. He almost grinned at her when she spun around to face him.

"Lord Francis?" she said. "Oh, it *is* you. Did he hurt you? How foolish of you to come up on him like that. He might have *killed* you." She took a couple of steps toward him.

"I suppose," he said, trying to set his coat and sleeves to rights on his shoulders and arms, "you had the situation quite under control, Miss Downes?"

"No." The confidence went from her voice and one of her hands crept up to clutch her pearls. "No, I was deceived. The child said he had a brother stuck up a tree. They had crept in here just to watch the festivities, he told me, and would be whipped if they were caught. But he had that—ruffian waiting here."

"You are all right?" Lord Francis asked her, trying to see her expression in the darkness. "No real harm has been done? They picked a perfect victim, of course, although I am sure it was accidental on their part. You never could pass by anyone in trouble, could you?"

"I am all right," she said. But he watched her shudder. "He was dirty. He smelled dirty. He touched me. He had a hand over my mouth. They were going to take Mama's pearls and my bracelet from Edgar. I feel—I feel dirty too."

The intrepid Miss Cora Downes was beginning to suffer from delayed shock. She was beginning to come to pieces. Lord Francis took a step toward her.

"They are gone now," he said, making his voice as soothing as he was able. "You are quite safe. I will not allow them to come back and harm you."

She closed the gap between them in sudden haste and grabbed for the labels of his coat. Her face came burrowing into the folds of his neckcloth that had taken his valet half an hour to perfect a few hours before. But that appeared not to be close enough. She straightened up, hid her face against his shoulder, wrapped her arms tightly about his neck, and pressed her body against his from shoulders to knees. Lord Francis was given the distinct impression that she would have climbed right inside him if it had been possible to do so.

"Hold me," she commanded him.

He held her. Tightly. And felt as if someone had moved the sun a few million miles closer to the earth and was beaming its heat directly at him. Good Lord—oh, devil take it! He furiously ignored his body's interest—a euphemistic word if ever he had thought of one—and concentrated all the power of his mind on giving her comfort.

"Sh," he told her softly, though she was making no noise. "I have you. You are quite safe, Cora."

He wished her bosom would not heave against his chest as if she had just run a mile or more.

"Ah." She sighed deeply into his shoulder. "You smell so good." Perhaps she needed to say it again in case he had not heard it the first time. Perhaps she merely needed to look into his face to make sure that she really was with someone with whom she could feel safe. She lifted her head and looked into his eyes—their noses and mouths were almost touching. "You smell so very good."

No one had ever before told him that he smelled good. Somehow Miss Cora Downes made the words sound quite blisteringly erotic. He tipped his head slightly to one side so that their noses would not collide, focused his eyes on her lips, muttered "Cora" from somewhere deep in his throat, and had his mouth perhaps a quarter of an inch from hers when hell broke loose.

"Well!"

That was the start of it. The word was uttered in the shocked, outraged, haughty voice of Lady Augusta Haville.

She had brought a whole army with her—or so it seemed in the dark, close confines of the path. The couple they had been walking with was there as was the couple Miss Downes had been with—as well as Greenwald and Lady Jane Munro and Corsham himself. There were a few other people too, people Lord Francis suspected he might know if only someone would come along with a branch of candles so that he could see better.

Apparently not one of the lot of them needed a branch of candles or even a single candle to know very well what he was up to. And of course they were very nearly right. Another quarter of a second and another quarter of an inch and he would have had no cause for outrage at all.

"Well, Kneller," Mr. Corsham said stiffly, "it is plain to see that they were right all along."

No one needed to be told who *they* were or what it was they had been right about all along.

"No sooner do I turn my back for the merest moment . . ." Mr. Corsham did not finish his sentence, but turned his back once more and stalked away.

"Cora," Lady Jane said, sounding tearful.

"Come, my love," her betrothed said. "This is none of our concern, I believe."

Except that Miss Cora Downes was his invited guest and might have been robbed and ravished and murdered, Lord Francis thought.

"And I thought to give you the benefit of the doubt," Lady Augusta said, a universe of scorn in her voice. She was presumably addressing herself to Lord Francis. "But you could not wait for the opportunity to rush to the arms of that *slut*."

"Oh," Cora Downes said, sounding more interested than shocked, "is that *me* she is talking about?"

"If the glove fits, wear it." Lady Augusta spat out the triumphant cliché with an equally clichéd toss of the head and turned to march away, taking the other couple from her party with her.

"I was almost *robbed*," Cora Downes said. "Lord Francis came to *rescue* me."

But they appeared to have lost the bulk of their audience except for a now sobbing Jane, an embarrassed-looking Greenwald—Lord Francis suspected that the two of them had been up to clandestine business in the woods when they should have been walking with Miss Downes and Corsham and keeping an eye on them—and the sheepish-looking couple who were members of the same party.

The rest of the audience were doubtless breaking speed records in their haste to get back to the pavilion and the crowds in order to spread the glad tidings.

"Hush," Lord Francis said, setting an arm about Miss

Downes's waist and drawing her against his side. "Come, I will escort you back to Greenwald's box. Her grace will take you home."

"They thought we were having a *tryst* here," she said, sounding dazed. "Did they not realize it was only me—and only you?"

Lord Francis suspected that they—every last one of the spectators—had known those facts very well indeed. They were the same couple who had been discovered in close embrace out on the deserted balcony of Lady Fuller's ballroom.

"Come," he said quietly. "Take my arm."

She took it. "This is ridiculous," she said. Her voice had gained strength. "How very foolish people are. Yes, take me back to the pavilion, Lord Francis, and we will tell everyone exactly what happened. Will they not be embarrassed to have so misjudged the situation?" She laughed suddenly and sounded genuinely amused. "You and I enjoying a secret tryst—what a delightful joke! Can they not see it?"

Probably not, Lord Francis thought, patting her hand soothingly. He could not see it himself. In fact, he felt about as far removed from laughter and jokes as he had ever felt in his life.

Cora had been shut up inside the Duchess of Bridgwater's house for four whole days even though the sun had shone brightly from a cloudless sky for all of those days and summer was upon them. And even though there had been plans and engagements for every morning and afternoon and evening of those days.

No one had called. She had been nowhere.

It seemed that she was in something of a scrape. Her grace and Jane and even Elizabeth were very kind about it, but they made no attempt to tell the world how ridiculous the situation was. And they did not encourage Cora to brazen it out by keeping her engagements.

It was definitely ridiculous. It had been from the start. When they had arrived back at the pavilion after that dreadful incident with the thieves—the woman must have been an accomplice too, Cora had realized in a moment of inspiration—it had appeared that everyone was looking at them and that an unnatural hush had fallen over the gathered revelers. Cora was not given to conceit. She was not one to imagine that everyone was looking at her when in fact everyone was not.

Cora would have stood in the middle of the dancing area before the pavilion and addressed the mob since she obviously had their attention anyway. She would have told what had happened. She would have explained how clever the woman and the boy had been and how evil-smelling the man had been. She would have described her struggles and told about how she and Lord Francis between them had vanquished the foe. She would even—since she was not conceited—have admitted to that moment of weakness when she had felt suddenly dirty and violated though no serious harm had been done and had needed the comfort of Lord Francis's arms.

She would have made them all lower their eyes in embarrassment at their mistake. And then she would have made them laugh and everything would have returned to normal. Not that she would ever again admit Mr. Corsham to her smiles and her conversation and her company. He had behaved with a shocking lack of gallantry. Good heavens, he had fallen into the trap quite as much as she had. And it had certainly not been he who had come galloping to her rescue.

But she had been given no chance to tell her story, and to her chagrin Lord Francis had made no attempt to tell it either—except in a hushed voice and in the barest of details to her grace, to whose side he had escorted her without pause. He had ended his explanation with the advice that her grace take Miss Downes home immediately and keep her there until he called the next morning.

And so Cora had known all the indignation and all the ignominy of being hustled out of Vauxhall, Lord Greenwald's party all behind her like silent whipped dogs, feeling as if somehow she was in deep disgrace.

She had been brought home—though it was not home at all, she had been only too aware for four whole days—and kept there. And Lord Francis had *not* come the day after Vauxhall or any day since. No one had come.

She wanted to go home, Cora decided. She wanted Papa and Edgar and her familiar world. A world that was ruled by sane laws of common sense. She wanted to have done with this world. It had been an exciting world and a gratifying world—she was not going to pretend that it had not been fun to be a heroine. But it was a silly world.

She had asked her grace if she might go home. She was only an embarrassment now to the family that had brought her here. Elizabeth and Jane still had commitments to honor and naturally enough the duchess must wish to concentrate on the progress of her daughters' betrothals. But the duchess was being gracious about the whole thing. Cora must stay and relax, she said. All would be well. She was very sorry that she had been the cause of all this unpleasantness. She should have found Cora a husband in Bath.

Cora felt like a nuisance even though she could feel no guilt over anything that had happened. *Nothing* had happened. She could not understand how anyone could have imagined that anything had—especially with Lord Francis Kneller of all people. But she felt a nuisance. She felt in the way. All she could do, she supposed, was to stay quietly here until everyone returned to the country next week and she could go home to Mobley Abbey. There would still be plenty of summer left.

Lady Augusta Haville had called her a *slut,* she kept thinking. Oh, how she would dearly love to slap that young lady's face for her. In *her* world, in Cora's world, women did not go about being so vulgarly insulting to one another. And this was supposed to be the genteel world? Ha, Cora thought.

Lord Francis had been about to *kiss* her, she kept thinking. On the lips. Papa and Edgar often kissed her—they were an openly affectionate family. They kissed her on birthdays and when one or other of them was coming or going. Always on the forehead or one of her cheeks. Sometimes she felt a little weak-kneed when she remembered that Lord Francis had been about to kiss her on the lips. And she wondered what it would have felt like. She smiled to herself when she caught herself in such wonderings. Like a brother's kiss, that was what. It would have been comforting just as his arms had been and his body had been—she had been a little surprised to find that there had been nothing at all soft or effeminate about either, though her eyes had given her the same message before. And he had been able to *carry* her before.

He had called her Cora. Her name had sounded softly feminine on his lips. She had always thought that her name had an unfortunate resemblance to the cawing of crows.

She was bored. For four whole days she was so bored she could have screamed. But even in Bristol and at Mobley she had learned that it was ungenteel for a lady to scream except in some dire emergency, like the sudden appearance of a mouse, for example. But whenever Cora saw a mouse, she forgot all about screaming in her curiosity to get closer to observe the little creature.

On the fifth day there was finally a diversion. Elizabeth and Jane were both at a garden party that Cora herself had been looking forward to. They were under the chaperonage of Lady Fuller. Her grace and Cora sat at their embroidery until the former was summoned to the downstairs salon by the arrival of a visitor.

Cora felt as if she were in quarantine for some deadly disease. The visitor would not be brought up to the drawing room, of course. She stitched on.

But then the butler returned with the request that Miss Downes join her grace in the lower salon. Cora put aside her embroidery and got to her feet with an eagerness that she despised. Someone had called and was willing to say how-d'ye-do to her? What a miracle!

She stepped through the salon door, which a footman had opened for her, and felt her spirits soar even higher. She beamed at Lord Francis Kneller as her grace got to her feet and came toward the door.

"Lord Francis wishes to have a word alone with you,

Cora," she said. "I shall be upstairs, dear, if you need me."
She left the room.

Cora scarcely heard her. She hurried across the room,
both hands outstretched, and smiled brightly at her visitor.

"Oh, Lord Francis," she said. "How *happy* I am to see
you."

She could see immediately, even before he had clasped
both her hands in his, why he had not called before. The
poor man had been ill. He was deathly pale.

Chapter 11

~

Her face had lit up with such total delight that for the moment she seemed startlingly, vividly beautiful. For a moment he felt dazzled.

The past four days must have been dreadful for her. She had not been out of the house, her grace had just told him, or received any visitors. Even his own visit here, the morning after Vauxhall, had not been made to her. And Bridgwater had not called on her either. The girl was in awe of him, he had told Lord Francis with a grimace just an hour ago. He had thought it better to stay away.

But Bridge felt terribly guilty about the whole thing. It was his mother who had brought her to town, his mother who had undertaken to introduce her to the *ton* and to find her a husband not too far above her in station. And he, Bridgwater, was the head of the family. Ultimately the girl's safety and reputation were his responsibility. And, to add to his guilt, there was the fact that it was *he* who had asked Kneller to dance with her at that first ball, to bring her into fashion.

But here she was, after four lonely days spent indoors, looking far more blooming than he felt. And as soon as the duchess left the room, she came hurrying toward him, her hands outstretched, and spoke as she always spoke—quite openly and without artifice. Cora Downes, he suspected, was incapable of calling a spade anything but a spade.

"Oh, Lord Francis," she said as he took her hands in his and clasped them tightly. "How *happy* I am to see you."

He felt doubly wretched, if that were possible.

She should have been pale and quiet. She should have hovered at the door, eyes downcast. But he realized something, and the realization amazed him. She had no idea why he was here. She had no idea what he had been doing for the past four days. She had no idea!

"I am so *glad* you have come." She rushed onward with further speech before he could properly marshal his thoughts. "I am so desperately in need of a good laugh. You would not believe how dreary it has been here for the past four days. I have been advised not to go out, not to see anyone. I am sure her grace and the girls mean well, but really it is so ridiculous. Do you know what is being *said?* It was being said that evening, of course, but to have had the myth continued with since then is the outside of enough. Tell me how foolish you think it all is, and we will have a good laugh together."

Her bright smile, delivered only inches away from his face, would have seemed coquettish with anyone else. With her, it was quite without guile. It was merely a bright smile.

He clasped her hands a little more tightly. "I am afraid," he said, "you are in something of a scrape, Miss Downes."

"Oh," she said, and her smile faded instantly. "That is just the word her grace used. Is it true, then, that everyone really believes that we slunk away together for a *tryst?* I have never known any more stupid body of people than the *ton*. And that is what has made you ill, is it not? You are dreadfully pale, you know. Because you are a member of the *ton*, it has bothered you. You do not want to have the reputation of being a gentleman who seduces ladies. But no matter. The *ton* will forget. I will be going home to Mobley Abbey at the end of this week and in another week I will have been forgotten about here. You need not worry. But I am sorry that I have made you ill. You came to rescue me in Vauxhall, which was extraordinarily brave of you when you might have been killed. But instead of being hailed as a hero, you have landed yourself in a *scrape*. It is very unfair."

She was looking at him with earnest sympathy. Good Lord, *she* was the one trying to get *him* out of the scrape.

"Miss Downes," he said, "I must apologize for keeping you waiting here for all of four days. I have not been ill in my bed, you know. I have just returned from a visit to Bristol and one to my brother."

Her eyes opened wide with amazement. "*Bristol?*" she said. "Oh, if only I had known you were going there. Mobley Abbey is only just outside Bristol, you know. I would have asked you to call on my father." But she flushed suddenly and bit her lip. "No, that would not have done, would it? A duke's son to call on a Bristol merchant. Perhaps it is as well I did not know. I would—"

"Miss Downes," he said firmly. "It was to Mobley Abbey I went, not to Bristol."

At last she was at a loss. "Oh," she said.

"I went to speak with your father," he said. "To offer for you. He approved my suit. A marriage contract, mutually agreeable to both of us, was drawn up. It will be signed as soon as I have had your consent. *If* I have your consent. Will you do me the honor of marrying me?"

Any other woman but Cora Downes would have been expecting this, he thought. Or desperately hoping for it. Or dreading that it might not happen. Any other woman would have realized that there could be only disgrace ahead of her if this did not happen. But Cora Downes stared at him for several silent moments with blank eyes and a slightly hanging jaw.

Then she threw back her head and laughed so merrily that he almost found himself joining her.

"Oh, that is priceless," she said when she finally sobered. "It is marvelous. I just *knew* that if only I could see you again I would laugh again. You are so *funny*. I almost believed you for a moment. Now, would not you have been surprised if my eyes had become starry and I had said yes? *Then* you would have known what it was to be in a scrape.

Oh, I wish I had thought fast enough and done it." She bit her lower lip and looked at him with sparkling eyes.

"It is no joke," he said quietly.

He watched her smile fade very gradually and her eyes become wary. She continued to clamp her teeth onto her lower lip.

"No," she whispered after a long while, and she drew her hands away from his. "Oh, no." She shook her head slowly from side to side. "You are being *gallant*. How foolish the *ton* is. How criminally foolish. But I am not a member of the *ton*, Lord Francis. I will not force you into anything so abhorrent to you."

It was tempting. So very tempting.

"You have been compromised twice in the last week and a half, Miss Downes," he said. "Both times by me. It will be better if we set it right—better for both of us. But let us not make it a negative thing. There are positives, are there not? I believe we like each other. We never seem to lack for conversation when we are together and we are comfortable together. We seem to have the ability to make each other laugh. Will it be so bad for us to be married? I think it might be rather pleasant."

He had convinced himself that it would. Surely friendship was an important ingredient of marriage.

"Pleasant," she said. "You think no such thing. You cannot possibly wish to *marry*."

"I am thirty years old," he said. "A dreadful age to be, is it not? It is high time I was married. I can think of no one else I would rather marry." No one else who was not already married, that was. Oh, Samantha!

"You would hate it," she said. She was looking sympathetic again. "Marriage, I mean. And to me of all people. I am not even a lady, Lord Francis. My father is not a gentleman. He is very wealthy, but he made his money in trade. You are more than a gentleman. You are a duke's son, a duke's brother. Good heavens, you have a *title*. I would be Lady Cora if I married you. That is absurd."

"You would be Lady Francis Kneller," he said, smiling, "not Lady Cora. Is it such a very daunting title?"

"You went to visit your brother," she said. "What did *he* say? I will wager he was not pleased."

That would be an understatement. Fairhurst had grown purple in the face. He had bellowed. He had reasoned and argued and cajoled and grown belligerent and thoroughly obnoxious. He had tried to lay down the law when there was no law to lay. He had stopped just short of disowning his brother, but he had made it perfectly clear that he would receive Lady Francis only with the greatest reluctance if she was not even a lady to start with."

"My brother is not my keeper," he said.

"You see?" Her voice was accusing. "You cannot say that he liked it, can you? You cannot say that he gave his blessing. What did *Papa* say?"

Her father had surprised him—pleasantly. He was not in any way vulgar. On the other hand, despite his wealth and his newly won status as a landowner, he was not pretentious. He was candid, down-to-earth, forceful. After a very brief acquaintance with the father, it had been easy for Lord Francis to know why the daughter was as she was. The brother had been a little trickier to deal with. Also a man without pretensions, he was indistinguishable in manner and appearance from a born gentleman. He was a handsome devil, Lord Francis had noticed, and also a rather hostile one. He had not thought that marriage into the aristocracy would suit his sister.

"Corey does not take well to rules and restrictions," he had said with eyes that had the same directness as his sister's. "If she has fallen afoul of the *ton* this time, it will happen again. I will wager she does not even know that it has happened. She will never know because she does not deal in petty intrigues or gossip. It will happen over and over again. Corey is a walking disaster."

Lord Francis had been unable to stop himself from grinning. "I have noticed," he had said, "that farce seems to dog her footsteps."

Rather than offending the younger Downes, he had seemed somehow to have pleased him. Relations between them had thawed somewhat after that.

"She needs someone who can find humor in her disasters," Edgar Downes had said. "My father and I can—usually. We are extremely fond of her, you know."

It had been both statement and warning. If he ever treated Cora badly, Lord Francis had understood, he could expect to be squashed to a pulp between the two of them. The father had questioned him just as closely about his means and prospects and had driven as hard a bargain on the marriage settlement as if he had been any Tom, Dick, or Harry who had stepped in off the street demanding to marry his daughter. He had not given his blessing lightly.

"He interrogated me for all of an hour," Lord Francis told Cora now, "and then agreed to give his blessing to our union—*if* you would agree to it. He warned me that you would be in no way influenced by the fact that you could become *Lady* Francis. Your brother looked as if he was about to hoist me with one hand and squeeze all the air out of me until I promised always to laugh at your disasters."

"You saw Edgar too?" she said. Then she bristled. "He has called me a walking disaster ever since I was a girl. That is most unfair. How dare he say it to you? What will you think of me?"

He leaned down slightly until his eyes were on a level with hers. "Do you care what I think of you, Cora?" he asked. "I will tell you if you like. I think you are a woman who has been unspoiled by life—by your father's wealth, by your privileged upbringing, by your unexpected fame as a heroine, by your introduction to the *crème de la crème* of society, even by the chance that has presented itself this morning to elevate yourself permanently to almost its highest ranks. I think you are a woman who thinks her own thoughts and is unafraid to be herself no matter what society demands of her. You are a woman I like, Cora Downes, a woman I respect."

He was rather surprised to realize that he meant what he said. He had never really considered what he thought of her until this moment.

"Oh," she said. She looked unusually forlorn. And even as he watched, her eyes filled with tears. "Please, will you go away now? I will always be grateful to you. I want you to believe that. This is the greatest kindness of all, what you have done during the last four days, what you are doing now. But I cannot marry you. I could not do that to you. You are too kind." She lifted a hand that was noticeably shaking and set her palm lightly against his cheek. "Thank you."

He should have left at a run. He should not have stopped running until he had put the breadth of London between them. Instead he stood where he was and felt very like crying himself.

"And what about you?" he asked. "You have not said that I could not do that to you. Would marriage to me be quite abhorrent to you?"

"No," she said softly. Her fingertips were caressing his cheek. She was going to say it in a moment, he thought in something of a panic, and then he would be forced to say it too and lie to her for the first time. *Don't say it.* "No, not abhorrent. I like you excessively. But—" She bit her lip for a moment. "But I am a romantic, you see. I have always thought that when I married, it would be for love. I want more than companionship and laughter. I want—oh, togetherness. I want children. Half a dozen children. Don't laugh." He was very far from laughing. "I want—well, the moon and every one of the stars. We could never have that, you and I, because we only like each other. I have always thought that I would not settle for less than my dream. But I suppose it is too much of a dream. It is too unrealistic."

What he felt mostly was relief. She was not in love with him, then? But it was too late to feel relief about such a thing. She must marry him, and it would be desirable that she love him, would it not?

He covered her hand against his cheek and turned his head to set his lips against her palm. There was nothing dainty about her hand, he thought irrelevantly. Although smooth and well manicured, it was a hand that looked capable of doing a good day's work.

"Let us settle for as much of the dream as we can make

come true, then, shall we?" he asked her. "Marry me, Cora, will you?"

"I cannot see the need," she said. "They were such stupid incidents, both of them—the one at Lady Fuller's ball and the one at Vauxhall. Good heavens, did no one else but you and me *see* that child? Why should we let them force us into a marriage neither of us wants?"

"Why?" he asked. "Because something like this has the unfortunate habit of following one about, Miss Downes. Not so much me. Doubtless I will be seen as one devil of a fellow for a while. It is not an image of myself I cultivate, but it will do my reputation no real harm. But you may find that even in Bristol and Bath society there will be whispers to the effect that you are *fast*. It is not a pleasant word for a lady to have attached to her name."

"It is a silly word," she said.

"Silly and unpleasant," he said.

There was a light knock on the door and it opened almost immediately. The Duchess of Bridgwater stepped inside without hesitation, though she looked rather apologetic.

"This interview is still in progress?" she asked, her eyebrows raised.

Lord Francis frowned. Was Cora Downes a green girl that she could not be left alone with him for longer than the ten or fifteen minutes they had been allowed? Had her grace feared that she would find them locked in a lascivious embrace?

"Yes," he said.

"I shall take Mr. Downes and Mr. Edgar Downes upstairs to the drawing room, then," she said. "You will find us there when you are finished."

Ah, yes. They had said they would follow him to London. He had not expected they would come before hearing from Cora. But he had understood from his meeting with them that they were very fond of her indeed.

"Papa?" She was close enough for her shriek to feel as if it was doing damage to Lord Francis's eardrums. "And Edgar? Here? Now? *Where?*"

They would have had to be stone deaf not to have heard

her even if they had been waiting in the attic. They appeared in the doorway behind the duchess, and her grace had to step smartly out of the way to avoid being bowled over by Cora Downes, who hurtled past her, still shrieking. Her father caught her in a bear hug that would surely have crushed every bone in the body of a lesser woman. Her brother did likewise when her father was finished with her, but he also lifted her off the floor and swung her in a complete circle.

The duchess looked vaguely amused. Lord Francis's nerves were too taut for humor.

"Well?" the elder Mr. Downes asked, looking from his prospective son-in-law to his daughter and back again.

She had been missing them dreadfully. She had not known quite how dreadfully until she heard they were just outside the door. Seeing their dear faces and the blessedly solid bulk of each of them—Papa and Edgar could actually make her feel *petite*—made Cora almost delirious with happiness.

All would be well now. They had come.

And then Papa asked the single word question—"Well?"

They had come to see if she would have Lord Francis. They had come for the wedding. She understood suddenly that if there was a wedding, it would be soon. There was a scandal to be squashed in the bud. They had come to buy her bride clothes and to give her their love and support. Papa had come to lead her tottering form down the aisle of some church so that she would reach the altar in time to say *I do* or *I will* or whatever it was a bride said to change her life forevermore.

It all seemed very real suddenly. *They expected her to marry Lord Francis.* Papa and Edgar always avoided London whenever they could. It was not a place they would visit purely for pleasure. They had come for a wedding.

Her eyes focused on Lord Francis from across the room, where she stood with Edgar's arm about her waist. And she tried to see him through their eyes. She was surprised that they had approved his suit—especially Edgar. Edgar had

one weakness if he had any at all. He could be rather cutting about men whom he deemed less than fully masculine.
Edgar, unlike herself, could not adopt the philosophy of
live and let live.

What she saw surprised her a little. Lord Francis was, as
usual, dressed quite immaculately. He must have gone
home after his long journey to bathe and change his clothes
before paying this call. But he was dressed uncharacteristi-
cally in a dark green superfine coat with buff breeches and
sparkling Hessians. His neckcloth was tied neatly, with no
suggestion of flamboyance. Suddenly he looked a fine figure of a man by anyone's standards. And handsome. Except
for his blue eyes, she had never really thought of him before as handsome. Or ugly either. She just had not passed
any particular judgment on his face or his dark hair.

If he had dressed like this at Mobley, Papa and Edgar
would have had no reason to *know*.

She felt something else too as she gazed at him in the
few seconds that elapsed between Papa's question and Lord
Francis's answer. She felt a sudden and unexpected and almost fierce protectiveness. She did not *want* them to know
and sneer. He was a very precious person. If he chose to
wear pink or lavender or turquoise coats at a time when
most men were turning to more sober black, then that was
his concern. Personally, she found black rather tedious and
hoped that the fashion would not last long.

Lord Francis smiled at her and then looked at Papa.

"You were quite right, sir," he said. "She is by no means
easy to persuade. I was almost at the point of trying a little
arm-twisting when you arrived."

Good heavens! Papa and Lord Francis had become well
enough acquainted to *joke* with each other? For Papa threw
back his head and uttered a short bark of laughter.

"She has not been dazzled by the prospect of a title, then,
has she?" he said. "Well, I warned you she may not have
you. She has not been willing to have anyone else yet, including a few eligible men at home and a few more here, I
have heard."

"You do not have to have anyone you do not want, Corey," Edgar said, giving her waist a little squeeze.

"I think perhaps she wants to devote herself to her father in his old age," Papa said, chuckling. "But we are much obliged to you, my lord, for being willing to do the decent thing by my daughter. We will look after her from this point on."

"We certainly will," Edgar said. "We will take you home tomorrow, Corey."

There were several points about the conversation that unexpectedly irritated Cora. For one thing, she was being spoken of in the third person—by three *men*. As soon as two or more men got together, of course, the superiority of their gender made a woman quite insignificant. Even if they loved and cherished her, she was merely a fragile toy to be protected. For another thing, she did not like to hear Lord Francis being lumped with all those other silly suitors whom she had rejected. There was no comparison whatsoever. And for another thing, much as she loved her father, there was something distinctly chilling about the prospect of devoting herself to him in his old age—no romantic love, no marriage, no home of her own, no children, none of *that other*, about which she was avidly and embarrassedly curious.

Of course, even if she married Lord Francis she would never know most of those things. But *some* of them— surely she would be able to expect some of them. Would *some* be enough? How much physical aversion did he feel for women? She squashed the very improper thought.

Oh, dear, she was so confused.

"Miss Downes?" Lord Francis was addressing her, ignoring Papa and Edgar for the moment, though in their usual manner they were proceeding to take charge. "You have not given me a final answer. Can you give it now? Or would you prefer that I return—perhaps tomorrow? Will you marry me?"

"Yes," she said. As meekly as that.

And *that* was that, she thought a few moments later while she was being subjected to hugs again—including one from the Duchess of Bridgwater.

Gracious heaven, what had she done?

Papa was slapping Lord Francis on the shoulder and pumping his hand at the same time.

And if his paleness had not been occasioned by illness, she thought suddenly when it was far too late to think at all, what *had* it been caused by? By the fact that he felt compelled to marry her?

Oh, the poor gentleman. The poor, dear man.

Chapter 12

❦

It was a surprisingly large wedding, considering the fact
that it took place only two weeks after the incident in
Vauxhall that had precipitated it.

The Duke of Fairhurst surprised Lord Francis by arriving
in London two days before the event and bringing his wife
with him. It was as well that they had opened the Fairhurst
town house. The following day Lord Francis's sisters both
arrived from the country with their husbands.

The groom gave them no chance to express to him their
opinions of his marriage. He paid them only a brief call and
took Cora with him. He did not suppose afterward that she
had made a particularly good impression on any of them—
she sat stiff and almost mute throughout tea, ate only half a
scone, and took only one sip of tea. Lord Francis realized
that she could drink no more as her hand was shaking. It
amused him that a woman who was so bold and fearless in
almost any situation that presented itself could be reduced
to shivering terror in the presence of aristocracy.

She did not make a good impression on them, perhaps,
but neither did she make a bad impression. She was dressed
elegantly and fortunately had left farce at home behind her
for once.

Of course, his family did not approve. He did not need
private words with any of them to confirm that impression.
The other three had all made excellent matches. They had
expected as much of him. At the very least they had ex-

pected him to marry a lady. But they were family, when all was said and done. They were not prepared to turn him off merely because he was insisting on marrying far beneath him.

Mr. Downes had a brother and numerous nephews and nieces living in Canterbury. All of them were prosperous businessmen or married to successful men. All of them were summoned to London for the wedding and all of them came except for one niece, who was in imminent expectation of a confinement. They took up collective residence in the Pulteney Hotel. Lord Francis and Cora took a second tea with them there after leaving Fairhurst's. This time Cora ate heartily and drank two cups of tea. She talked and joked and laughed.

And of course the Duke of Bridgwater, with his mother and his two sisters, attended the wedding. Indeed, her grace offered to have the wedding breakfast prepared at her town house, but she had two rivals. Fairhurst offered to host it. Mr. Downes did not *offer* to have it at the Pulteney—he insisted. And so a private banqueting room was reserved and a private banquet ordered.

Bridgwater had agreed to be Lord Francis's best man. He seemed rather abjectly apologetic about the whole thing, as if it had all been his fault.

"This is the devil of a thing, Kneller," he said. "It makes one realize how fragile a thing one's freedom is and how unexpectedly limited one can suddenly be in one's choices. It gives me the jitters, to be quite frank with you." He took snuff with slow deliberation. "After this and after I have got Lizzie and Jane safely wed, I am going to retire from the world and become a recluse. No marriage is better than a forced marriage, after all. I am most terribly sorry for my part in this, old chap."

Lord Francis felt compelled to assure his grace that this marriage *was* of his own choosing, though perhaps the timing was not. He felt compelled to declare that he was fond of Miss Downes—"damned fond," as he put it, not to appear too lukewarm.

But his grace went away still declaring that never *never*

would he risk matrimony or the danger of matrimony himself. No more looking about him in the hope that his eye would suddenly alight on that one woman who had been created for his eternal delight. No looking about him at all from this moment on. No eye contact with any single female below the age of forty or with the mama of any single female.

The Earl of Greenwald attended the wedding with Lady Jane. Lord Francis had also invited a few of his friends as well as his young cousin, Lord Hawthorne. Lady Kellington, who still declared she would be eternally grateful to Cora for snatching her dogs from the clutches of death, more or less invited herself. Lord Francis had written to the Earl of Thornhill to announce his coming nuptials, but there would be no time for his friend to come from Yorkshire. Besides, Lady Thornhill was with child, and Gabe was strict about not allowing her to travel at such times. They had not even come for Samantha's wedding for that reason, though Samantha was more like a sister than a cousin to Lady Thornhill.

Even in the days leading up to his wedding Lord Francis could not stop thinking of Samantha. If someone could have told him at her wedding to Carew that he himself would be marrying a mere few weeks later, he would have . . . Well, he did not care to think of it. It seemed disloyal to his love for Samantha to be marrying so soon after losing her. And yet it *was* disloyal to Cora to be thinking such thoughts.

Cora was blameless in this whole mess. So was he. But mess there was, and there was only one way in which to set all to rights. At least he did not dislike the woman. Quite the contrary. And at least he did not find her unattractive. If anything, he found her too attractive. No gentleman, he thought, should have such lustful thoughts about the woman he was about to marry. Not, at least, when he did not love her. Not when he loved another woman.

He was going to have to try, at least, he decided, to grow fond of Cora. It should not be impossible. Indeed, he already was fond of her to a certain degree. And he was going to be faithful to her. Not just in body—although he had kept his fair share of mistresses, he had never approved of married men doing so. He was going to have to be faithful to Cora in mind too. That meant forgetting that his heart had been broken, forgetting that he was being forced into marrying the wrong woman.

Yet even as he made the decision, he wondered how soon it would be before Samantha heard the news from Thornhill—or from Bridgwater. And how she would feel about it. Or if she would feel anything at all.

His wedding was not at the fashionable St. George's with half the *ton* in attendance. It was at a smaller church with his family and hers and some of their friends. Larger than might have been expected, yes, but still a far more intimate wedding than Samantha's had been. It was very sweet and very solemn and very, very real.

Cora was dressed in spring green muslin and looked rather like an earth goddess, he thought. He was glad she had not dressed in white, as most brides did. White did not suit her. In her own way, he thought, taking her hand in his when the vicar instructed him to do so—in her own way, despite her bold features and heavy hair and overgenerous figure and unusual height, she was beautiful. Or perhaps it was because of those attributes. Cora Downes was very much her own person, in both appearance and behavior.

Cora Downes. He repeated words after the vicar when instructed to do so, and she repeated words. He took the ring from Bridgwater and slid it onto her finger. And then strangely, mysteriously, irrevocably, she was no longer Cora Downes. She was Lady Francis Kneller.

She was his wife.

He remembered to smile at her.

And so it was done. He was a married man. The register duly signed, he led her outside into the heat and the sunshine and paused on the church steps with her so that they could be greeted by their guests before driving away in his carriage. In the course of just a very few minutes, his life had been changed into a course that was so new and so unknown that he was bewildered by the prospect of proceeding with it at all.

"Lord Francis," she said, squeezing his arm. "You do look splendid. That is a lovely pale shade of green. It makes my dress seem almost garish."

She had saved him from meaningless panic by bringing him laughter instead. It had been *his* place to compliment *her* on her appearance and give her that little reassuring squeeze of the arm.

"Cora," he said, chuckling, "as usual, you render me speechless. But not garish, my dear. Glorious, vivid, like spring turning to summer. But then perhaps I mean the woman inside the dress more than just the dress itself."

She laughed merrily. "Oh," she said, "you are so *good* with words. You make me feel almost beautiful."

They were the last private words they exchanged until they were alone together after the wedding breakfast, on their way to Sidley, his estate in Wiltshire.

All day, since the moment she woke up to find the Duchess of Bridgwater's maid drawing back the curtains at her window, she had pretended to herself that this was the wedding day she had always dreamed of.

It had not been so very difficult. As soon as the curtains were back, she had seen that yet again the sky was cloudless. And as soon as she had set foot inside her dressing room she had seen the wedding dress spread out there that she had insisted upon even though her grace and Jane had tried gently to persuade her to choose white, since white was what most brides were now wearing. But she loved her dress. To her, green was the perfect color for a bride, suggestive as it was of life and warmth and energy—and springtime.

Then downstairs in the breakfast room and later back in her dressing room, her grace and Elizabeth and Jane had all been determinedly gay. Dressing for her wedding had been a communal exercise, involving the three of them and two maids—and involving too a great deal of chatter and laughter.

And then Papa and Edgar had arrived—Edgar had insisted on coming too rather than proceeding to the church alone—to take her to her wedding and had aroused both excitement and nervousness in her—and even tears.

Inside the church, while her papa had escorted her to the altar rail, she had noticed immediately the contrast between the sober colors worn by her male relatives—solid middle-class citizens, all—and even of the other male guests, including the Duke of Bridgwater, who was the best man, and the light green worn by Lord Francis. And fixing her eyes on him as he stood waiting for her and watching her, she had felt again that rush of protectiveness for him. Let her hear or see just one suggestion of a sneer over him for the rest of this morning and she would make her feelings known and no mistake about it.

He also had copious amounts of lace at his wrists and throat and his neckcloth was a work of art to surpass all others.

And then there had been the wedding service itself. She had listened to every word, watched every gesture, felt every nuance of atmosphere. It had been her wedding—her wonderful wedding, her dream wedding—and she had been determined to commit every detail of it to memory. Including the paleness of her groom's face and the nervousness in his voice and the slight trembling in his hand as he put her ring on her finger and the same slight tremble in his lips when he kissed her. And his smile afterward, telling her that he did not blame her for all this, that together they would make the best of it.

In his own way, she had thought, he was very handsome, and she would take on anyone who dared to hint otherwise. Even Edgar. It would not be the first time she had gone at Edgar with her fists—she had always scorned to use her fingernails—and their battles had never been as uneven as they might have been because he never felt at liberty to come back at her with *his* fists. She would black both of his eyes if he ever so much as pursed his lips in criticism of Lord Francis.

Her husband.

Despite the close attention she had paid the wedding service, the realization had still jolted her with surprise.

He was her husband. She was Lady Francis Kneller.

And then, outside the church and at the Pulteney, she had been hugged and kissed to death—her uncle and her male cousins and even the female cousins' husbands all seemed to be large men like Papa and Edgar. Even the Duke of Fairhurst had hugged her, and her new sisters-in-law had pecked her cheeks, though Cora suspected that none of them really liked her at all. The duchess of Bridgwater had been kind enough to shed tears over her and Jane might have crushed every bone in her body had she only been a little larger and a great deal stronger.

Oh, yes, it had not been so very difficult to imagine that this was the wedding day of her dreams. In many ways it really had been wonderful. Lord Francis had kept her at his side at the Pulteney and had refused to allow either her family to pry her away from him or his family to do the like for him. He had behaved as if they were any normal bride and groom—unwilling to be parted for a moment. It had been easy to believe that it was so.

But finally, after another round of hugs and kisses and handshakes and back slappings, they were in his carriage, alone this time—the Duke and Duchess of Bridgwater had ridden with them from the church to the Pulteney. They were on their way to Wiltshire, to Sidley, his home there. They would arrive before dark, he had assured her.

They were alone together, and she had to admit to herself finally that this was no normal marriage after all. Was it?

Her grace had had a talk with her last evening after ascertaining that her Aunt Downes from Canterbury had not already done so. She had tried her best to sound reassuring, though there really had been no need. Cora had already known or guessed most of what she had had to say, but the knowing had never frightened her, as it was perhaps supposed to do. It had only aroused her curiosity to experience it for herself. And a little more than curiosity. She had always *wanted* it and was unable to imagine how any woman could cringe from the very thought of it.

But the trouble was that she was not going to have it with this marriage. Was she? She was really not at all sure, but she rather thought not. And she would prefer not to expect it rather than be disappointed over the coming days and weeks. But if she was not to experience it in her marriage, then she was never going to experience it at all. The thought saddened her immensely. Even apart from the loss of her half a dozen children she was sad.

But it was not his fault. She was never going to blame him.

She turned to him. But he had turned to her at the same moment and was taking her hand and lacing his fingers with hers and smiling at her.

"Well, Cora," he said, "the deed is done and we have survived it. Do you think we can rub along together tolerably well?"

"I think so," she said. She squared her shoulders and found that her left shoulder was now touching his right one. Neither of them sprang away from the contact. "I daresay your home is large and splendid and has a whole army of servants, but you will find that I will not be at a loss. I have managed Mobley Abbey for a few years and have been Papa's hostess on a number of occasions. I will not shame you before your servants and neighbors, I can assure you. And I am quite prepared to take on my responsibilities on the estate and in the parish. I will do all that is expected of any wife. I will not shame you. And I—"

He was laughing softly. What had she said wrong?

"Cora," he said, "you are not about to go into battle, dear. You need not look quite so determinedly belligerent. And what about me? Will your busy schedule allow you to grant me any of your time?"

"When you wish it, of course," she said. "But I shall not expect to live in your pocket, you may rest assured. I know that ladies are not expected to cling to their husbands. Even in *my* world that is so. Men think they have to spend their time about the important things in this world. They are quite misguided, of course. They look after only the mundane matters, like the making of money, while the women look after the really important things, like the well-being of people. But women have learned to pamper men and make them feel important even when they are not particularly so. I will not interfere with your life."

He was shaking with laughter now.

"Cora," he said, "you never fail me. What a delight you are. You have just dealt me the most excruciatingly cutting set-down of my life, and you do not even realize you have done so, do you?"

The trouble was that she did not think of him as an ordinary man. But she had just implied that she would leave him alone to his useless, self-important life of business while she looked after the truly important things.

She bit her lip and looked at him—and exploded into laughter. They leaned against each other's shoulder and indulged their amusement far longer than was necessary.

If she had said such a thing to Edgar—and she sometimes did, when goaded—she would have had a blistering argument on her hands. There would have been no glimmering of humor in the matter.

"Will I have to plead for some of your time?" Lord Francis asked.

"No," she said, her laughter fading. "But what I meant to say is that you must not feel obliged to entertain me. I will soon learn to entertain myself. I am not a cowering, helpless person."

"Only when you are in the presence of princes and dukes," he said.

"That was unkind," she told him. "You would too if you had never met any before in your life. But really you must feel no responsibility toward me. I know this marriage was not of your choosing. I know that left to yourself, you would not have chosen marriage at all. Well, if you *had* to marry, perhaps it is as well you married me. I will be quite happy to allow you to be free, you see. I will be quite happy to be free myself."

She felt more miserable saying so than she cared to admit to herself. Was that what she had undertaken by marrying Lord Francis? Was she going to lead a lonely life?

He clasped her hand a little more tightly. There was no laughter in his face now, she saw when she glanced at him.

"What are you saying Cora?" he asked. "Are you saying that you married me because you saw the necessity of doing so, but that you would rather it be a marriage in name only? That perhaps it would even be better for us to live apart?"

Oh, no, she would not *rather* it be any such thing. And live apart? She had not expected this. Oh, not quite this. They were going to live apart? Panic made the air in her nostrils feel icy.

"If you wish it," she said.

"I do not wish it." His words were curt. There was coldness, even anger, in his voice. "And I will tell you now, Cora, that if it is what you wish, if it is what you think to insist upon, then you may find yourself in for a shock. I may not be the husband of your choice and you may not be the wife of mine—I will pay you the respect of being honest with you, you see—but we are husband and wife. I intend that we remain so—for the rest of our lives. Fight me if you wish. I promise you it will be a fight you cannot and will not win."

She should be feeling outrage at this blatant evidence that even Lord Francis Kneller could play at being lord and master when he thought he was being challenged. She waited for the familiar fury against *those males*. But all she could feel was something quite unfamiliar. Not anger. Certainly not meekness or fear. Desire? If that was really what she was feeling, she had better squash it without further ado. She could not possibly feel desire for Lord Francis. It would be emotional suicide to feel any such thing.

But what did he mean? *What did he mean?*

"Capitulation, Cora?" he asked. "Without a shot fired? You disappoint me." The anger—if that was what it had been—had gone from his voice. "Come, talk to me."

"I really did not want us to live apart," she said. "That was not what I meant. I merely meant . . . Oh, it does not matter."

"I know what you meant," he said. The familiar amusement was back. "You meant that you did not want me to feel the burden of having been forced into offering for you and marrying you. You were being *noble,* Cora. You were being *gallant.* You do like to turn our roles upside down and inside out, do you not, dear? I am supposed to be the noble one. I am supposed to be the one reassuring *you.* Instead of which I have been ripping up at you. I *never* rip up at people. You see what an effect you have on me?"

She looked at him sideways. His eyes were smiling.

"I suspect that after a week of marriage to you, I will not know whether I am on my head or my feet," he said. "And I will predict now, Cora, that life with you is not going to be dull."

"I do hope not, Lord Francis," she said. "I cannot abide a dull life."

"Cora," he said, "since you live in terror of lordships, would it be wise to drop mine? Shall I be plain Francis?"

"I am not terrified," she said indignantly. "Merely—"

"—terrified," he said when she was unwise enough to pause to seek for the best word. "Call me Francis."

"Francis," she said.

They lapsed into silence. He wriggled a little lower on the seat and set one foot on the opposite seat. Before many minutes had passed, she knew that he was sleeping. He was breathing deeply and evenly. Her fingers were still laced firmly with his.

What had he meant? The question turned itself over and over in her mind without bringing any answers along behind it. What had he meant when he said that they were husband and wife and would remain so for the rest of their lives?

What had he meant?

Chapter 13

❦

She stared out into darkness, though in her mind's eye she could see the cobbled terrace below her window and the sharply sloping terraced bank of shrubs and flowers beyond it. At the foot of the slope there were formal gardens with grass, low box hedges, and gravel arranged into immaculately kept geometric shapes. There was a fountain at the center, with jets of water spouting from the mouth of a winged cherub.

She had fallen in love with the park and the gardens even before noticing the house, neat and solid and classical in design. She was so very glad he did not intend that they live apart. Her heart had gone out to her new home from the start. Though he had told her he did not spend a great deal of time here. Perhaps she could change that now that she was with him to give him some companionship.

Would they be able to rub along together tolerably well, he had asked her in the carriage. Oh, she really thought they might. After all the fuss of their arrival and her presentation to the staff, who had been lined up rather dauntingly in the hall, and after the housekeeper had shown her to her apartments and she had bathed and changed and had her hair dressed—after it all they had sat down together for dinner and then had gone together to the drawing room. They had not stopped talking except when the need to laugh had given them pause. They had laughed a great deal. She had told him some stories from her childhood and he had reciprocated with tales from his. They had both chosen amusing stories that they knew would tickle the other.

He *did* like her, she thought, as she liked him. She liked him exceedingly well. She drew her single braid over her shoulder and ran her fingers absently along it. He had been very kind to marry her. She was going to make sure that he never regretted doing so. He did not dislike her—else he would have jumped at the chance for near-freedom she had offered him in the carriage. Instead he had appeared quite offended.

And would she ever regret it? She drew a slow breath and let it out just as slowly. She thought of all her dreams of marriage and of the men she had refused because none of them had fit the dream. She thought of what the Duchess of Bridgwater had told her yesterday, expecting that she was putting fear into Cora, assuring her that it was really not so fearsome after all, that once she grew accustomed to it she might even come to like it. Cora had always expected to like it—in her dream marriage. And she thought of today and the way she had deliberately tried to enjoy her wedding day. She *had* enjoyed it. Right up until the moment when Lord Francis—she must remember to drop the *Lord*—had escorted her upstairs and paused outside her dressing room to kiss her hand and open the door for her.

She had felt lonely since then. There was no reason to feel lonely. Every night since her infancy she had gone to bed alone, and she had frequently stayed alone in strange houses. There was nothing different from usual about tonight. Except that it was her wedding night and it should—if this had been a normal marriage—have been gloriously different from any other that had gone before it.

She wondered if companionship was going to be enough. Not that she had any choice in the matter now. The deed, as Francis had put it, was done.

And then there was a tap on the door of her bedchamber and the door opened almost before she could spin about and long before she could think of calling to whoever it was to come in.

It was Francis, looking very gorgeous indeed in a scarlet silk dressing gown.

"Oh, Francis," she said, smiling brightly, wondering why she sounded breathless, "did you want something?"

He paused with his hand still on the knob of the door after closing it. He looked at her with raised eyebrows. "Cora, my dear," he said, "you leave me near speechless, as usual." He relinquished his hold of the knob and came toward her. "Now what could I possibly want with my wife on my wedding night?"

Her knees almost buckled. Certainly her stomach performed a headstand and then rolled into a tumble toss.

"Oh," she said, gripping her braid as if only by doing so could she keep herself upright. "Oh, Francis, how kind of you. But there is really no need, you know. You must not feel you *have* to, just for my sake. I shall be quite content . . ." She swallowed. He had come close and had set his hands on her shoulders. He was looking into her eyes.

"Kind?" he said. "I must not feel I have to? That is remarkably generous of you, Cora. Are you frightened, by any chance?"

"Frightened? Me?" she said. "No, of course not." They were going to have a *wedding night?* "I just meant that you must not feel obliged to do this if it is distasteful to you. I will understand. I did not expect it." She should not be too persuasive, she thought. She did not want him to go away. If she could experience this—even just once in her life— she would be content. Even if it must be with a man she did not love. She *liked* him enormously. That would suffice.

One of his hands was cupping her cheek. His eyes really were decidedly blue, she thought. They were not the sort of gray that wishful thinking pretended was blue. "Because we married in haste and under some compulsion?" he said. "You expected I would think all my obligations to you fulfilled once I had given you the protection of my name, Cora? No, dear, we will be man and wife in more than just name."

Her knees really did go then and he had to catch her in his arms.

"Oops," she said and laughed. Suddenly she really did feel both nervous and self-conscious. She was so very unattractive. She was so very large. He was both elegant and graceful. And she had not thought of wearing a dressing gown over her nightgown. She had *braided* her hair. She must look like an overgrown twelve-year-old.

"Cora." His voice was very low. "It is just me, dear. We have talked and laughed and been comfortable together all afternoon and evening. And I am not one of those nasty princes or dukes or marquesses to terrify you."

"I am not terrified of them," she said, "or of you. I am not, Francis."

He smiled and loosened his hold of her. "Unbraid your hair for me, if you please," he said. "I have always wondered what it looks like down."

"Just as unruly as it looks when it is up," she said, lifting her arms to comply with his request. "I should have had it cut. I know short hair is all the crack. But I keep thinking that if I do not like it short I will have to wait years before it is long again. Besides, Papa thinks there is something rather sinful about short hair on women. If God had wanted them with short hair, he always says, he would have made it so that it would not grow. But he never thinks that the same argument could be used of men. And of men's beards, too."

She was prattling. She wished now she had not persuaded herself that he would not come. She wished she had prepared her mind, planned what she would say.

He took her hands away from her hair when she had unbraided it and was combing through it with her fingers. He did it himself. She could feel herself blushing. She had never thought to blush before Francis.

"Oh, Cora," he said, "it is beautiful. It is a shame you cannot always wear it down. Though I must admit I feel smug at the thought that only I will see it thus. I can sympathize with sultans and their harems. Don't ever have it cut. If you ever do, I shall take you over my knee and beat you for gross disobedience."

She threw back her head and laughed merrily. "You may

try it if you fancy the idea of two black eyes and a broken nose and smashed teeth," she said.

He was grinning too and then chuckling. "This is better," he said. "I thought your eyes were about to start from your head, Cora, and your cheeks were about to burst into flame. Come to bed."

It was a good antidote to laughter, that last sentence. She wondered if he really wanted her or if this was very much a matter of duty to him. It made little difference, she supposed. It was something he had decided to do and she was not going to argue further. She was going to enjoy the experience while it was being offered. Perhaps this would be the one and only time. She climbed into bed while he removed his dressing gown and blew out the candles.

This was her wedding night, she thought. She set herself deliberately to enjoy it, as she had set herself earlier to enjoy her wedding day.

It was a necessity to desire her enough to consummate their marriage. He had married her that day and owed her certain duties. He owed her his body and his seed. It was necessary that he make love to her often enough to enable her to perform *her* duty of filling his nursery and getting his heir.

But he felt almost ashamed of the extent of his desire for her. She was—or had been—Cora Downes, he reminded himself when he entered her room and saw her standing at the window, dressed only in a thin cotton nightgown. She was the woman he had agreed to bring into fashion, the woman for whom he had set himself to find a husband. She was the woman whom farce followed closely. The woman he had been forced, much against his inclination, into marrying because twice he had inadvertently compromised her. She was *not* the woman he loved.

And yet, as he dealt with her nervousness, he found himself wanting her very much indeed. And as he watched her unbraid her hair and then pushed aside her hands so that he could smooth it out with his own fingers, he felt himself harden into arousal far sooner than he would have wanted to do so. Her long, loose hair was the one extra ingredient, missing until now, that made her finally and magnificently beautiful. Not in any remotely delicate way. He found himself thinking of Amazons—and then she was threatening to black his eyes and break his nose and his teeth in response to his teasing threat to spank her.

She was wonderful.

She was also a virgin and very, very innocent, he suspected. His mind went to determined war with his body as he climbed into bed beside her and slid one arm beneath her neck to turn her against him. He must be gentle with her. He must not frighten or disgust her. He must hurt her as little as he possibly could. He must be patient.

He did not kiss her. With his free hand he caressed her face and her neck.

"Mm," she said, and she put her arm about his waist and wriggled closer to him. He paused and drew a few deep breaths. His mind was threatening to lose the battle.

He slid his hand down her back, pausing at her waist, continuing more lightly to her buttocks, moving up over her hip to her breast. She moved back a little from him not to impede his progress.

He felt as if he had been plunged into a bath of steam. She was warm and shapely, generously curved in all the right places, soft where she was supposed to be soft, firm where she was supposed to be firm. Her breasts were large and youthfully firm. He cupped one in his hand, tested the nipple with the pad of his thumb. It hardened under his touch.

"Oh," she said and she started panting quite audibly.

He opened the buttons of her nightgown, going slowly in order to give himself a chance to impose control on himself and to give her a chance to know what he was about to do. He fondled her other breast beneath the fabric of her gown.

"Ah," she said. "Ah."

She had forgotten her nervousness. He moved his hand down inside the gown, flat over her stomach, down over the warm hair to curl into warmer depths. He did not attempt any more intimate exploration. She was breathing in gasps against his shoulder.

It was time, he thought. He could teach her gradually over time more about foreplay. But he would not frighten her again tonight. He removed his hand and reached down to draw up her nightgown—up over her legs to her hips. He paused there, but he gave in to desire and raised it up over her breasts and turned her onto her back.

He could hear the blood thundering in his ears. He could not remember a time when he had been so hotly aroused—not that he spent a great deal of time trying to remember such an occasion.

She was all magnificent, warm woman, he thought as he came on top of her, nudged his knees between hers, and spread her legs wide. There was no resistance. He gritted his teeth, pressed his eyes shut, and imposed iron control on himself as he slid his hands beneath her to hold her firm while he mounted her. He moved slowly, pushing inward to the barrier and slowly yet firmly beyond it to embed himself deeply in her. She whimpered once, quietly. He lifted some of his weight onto his forearms so that she would be able to breathe beneath him. He waited, gathering his breath and control.

And then she took charge.

He felt her legs slide up the outsides of his own—long, slim, smooth legs, which raised his temperature as they moved. And then she lifted them to twine about his own. And tilted her hips and pushed against him so that he seemed even deeper. He was alarmed at the sensations she aroused in him. He raised his head and looked down at her. His eyes had accustomed themselves enough to the darkness that he could see her head thrown back on the pillow, her eyes closed, her hair all about her face and shoulders. Her mouth was open. Even as he watched she pressed her shoulders back into the pillow and thrust up her bosom to touch his chest with her hardened nipples.

Something snapped in him—his control. His body had won the war.

"Cora," he said with a groan, lowering his face into her hair, gritting his teeth again, shutting his eyes tightly again. But nothing helped. His hands came beneath her once again and he moved in her with deep, convulsive, swift strokes.

It was all over in moments. He thrust deeply and spilled and gushed into her.

Like a schoolboy with his first woman, he thought when thought returned after a few seconds of oblivion. No, that was insulting to schoolboys. His first woman had had to coax him, gauche and terrified, to climax.

He felt deeply ashamed. He disengaged from her, lifted himself off her to lie beside her. He rested one arm across his eyes and tried to stop panting.

"I am sorry," he said. "I am so very sorry, Cora."

He hoped he had not hurt her badly or shocked her too deeply. But he must have done both. At the age of thirty he had been gauchely excited by a woman's well-endowed body. His wife's. He had had women who were marvelously skilled at their profession, and had never relinquished his control. No, he had had to reserve that ignominy for his wife's bed. On their wedding night. While he was in the process of taking her virginity.

Her hand burrowed its way into his. "It is all right, Francis," she said. "Don't distress yourself. I understand. I do." She lifted his hand and held it against her cheek. She turned her head and kissed the back of it. "I do understand," she said. "And I do not mind at all. You must not think I do. I am very fond of you just as you are of me. You do not have to pretend for me. I understand."

He was not sure he understood what it was *she* understood or what it was he need not pretend to. Sexual expertise? Well, he had just proved that he was sadly lacking on that score. He could not reply immediately. He merely squeezed her hand slightly.

She was quite magnificent, he thought. If only he could get his desire for such a sexual feast under control, he would be the most fortunate of husbands. This was his for a lifetime. *She* was his for a lifetime. It somehow did not seem right that he did not love her. He thought fleetingly of Samantha, but ruthlessly suppressed the thought. It was certainly not right to think about *her*. He would be far better employed cultivating an affection for his wife to match his physical desire for her. He already was fond of her. He had never been in any doubt about that.

He did not want to come to crave her only like this. He had never wanted a marriage of just this. He wanted friendship and emotional intimacy and partnership and parenthood as well as sexual satisfaction. None of which were impossible with Cora, except perhaps the second. He must work on the second.

He should have left her bed and returned to his own, he thought when it was too late to act on the thought. He was warm and comfortable and very close to sleep.

What was it that she understood? What was it that she did not mind? What was it he need not pretend to?

Lord Francis slept, his one arm still over his eyes, his other hand held against Cora's cheek.

For a few minutes she was horribly disappointed. It was all over—so soon. Almost before she had started to enjoy it. And it might never happen again. He would not wish to do it with her ever again.

She had been too eager, perhaps. She had scared him, disgusted him. But she had not been able to help herself. He had lain down beside her and set his arm about her and she had been instantly aware of his warmth and his firmly muscled, splendidly proportioned body. He had felt so very masculine. And his hand, moving first over her face, and then over her body, and finally over the most private parts beneath her nightgown had excited her almost beyond thought. She had forgotten entirely that he was—well, that he was not as other men were.

She had wanted the rest of it so eagerly, so hungrily. When he had lifted her nightgown and come on top of her, she had hardly waited, as any modest bride would, for him to part her legs. She had opened for him. What had fol-

lowed had been indescribably wonderful. She had expected
it to feel good. But she had never imagined the sensation of
stretching, as if she was really too narrow but he would
forge a passage anyway. The pain she had expected. But it
had been over in a moment almost before she had been able
to feel it as pain. And he had come deeper. That had been
the most wonderful part of all. She had never imagined
such depth. She really had not dreamed there could be that
much room inside her. But there was—she had even coaxed
him deeper.

She had been so very excited. She had known there was
more to come. She had known there was ecstasy to come.
From sheer instinct she had moved her body into position
to feel the ecstasy. She had expected it to take a long time.
She had heard that men derived great pleasure from this.
There had been little time for much pleasure yet.

Then he had started to move, again with unimagined
force. But before she had even begun to enjoy it or to
somehow fit herself to it so that she could partake of the
pleasure, it was all over. He had stopped suddenly, pushing
even more deeply into her, she had felt increased heat deep
inside, and he had gradually relaxed on top of her.

It had all been over. She had felt deeply disappointed.

Until she had heard his apology. Until she remembered.
It had not been possible to remember while it was happen-
ing. He had such a very masculine body—not that she had
any with which to compare it.

She pushed disappointment aside in her concern for his
feelings. She felt a welling of the now-familiar tenderness
and protectiveness. He had done this for her. All of it. He
had married her and brought her here and done this to her
all because he wanted to protect her from disgrace with the
ton. Really it had been all her fault. If she had not been so
foolishly terrified at meeting the Prince of Wales, Francis
would not have had to take her out onto that balcony when
there was no one out there to act as chaperon. If she had not
so foolishly fallen for that little boy's pathetic story at

Vauxhall, he would not have had to come after her and comfort her and be caught with his arms about her.

It was all her fault.

And through it all he had acted as the perfect gentleman. Not only for the sake of society, but for her sake too. He had known that without a consummated marriage she would feel less of a woman and a failure as a wife. And so he had consummated it. And had hated every moment of it.

She was so very unattractive. She was too tall and too large everywhere. It was no wonder . . . But then even an attractive woman would not appeal to Francis.

She would not allow it to happen again. She would somehow convince him that it really did not matter to her. But the very thought brought unexpected tears welling to her eyes. Just a matter of minutes ago she had told herself that if she could experience this but once in her life she would be contented. But she knew now how wrong she had been to think that. It had been so wonderful, so very, very wonderful even if it had ended in disappointment. The prospect of never experiencing it again made her feel dreadfully bleak. She sighed aloud and turned her head to lay her lips against Francis's hand again.

She could not sleep. And she could not get comfortable. She turned onto her side facing him and onto her back again. And again onto her side, all the while holding his hand. And then the thought came to her in a flash of unwelcome insight—the thought that would doom her to an entirely sleepless night, she knew.

She had fallen in love with him.

All this time she had been telling herself that she enjoyed his company, that he was easy to talk with and laugh with, that she was a little fond of him. And all the while she had been falling in love with him.

But being in love under the circumstances was a little painful.

No, really it was quite, quite painful.

What a stupid, brainless thing to have allowed herself to do.

Cora sighed once more and tried to find comfort for her cheek against his hand.

Chapter 14

~

L ord Francis woke up when a sunbeam and his right eye decided to occupy the same spot on the bed. He blinked and moved his head—and realized with a start that he was at Sidley and, more specifically, in his wife's bed. At surely a far later hour than the one at which he usually got up. He was surprised to find that he had slept deeply through the night.

He turned his head gingerly, hoping that his sudden movement had not woken Cora. Perhaps he could get himself out of her bed and out of her room without disturbing her.

She was not there.

He sat up, feeling remarkably foolish. His wife had got up on the morning after her wedding, leaving him to sleep on? Was not the situation usually reversed? But he might have known that Cora would turn the tables on him. She was probably out and about by now, running the estate.

He hated the thought of meeting her face-to-face this morning.

She had had an early breakfast, he discovered when he had dressed and went downstairs. She had eaten just toast and coffee—she had been unwilling to wait for anything to be cooked. They just had not expected her ladyship to be down so early this morning, the butler said, sounding almost aggrieved. And was he looking reproachfully at his master? Lord Francis wondered, hoping that he was not blushing. As if to ask what on earth a bride was doing up early on the morning after her wedding night.

The whole thing seemed about to become a public as well as a private disaster.

She had spoken with the housekeeper and made arrangements to consult with her and to examine the household accounts later in the morning. She had appeared in the kitchen—a domain on which he had never trespassed since he knew it to be ruled by a somewhat tyrannical cook—in order to bid everyone a sunny good morning and ask Alice how her cold was healing. Alice had been unfortunate enough to sneeze while standing in line for inspection in the hall yesterday afternoon. Cora had suggested coming back later to discuss the day's menu since Cook was busy getting his lordship's breakfast.

The devil. Cook would not like that, Lord Francis thought, almost nervously.

And then she had taken herself outside to enjoy the morning air and to explore the gardens. That was what she had told the butler, anyway. She was nowhere to be seen by the time Lord Francis went out there, breakfastless.

He found her in the stables, bent over the raised hoof of one of his carriage horses with his head groom. She was wearing a simple cotton morning gown. Her hair was up but dressed loosely and simply. He guessed that she had dressed without benefit of her maid. She wore neither shawl nor bonnet.

She turned her head and smiled brightly when he appeared. No blushes at the sight of him—and no grimace of distaste either.

"You suspected yesterday that one of the horses was not quite fit, did you not, Francis?" she said. "It is this one. I mentioned it to Mr. Latterly and he looked and sure enough there was a stone and it has chafed the poor horse's hoof. It is a good thing we do not plan to travel today."

She had mentioned it to Latterly. Not either he or his coachman. Lady Francis Kneller, he thought, was going to take some careful handling. But he could not stop himself from seeing the humor of the situation. His bride had been

out and busy while the exhausted bridegroom had kept to
his bed in order to sleep off the effects of his wedding
night. He grinned.

"Good morning, my dear," he said. "Good morning, Latterly." He too bent over the horse's hoof attentively in
order to confirm with his own eyes what he had already
been told.

A few minutes later he was leading his wife from the stables, her arm linked through his. She was chattering to him
about horses. She had learned to ride as a child, but there
had not been nearly enough opportunity to practice her
skills until the move to Mobley Abbey. She loved riding.
There was no exercise quite so exhilarating. She was talking very brightly, he noticed. Too brightly? She was looking ahead instead of at him.

"I hear that you have a busy morning planned," he said.
"Can you spare half an hour for a mere husband, my dear?"
It would have been easier to have gone inside for breakfast
and to have allowed her to disappear with the housekeeper.
But he had the feeling that if he did not talk to her now,
they might never talk again. Not really talk, that was. And
he might turn forever craven.

"Of course." She smiled quickly at him, turning her head
and lifting her eyes to his chin before looking ahead again.
"What a foolish question, Francis. I will always have time
for you. You are my husband."

"There is a scenic walk," he said, pointing to the trees at
the far side of the terrace. "A planned route that circles up
behind the house and comes out close to the stables again.
It was created for maximum picturesque effect and to give
the illusion of peace and seclusion. The whole park has
been very carefully designed."

"And yet you have spent little of your time here," she
said. "Perhaps things will change, Francis, now that you
have me as a companion."

A companion. Not a wife. She even seemed to throw
special emphasis on the word. The subject had to be dealt
with.

"Cora." He covered her hand on his arm and patted it. "I

must apologize for last night. It must have been a less than pleasant experience for you."

"It was not unpleasant," she said briskly, "and I thank you for it. It was extremely kind of you. But it is over now. We can put it behind us. It was not necessary, but I was and am grateful."

Had he understood her correctly? Was she saying that the sexual aspect of their marriage was unnecessary? Had he been that bad? He winced inwardly.

"*What* was extremely kind of me?" he asked. "Hurting you and then leaving you wanting, Cora? It was unpardonable."

Her cheeks were rosy, he saw. She walked onto the path between rhododendron trees without looking to the right or to the left.

"You knew," she said, her voice trembling slightly, "that it was something I wished to experience at least once in my life, and so you made an effort for my sake. I am very grateful to you. My curiosity has been satisfied and it was—well, really it was pleasant even though it ended sooner than I hoped. It is something I will always remember. But it is not something you need feel duty-bound to repeat. I understand. I truly do. And it will never make me think any the less of you. I like you and I respect you just as you are."

He felt the insane urge to laugh. Her voice had become so very earnest as she had proceeded in her speech. They were approaching a marble statute of Pan blowing his pipes, but she had not even glanced at it. She was staring determinedly into the middle distance.

"Cora." He drew her to a halt with a hand over hers. They had been moving along almost at a run. "I am relieved to hear that I did not utterly shock you last night. But are you assuming that I have no wish to repeat what we did together? Do you not think I would wish to redeem myself by doing better tonight and in the coming nights? Do you not think perhaps it will be a matter of pride with me to see to it that it does not end sooner than you hoped tonight?"

"Oh, Francis." She caught at his hands and leaned toward

him, looking so directly into his eyes that he felt robbed of breath. "No. No, really you must not. I understood even before we married, before I agreed to marry you. I accepted it then. It is all right. I will find plenty with which to fill my life and give it happiness. I want you to relax now and find happiness in your own way. You owe me nothing—except perhaps a little companionship. But that will not be difficult, will it? I think you like me." She smiled at him.

She kept saying that. She had said it last night. He frowned, feeling as if she were privy to some secret that had been withheld from him.

"Cora," he said, "*what* is it that you understand, pray? I must confess myself mystified."

Her face, which had recovered its normal color a few minutes before, flushed crimson again. Even her ears were red-tipped. "*You* know," she said.

"No." Even her neck was red. "I am afraid I do not, dear. Why do you believe so earnestly that I do not wish to make love to my own wife?"

"*Because,*" she said.

"Which is a marvelously eloquent reason," he said, "to someone who can read minds."

But she would say no more. She stared at him, clinging to his hands, as though it were impossible to look away or to move at all. She had said nothing intelligible to give him an inkling of her meaning. But it flashed on him suddenly anyway. He stared back.

"Cora," he said, "do you believe that I prefer—men to women?"

Her continued silence gave him his answer.

Good Lord! Whatever had given her . . . ? What the deuce?

He should have felt anger, outrage. It was not a tolerant age in which they lived. What she suggested was a capital offense. He should have been white with fury.

Only Cora could possibly have come up with such a preposterous theory. And she had married him believing it.

The thought saved him. Only Cora!

He threw back his head and shouted with laughter. He

roared with it. He dropped her hands, turned away from her, and doubled over with it, clutching an aching side.

"Oops," she said from behind him at just the moment he had decided to turn to find out why she was not laughing with him, as she usually was. She sounded quite sober. "Have I been mistaken? Have I made an utter cake of myself?"

He turned to look at her. She was standing very still, one hand over her mouth. Her eyes were as wide as saucers and were filled with dismay.

"One might say that," he said, "if one wished to be unkind. Cora, whatever gave you that ridiculous idea? Why would I have married you? Why would I have—consummated our marriage?"

"I thought you were being kind," she said. "You said yourself that I was in something of a scrape."

"Kind indeed," he said, tipping back his head and laughing again. "But what made you think it?"

"Well, your coa— Your app—" She bit her upper lip. She was looking very unhappy. That fact only added to his amusement. "Papa and Edgar and all the men with whom they associate always dress in the soberest of dark colors. They never wear lace or fancy knots in their neckcloths or a great deal of jewels, even in their *quizzing* glasses. Edgar always says that men who wear bright colors are . . . Well, Francis, you *do* wear turquoise coats, you must confess. And lavender ones. And *pink*. I do not mind at all. I like to see you dressed that way. Fashions for men are becoming all too sober. But . . ." Her voice trailed away.

"Cora." He set his head to one side and looked at her. He was still brimming with laughter. "I wear pink coats and you *think*. Merely because your brother *said*. It is my experience that people are not so easily classified. A man who prefers men is just as likely to be large and brawny and dressed all in sober black as to wear pink coats and lace. More so. Most men would not be eager to advertise such a preference. It would be dangerous. And you have thought this of me from the start? But why did you marry me? Your father and brother, I remember, were quite willing to take you home with them and look after you. They were exerting no pressure on you to have me. Why did you?"

Unexpectedly her eyes filled with tears and he felt sorry for his laughter. "Because," she whispered. Then she caught at her skirts with both hands. "I have never been so mortified in my life. I wish I could *die*. I will never *ever* be able to look you in the eye again. Excuse me. I have appointments I must keep at the house. I must be busy. I have a home to run."

And she was gone, flying down the path the way they had come, all pretty ankles and shapely derrière and hair falling out of its loose knot.

He did not try to stop her or go after her. He stayed where he was, feeling sorry that he had laughed so hard and humiliated her so deeply. And yet he continued to feel amused. He had been teased mercilessly enough over the years about his preference for bright colors and pastel shades in his clothing. But he had always felt secure enough in his masculinity to follow his own inclination. He had even done so deliberately to amuse others. He could remember choosing his pink coat with the conscious thought that it would amuse Samantha.

But Cora came from a middle-class world, where men were perhaps not so free to display their individuality. Not if they wanted to rise in the world, anyway. She had seen him through middle-class eyes and had judged him accordingly. And yet she had liked him. And she had married him.

That last thought sobered him finally. Why had she married him, thinking what she had thought? She had not really needed to do so. Although there had been scandal and doubtless it would have clung to her for a long time if she were really a lady of *ton,* her father had not seemed to feel that it was imperative for her to marry. She was part of a close and loving family, and they had been quite prepared to take her home with them. The compulsion on her to accept him had not been as strong as it had been on him to offer.

Why had she married him, then? He thought now of the impression he had once had that she loved him. It was an amusing memory, considering what she had believed of him, or would have been amusing if he were still in the mood to be amused. Obviously *that* had not been the reason.

There could be only one. She had wanted a home of her own, a world of her own in which she was mistress. She had wanted companionship with him, some conversation, some laughter. She had been content to enter a marriage that she had expected not to be a marriage at all.

She did not really want him. Not in that way. And yet she had thanked him for what had happened last night, fumbling and gauche a performance as it had been. He wondered if she *wanted* it again. Perhaps not. Perhaps her assurances that she really did not mind the situation as it was—or as she had perceived it to be—also expressed her preference.

But it was out of the question. He did not love her and she was not the bride of his choice. But she was his wife and he had discovered last night the full power of his sexual attraction to her. He had not wanted to marry her, but the fact was that he *was* married to her. She would have to grow accustomed to a marriage far different from the one she had expected. Even if she did not like it.

It was a chilling thought to have less than twenty-four hours after they had been irrevocably bound together for life.

It was an extremely busy day. She had scarcely a moment to herself. After coming back into the house from her walk with Francis, she went down to the kitchen and chatted with the cook. Her first impression that Cook was not pleased to see her quickly dissolved as she listened to the woman's plans for the day's menu and showed admiring interest in the recipes for various dishes and told Cook about some of her favorite recipes and offered to write them out and bring them down one day. She found herself within half an hour seated at the large wooden work table, eating a hearty cooked breakfast merely because she had breathed in deeply and made appreciative comments on the appetizing smells.

By the time she left the kitchen, having discussed at satisfying length all the various herbs known to man and all the familiar and unfamiliar remedies for every ailment either of them had ever encountered or treated, Cora had the impression that she had won the approval of her cook.

And then she spent several hours with the housekeeper, looking at every room in the house, commenting on how neat and clean everything appeared even though Lord Francis was not a great deal at home. She pored over the household accounts and commended the housekeeper on her management and bookkeeping skills. She gave her approval of the purchase of new bed linens, which was apparently long overdue. She checked carefully first in the books to see that the housekeeping budget would stretch to such an expense.

Then she went walking with her maid into the village of Sidley Bank, having discovered with some relief that her husband was busy with his steward. She went to look at the church and there met the rector, who bowed and rubbed his hands together as if washing them and murmured about the honor her ladyship was doing him and his humble church. He took her into the rectory to meet his wife and she stayed to take tea with the two of them. Then the rector's wife took her to call on the late rector's widow and on two spinster sisters, who were clearly gentlewomen living on limited means. She took more tea at each visit.

It was only at a late dinner that she was finally forced to be with Francis again. She recounted at tedious length every minute detail of her day for his entertainment and was quite prepared to begin all over again if necessary. She did not allow even the smallest moment of silence. She did not once look him in the eye.

She looked regretfully at the pianoforte when they retired to the drawing room, but even Miss Graham, who had been the most patient and persistent governess ever to be born, had been forced to admit many years ago that Cora had been gifted with ten thumbs instead of only the usual two and eight nimble fingers. It seemed that conversation must be engaged in again. But she made the amazing discovery that *Francis* played. He played very well. He played all evening at her request and sang too with a very pleasing tenor voice. She joined him in a few songs since the musical ineptness of her fingers did not extend to her voice as well.

Finally the day was over. She had lived through it without having to do any thinking at all. Though that was a lie, she thought as she got into bed and raised the bedclothes up over her head and hoped that she could be alone with her shame until tomorrow. Of course it was a lie. The truth was she had done nothing but think all day.

She wished she could die.

How could she *possibly* have made such a ghastly, ghastly error? And how could she have let him *know* what she suspected? She admitted, now that it was far too late, that she had had no evidence at all—none whatsoever—for thinking what she had thought except for the pathetically unconvincing fact that he wore pretty coats. There had been nothing in his behavior, nothing in the behavior of anyone else toward him. Only that silly fact that she had seen him at her first ball dressed in turquoise and had immediately thought of peacocks. Her mind had been made up and firmly closed from that moment on.

Oh, the humiliation was too much to bear. She burrowed farther beneath the bedclothes.

She cringed into total immobility when she heard the same tap on the door she had heard last night and the door opened.

And now to cap everything she had been caught hiding beneath the bedclothes. She was too mortified to come out. She listened to the silence until she felt a weight depress the mattress close to her head and felt a hand come to rest on her rump.

"Cora," he said quietly, "it is just me, dear."

Which was an extremely foolish thing for an intelligent man to say. Did he not realize that that was the whole trouble?

"There is no need to hide from me," he said. "I am not going to ridicule you or tell anyone else about your error. It really does not matter. I am sorry I laughed. It struck me as funny, but I know it was humiliating for you."

"I am not hiding," she said. "I am cold." On a night so warm that all the windows had been left wide open in the hope of catching some cooling breeze.

"Then come out and let me warm you," he said.

She felt a stabbing of longing, of desire. But she wished he would go away and never come back.

"Cora." He was patting his hand on her derrière. "Come, my dear. We cannot go on like this for the next forty or fifty years."

There was laughter in his voice again. Oh, how dare he! She threw back the covers and looked deliberately into his eyes. It was, she thought, as difficult to do as it must be to persuade oneself to jump off a cliff. His blue eyes were twinkling.

"Well, it was all your fault," she said, glaring at him. "Turquoise coat, lace everywhere, a work of art at your neck, a sapphire ring on your finger, sapphires all over your quizzing glass, such elegant manners. What was I *supposed* to think?"

"That is the spirit," he said. "Rip up at me if doing so will make you feel better." He bent his head and kissed her.

She turned to jelly all the way down to her toes. His lips were not even *closed*. "And leather pantaloons," she said when she had her mouth back to herself, "and a dark pink coat."

"Quite so." he had stood up to remove his dressing gown, and then he sat down again and was opening the buttons at the front of her nightgown. With the candles still burning. And he was looking at what he was doing.

Her insides were performing intricate acrobatic feats.

"And a blue-and-yellow phaeton," she said. "What kind of man drives around in a blue-and-yellow phaeton?"

"This kind, apparently," he said. He opened back her gown so that she was exposed to below the waist. He looked at her and then he lowered his head to feather kisses over her breasts. He opened his mouth over the peak of one of them, licked at it, and then closed his lips over it and sucked.

There was such an ache in the place he had been last night that it was indistinguishable from pain. And then his hand was down there, inside her nightgown, and his fingers were doing something that should have been horribly embarrassing. But the ache and the pain and the sharp longing drowned out the embarrassment.

"You dressed soberly for Papa and Edgar," she said. "That was not fair. Not fair at all. Ooh!"

"Life is not always fair," he said. He had taken her nightgown by the shoulders and was stripping it right off her, down over her feet. And the bedclothes were right off her too. And the candles were still burning.

"You should have *told* me," she said. "You might have guessed what I thought. But you kept quiet. Just so that I would make a thorough cake of myself and you could laugh your head off."

He grinned at her as he stood again to pull his nightshirt off over his head. Now if only she had *seen* him, she thought, gulping, she would surely have known herself. Though she had always known that he had a magnificent body. She had fallen against it, had she not, that very first evening?

"Francis," she said, "do not *laugh* at me. I cannot abide being laughed at when I am feeling so very mortified. Especially when it is all your fault."

He was coming on top of her as he had last night. He was pushing her legs wide as he had then. She looked down and marveled anew that there was room enough inside her. It was going to happen again, she thought. Oh, she was so *glad* it was going to happen again.

"It is all my fault," he said. "Let me see if I can do better than last night, dear. Let me see if I can prevent it ending too soon for you."

She closed her eyes and bit hard on her lower lip as he came inside. There was no pain tonight. There was all the marvelous stretching and all the deep penetration, but none of the pain.

Let there be time, she thought as he began to move—slowly, quite unlike the hurried pounding of last night. *Please let there be time.*

There was all the time in the world. It was gloriously, deliriously wonderful. She twined herself about him, lifted herself against him, moved with him, experimented with muscles she had not known she had, ached her way toward what must surely be unbearable pain, and then eased her way beyond it to total pleasure and relaxation.

When she finally relaxed, she felt him quicken as he had at the start last night. And she felt again that increased heat deep within just before he relaxed his weight on top of her.

Oh, thank you. Thank you. Thank you.

Thank you, Francis, she told him silently when he had moved off her and was tucking the upper sheet about her.

Don't leave. Please don't leave.

He had got out of bed, but he was just blowing out the candles. He climbed in beside her again and took her hand in his.

Good night, Francis. Thank you.

"You are so very beautiful," he said softly to her. "Thank you, dear."

But she was fast asleep.

Chapter 15

❧

He need not have worried, as he had done briefly that first morning in the stables, that she would turn out to be such a managing female that she would try to run the estate for him. She did not.

She turned out to be an extremely busy and efficient mistress of Sidley. There was no doubt in anyone's mind after the first two or three days who was in charge of the household. And yet she was surprisingly well-liked. One might have expected that servants who had run the house without any interference for years would resent a mistress who insisted on having a finger in every pie. But they did not.

His wife had a way about her, Lord Francis discovered. She was never overfamiliar with the servants—there was never any doubt that she was the mistress and they were the employees. And yet she talked with them, smiled with them, joked with them, advised them, listened to their advice. He was amazed one day when he sent his compliments to the cook on the new and delicious dessert that had been served to discover that it had been made from a recipe given Cook by Cora.

Cook had allowed his wife to supply her with a recipe? *And had used it?*

His wife never trespassed on his domain—with the possible exception of that morning in the stables. But she took charge of her own with a competence that could only have come from training and long experience.

Lord Francis began to feel very comfortable in his home.

She spent almost all of every afternoon visiting or being visited. She visited laborers' cottages and tenants' homes alone. He usually accompanied her when she called upon the neighboring gentry and attended her in the drawing room when she was entertaining them. She was at ease and friendly without being in any way vulgar. Not that he looked for vulgarity in her. He had never seen any.

In the evenings they often visited or entertained. Sometimes they stayed home alone and whiled away the time with music or with reading. She liked to have him read aloud to her while she stitched away at her embroidery. She was not a particularly skilled needlewoman, but as she herself said, she could hardly sit and twiddle her thumbs when she was at leisure, could she?

At night they made love. Only once each night. It seemed somehow distasteful to him to think of doing it more frequently. Perhaps if his appetite for her had been less voracious, he would have allowed himself to have her more often. Or if he had loved her. As it was, he did not wish to use her as he would use a mistress, merely to satisfy his lust. He had too great a respect for her.

Not that she showed any distaste for what they did together in her bed each night, despite his fears that first morning. Quite the contrary. She was a willing and eager participant in what happened. She never spoke her satisfaction, but her actions spoke it for her as well as the little sigh of completion with which her own participation always ended—the signal for him finally to let go of the control he had never lost involuntarily since their wedding night.

They had a good marriage, he decided after three weeks. Far better than he could possibly have expected. They had settled into a comfortable routine at Sidley. They were firm friends. They laughed together frequently. They were good together in bed.

It was a good marriage. What more could a man ask for?

Unfortunately, it was a question he kept asking himself. A question he could not stop asking himself. For there was something—an indefinable something—that prevented them from relaxing into true happiness. Both of them.

From the beginning he had been startlingly aware of Cora's openness and candor. He could remember thinking that it would be impossible for her to call a spade anything but a spade. And it was still true. She still looked him more directly in the eye when she spoke to him than anyone else he had ever known. And she still spoke to him freely on any topic he cared to introduce. There was no evidence whatsoever that she kept anything from him or harbored any dark secrets.

And yet . . .

And yet there was something. He could not put a finger on it or even begin to grasp it with his mind. It was nothing he felt he could ask her about. It was nothing.

But he knew it was something. There was *something*.

Just as there was with him, of course. He could not help sometimes looking at her—often at moments of deepest contentment—and remembering that she was not the woman of his choice. He could not help remembering the dream he had had of love and the sort of marriage that would grow out of a mutual love. The dream had gone and he was settling for contentment, it seemed. Was that what happened to most people, if not all? Did dreams always give place to reality?

And yet he *was* content. He had a good life, one about which it would be wicked to complain. But he felt as if he were waiting. As if there were a completion that had not yet come.

This could not be all, he sometimes thought. And it saddened him to know that he could not be thoroughly happy with contentment. Or with a wife who was good to him.

He kept remembering the dream and wondering if even that was illusory. *Had* it been so very wonderful? Had he loved Samantha as deeply as he had thought? Was she as beautiful and as perfect as he remembered her? Would he have lived happily ever after with her if she had only returned his love, or if she had not met Carew?

He did not want to think of her or of his love for her. He

did not want to be disloyal to Cora even in his thoughts. She deserved better. She was a very likable person and she was a very good wife to him.

Contentment could have kept him at home for the rest of their lives. Sidley had never been a more pleasant place to live. And yet contentment itself became suspect. Was he going to settle for this for the rest of his life? Was there nothing more?

And so he stared at his letter at the breakfast table one morning long after he had finished reading it, feeling tempted.

"What is it?" she asked. Her hand came across the table to touch his arm. "Bad news, Francis?"

And he knew that he had hoped she would ask just such questions, and was ashamed of himself.

"No, not at all." He smiled at her. He always thought her most beautiful in the mornings—if he discounted the nights—when her hair was looped loosely over her ears and knotted simply at her neck. "It is from Gabe."

"The Earl of Thornhill?" she said. "Your friend from Yorkshire?"

"They want us to come for a few weeks," he said. "I have been a regular visitor there since their marriage six years ago. They were expecting me this summer."

She did not respond as he knew he hoped she would. She said nothing at all, but merely looked at him.

"What do you think?" he asked.

He had seen that pale, trapped look a few times before and knew what it meant. "Francis," she said almost in a whisper, "he is an *earl*."

"And so he is." He could not resist teasing her. "You would be in illustrious company, dear. Going to visit an earl and a countess in company with a duke's son and brother. As the wife of the said duke's son and brother." It always amused him that she had never been terrified of his own title.

"They must disapprove of me," she said. "They must have been disappointed for you, Francis. They must have thought, as your brother and sisters did, that you married far beneath yourself. And they were right. We should never have married. I would not have done so if I had known . . ."

He smiled at her confusion and covered her hand with his on the table. "I doubt they think any such thing, Cora," he said. "And if they do, the problem is theirs. You are my wife and I am not sorry I married you. You are in no way my inferior. In no way that matters even one iota."

"That is all very well to say as long as we stay here," she said, drawing her hand from his and getting to her feet. "But as soon as we leave here, you will realize that in everyone else's eyes I *am* inferior, Francis. I want to stay here, please. I am happy here."

And yet she looked anything but happy as she hurried from the breakfast parlor, muttering something about an appointment with Cook. Was that the problem? Was that what was between them on her part? She felt that the social differences between them would cause only problems for them as the future unfolded?

They would stay home, he thought with both regret and relief. She had saved him from temptation. He would stay home and carefully build on the contentment they had found in three weeks of marriage and residence at Sidley.

It was Cora, after all, who came first in his life. Before even himself.

She hurried into the scenic walk, the one Francis had introduced her to on the first morning. She pulled her shawl more tightly about her. It had rained during the night and the clouds were still low and threatening. There was a chill breeze. Summer seemed temporarily to have deserted them.

She had just been very selfish.

She had vowed to herself when she married him to devote herself wholly to his contentment, to forget about herself. To deny herself, as the Bible would have it. It was a horridly difficult thing to do.

And now she had disappointed him. The Earl of Thornhill, she understood, was his closest friend but they lived far apart. He must have been very happy to read that invitation this morning. He must have expected that she would be delighted by the prospect of traveling into Yorkshire.

Instead of which she had been peevish and self-pitying and selfish. If truth were known, she did not care the snap of two fingers what people said of her. But she did care what they said of him. She did not want his closest friend to censure or pity him because he had married her. He was probably doing so anyway, but if he saw her it would be worse. She was such a large *lump*.

She sat down on a wrought iron bench beneath a beech tree after first making sure that the seat was not wet. She drew her shawl close.

She *wished* she could be attractive for him. It had not mattered so very much when she had believed—she still grew hot and uncomfortable when she remembered that she had believed it—that he was not attracted to women. But it had mattered very much since. If only she could be a little smaller. If only her breasts were not so embarrassingly large. If only her face were pretty. If only her hair were fine and wavy. If only . . .

She wanted desperately to be beautiful for Francis.

She tried to compensate for her ugliness and her ungainliness by making his life comfortable. When she was busy making his home more cozy and livable, when she was visiting his people, seeing to their contentment, when she was visiting his neighbors or entertaining them, then she was almost happy. She convinced herself that she was being a good wife to him.

She tried to be a good wife in bed. Sometimes—most times—she lost herself in her own pleasure. It was difficult not to. He was so very—beautiful, so very masculine and virile. But she always determined not to lose herself but to lie still and passive for his pleasure. She had never yet succeeded.

She thought he enjoyed being in bed with her. But that was no occasion for pride. Men always enjoyed being in bed with a woman. She had heard that somewhere, though she could not for the life of her remember where—it was not a typical drawing room conversational topic. She had heard that sentiment did not matter to men as it did to women, that physical satisfaction was everything. She satisfied Francis physically, she believed.

But oh, she wished she could be beautiful for him. How he must wish he had a beautiful woman with whom to do that each night.

At first, once she had recovered from her embarrassment at discovering her error—not that she would *ever* fully recover—she had been overjoyed. It was to be a real marriage. She had physical closeness and intimacy to look forward to for a lifetime, or at least until they grew old. She could look forward to having children. She might be a *mother*. But her elation had not lasted long.

All too soon she had realized with cruel clarity exactly what she had done. She had married him and forever deprived him of the chance to marry a woman of his choice. She could not even comfort herself with the realization that he had done the same to her. There was a difference. He had been honor-bound to offer for her. As a gentleman— there was no truer gentleman than Francis—he had had no choice whatsoever. She had. Papa and Edgar had not thought it so imperative for her to marry him. It was unlikely that the scandal would have followed her so ruthlessly into her own world that it would have ruined her life.

He had had to offer for her. She had not had to accept. But she had.

And now he was trapped in a marriage that would never bring him true happiness. Or her either. If she had not loved him so painfully, perhaps she could have concentrated on making him comfortable and could have found contentment for herself. But she did love him.

And she had remembered something she would sooner not have remembered at all. That horrid woman in London—the Honorable Miss Pamela Fletcher—had said that he had loved some other woman who had married earlier in the Season. She had said that he was thought to be nursing a broken heart. Cora had dismissed the idea at the time as rather hilarious. But now . . .

Was it true? Had Francis loved another woman such a

short while ago? Had she broken his heart? Was it still broken? Cora frowned and bit the inside of her cheek and thought and thought, but she could not remember the woman's name or the name of the man she had married. Perhaps it was as well. She would always dread meeting the woman and seeing a confirmation in Francis's eyes that it was all true.

Was the other woman beautiful? she wondered. She would wager a quarter's allowance that she was.

And he was stuck with her, Cora.

She got to her feet and hurried back to the house. He was with his steward in the office wing, the butler told her after she had asked if his new, wider shoes were helping his bunion.

The steward himself answered her tap on his door, but Francis was visible beyond his shoulder. He came striding toward her and took her hands.

"What is it, dear?" he asked her. "Do you need me?" He stepped outside the door and closed it behind him after she had nodded.

"Francis," she said, "do reply to the Earl of Thornhill's letter and say we will come."

He bent his head to look more closely into her eyes. "But you do not wish to go," he said. "You want to stay here. Your wishes are mine, Cora."

She shook her head and smiled determinedly. "It was as you thought," she said. "I am terrified of his title. But that is ridiculous, is it not? You are better born than he since his father must have been an earl and yours was a duke. And I am not terrified of you. It is something I am determined to fight. I am no cringing creature."

He chuckled. "I had noticed," he said.

"Then we will go," she said briskly. "Write and tell him so."

"You are sure?" He searched her eyes with his own.

She nodded again. "What is the countess like?" she asked.

"She is very sweet and very amiable," he said. "You will like her, Cora."

She very much doubted it. And the countess would not like her either. "Yes," she said, "of course I will."

"They have two young children," he said. She could tell he was pleased, happy. "I always play with them. I like children."

It was something she had not known about him. Something that made her fall a little deeper still in love with him.

"We will go soon?" she said. "I will give instructions now, without further delay. I am looking forward to it, Francis."

"Liar," he said, his expression softening. "But you *will* like them. And thank you, dear."

She felt a silly rush of tears to her eyes and did what she had never done outside of her bed. She lifted her chin and kissed him on the mouth. And felt herself blush—after three weeks of intimacies at night. What sort of chucklehead would he think her?

He smiled and squeezed her hands.

He knew that she was very nervous. As was he. Nervous and guilty. He would have wanted to come to visit Gabe and Lady Thornhill even without other inducement. He had always enjoyed visiting them. He would have wanted them to meet Cora, since she was now such an intimate part of his life. He had kept telling himself these things ever since she had come to him in his steward's office almost a week ago.

He would have wanted to come regardless.

But of course there had been that other reason. He knew that for a fleeting moment fifteen minutes or so before they reached Chalcote, there would be a view of Highmoor Abbey from the road. He knew exactly between which hedgerows he would have to look, though he was surprised by his own knowledge since he had never before had any particular reason to look at the house from the road. The last time he had driven this route, back in the early spring, she had not even met Carew.

They would be passing that gap in the hedgerows in about five minutes time. His heart thumped dully against his chest and in his ears. He tightened his hold on Cora's hand.

"They married out of necessity, you know," he said. He had been talking about Gabe and his wife, trying to distract both her attention and his own. "Their marriage had an inauspicious beginning too." *Too*. Had he had to add that word?

"What happened?" She turned her head to look directly into his eyes.

And so he told her how six years ago Gabe had returned from the Continent, where he had left his stepmother, and had sought revenge against the man who had ruined her. The man to whom Miss Jennifer Winwood, now the Countess of Thornhill, had been betrothed. He had tried to get at his enemy through her, wooing her himself. But the villain had been only too eager to rid himself of her and had plotted quite ruthlessly to make it appear as if she were having a clandestine affair with Thornhill. He had succeeded all too well—a forged letter purportedly from Thornhill to Miss Winwood was read aloud to the whole *ton* assembled for her betrothal ball. Thornhill had been forced to rush her into marriage.

"A very inauspicious beginning," Lord Francis said now. "She hated him and he had meant only to use her. For a while our friendship was on very shaky ground. Gabe had not behaved admirably."

"No," she said. "What happened to the other man?"

The other man had been exiled when his father had discovered the truth. He had returned this spring and tried to seduce Samantha. Until Carew had found out and challenged him and beaten him to a pulp at Jackson's boxing saloon despite a deformed hand and foot. Lord Francis had not experienced anything quite so satisfying in a long while. He had been one of Carew's seconds. Bridgwater had been the other.

"He has left England for good," he said. "And good riddance to him. You will see soon, Cora, that bad beginnings sometimes have happy endings. There is a close attachment between Gabe and his lady."

He did not know whether he was trying to tell her that the same thing could happen with their marriage. But then their marriage had not had a *bad* beginning exactly. He deliberately did not turn his head to see the distant prospect of Highmoor Abbey. He watched his wife instead. She was biting the inside of her cheek, a habit with her that made him wince. It seemed such a painful habit.

The Earl and Countess of Thornhill were out on the terrace with their two children. It looked as if they had been out walking, Lord Francis thought, and had seen the carriage approaching. Gabe and his wife spent far more time with their children than was fashionable. Lady Thornhill, he noticed as the steps were put down and the door opened, was quite noticeably rounded with child again.

"Oh dear," Cora muttered to herself, sounding quite breathless.

He threw her a reassuring smile as he vaulted out of the carriage. He directed a quick grin at Gabe and the others and turned to hand her out. She need not worry, he thought. She was looking very smart indeed in a spring green carriage dress and straw bonnet. They would love her.

He did not know quite what happened—whether she stepped on the hem of her dress or whether her foot skidded on the wooden step or whether it was one of those invisible specks of dust that had brought her to grief at the Markley ball. However it was, she stumbled awkwardly, shrieked, and came tumbling forward to land in his arms, sending him staggering backward while breath whooshed audibly out of his lungs. Only by some superhuman effort did he succeed in keeping his footing.

"Oops!" she said loudly. And giggled.

"Oh, dear me," Lady Thornhill said, hurrying forward. "Did you hurt yourself?"

Gabe hung back, looking embarrassed. Lord Francis met his eyes over the top of Cora's bonnet. He grinned. He might have known that once they left the sanctuary of Sidley farce would catch up to her.

Cora was straightening her bonnet, which had skidded

round to half cover one eye. She had flushed scarlet and was looking acutely uncomfortable.

"I wish I could do this all over again," she said. And giggled once more.

Lord Francis set an arm about her waist, something he would not normally have done in public. "Cora," he said, "meet Lady Thornhill. And the Earl of Thornhill. Gabriel. Gabe. This is Cora, my wife." He felt an unexpected, almost fierce protectiveness for her. If they wished to continue the friendship, let there not be even a suggestion now of laughter or contempt.

Of course there was not. *Of course* there was not.

"I am so pleased to meet you." Lady Thornhill clasped her hands to her bosom and smiled warmly at Cora. "We have scarce been able to wait, have we, Gabriel? I thought you might arrive yesterday though Gabriel said it could not possibly be until today."

"Jennifer made every excuse she could muster yesterday," the earl said, chuckling, "to be at the front of the house, looking out the windows just in case. Lady Francis"—he held out his right hand—"welcome to our home. We will do our best to make your stay here a pleasant one."

"I am not normally so clumsy, my lord," Cora said, placing her hand on his. "Am I, Francis? Oh dear. But I tripped and fell—over *nothing*—the very first time I saw you, did I not?"

The earl smiled kindly and held on to her hand. "You fell for Frank at first sight, did you?" he said and laughed.

"I believe," Lord Francis said, "it was the effect of seeing my turquoise coat, Gabe."

Lady Thornhill laughed. "That must be a new one," she said. "Turquoise? Dear me. I do not blame you, Lady Francis. Though they are always very gorgeous coats, of course."

Fortunately Cora found the remark funny and they all had a good laugh. Good old Gabe and his wife, Lord Francis thought. They had worked hard, seemingly without effort, to take Cora's mind off her embarrassing entry into their lives.

"Uncle Frank." An insistent little hand was pulling at his coattail. "Uncle Frank, I bowled Papa out in cricket this morning. The wickets went *crash*."

"That's the boy, Michael," Lord Francis said. "You must try me tomorrow. I shall see if I can guard my wickets better than your papa can."

"Uncle Frank." Another little hand was patting one leg of his pantaloons. "Uncle Frank, may I sit up there."

"Certainly, Mary," he said and swung the child up to sit on one of his shoulders. He set one hand on the little boy's head. "Meet your new honorary aunt. Aunt Cora."

"Aunt Cora," Mary said and reached for a hand hold on one of Lord Francis's ears.

"Mary trips and falls lots too," Michael said, looking up at Cora. "Papa says she has two left feet and twenty toes on each one."

"Which is a matter entirely between Mary and me, my lad," his father said hastily.

"Lady Francis"—the countess took her arm—"do come inside. You will want to freshen up before tea. Let me show you your room. Your husband can find his own way. He knows it well enough. How *pleased* I am at the prospect of having your company for a few weeks."

"Well, Frank." The earl was holding out his right hand again. "Congratulations. There is nothing so satisfying as the married state. You will discover the truth of that for yourself soon enough if you have not already done so. She will soon be less nervous about being here. Jennifer will see to that."

Lord Francis could think of only one thing now that his wife had gone inside. He tried to suppress the thought but it was impossible. She was only a few miles away, he thought. No more than three or four as the crow flies.

And she was on close visiting terms with her cousin, the Countess of Thornhill.

Chapter 16

~

At first Cora was intimidated. The Earl of Thornhill was a tall, darkly handsome man. The countess was tall by any normal standard, though not nearly as tall as Cora, with silky dark red hair. She was elegant and slender—at least her frame suggested slenderness even though she was quite noticeably with child.

They were the perfect couple, perfectly well-bred, perfectly devoted to each other and their children.

But they were perfect in another way too. They were perfectly amiable and kind. Cora knew very well that they must have been dismayed to hear that Francis had been forced into a marriage with a merchant's daughter. She knew that her appearance could have done nothing to reassure them—she was the ugly smudge among three beautiful people, five if she counted the children. And she knew that her shudderingly embarrassing descent from the carriage must have confirmed them in all their worst expectations.

But the countess spoke with her as if she were an eagerly anticipated, newly acquired friend. Before they came downstairs for tea on that first day, Lady Francis was Cora and the countess was Jennifer. And before tea was over Francis had been assured that after six years he must finally capitulate and drop the formality with which he had always insisted on addressing the countess. Whether he would or no, *she* was going to call him Francis. And then suddenly Cora was Cora and the earl was Gabriel.

Before the day was over Cora had relaxed. They really were very pleasant people. She told Francis so when they were in bed together that night, before they got too mindlessly involved in lovemaking.

"They are just like normal people," she said.

He chuckled. "I shall pass the compliment on to them tomorrow at breakfast," he said.

"Don't you dare!" she said in horror.

He chuckled again and kissed her. She shivered with pleasurable anticipation when he rubbed the tip of his tongue lightly back and forth across her upper lip.

"I was not even wearing shoes that were too small for me," she said, wincing again at the memory that had plagued her all evening. "Oh, Francis, I could have *died*. Why do things like that always happen to me?"

"I think perhaps for my eternal delight, dear," he said.

Which was a remarkably gallant thing to say when he must have been *so* ashamed of her.

The following morning they all went riding. Even the children went, young Michael on his own pony, Mary up before her father on his horse. And then the men played cricket with Michael while the ladies rolled a ball with Mary and Cora helped her make a daisy chain. Cora paid some afternoon calls with Jennifer while Gabriel took Francis to see some new development on one of his farms. In the evening they played cards after the children were in bed.

It was all very pleasant. A very enjoyable holiday. Francis did not seem unhappy—but then he had not seemed so at Sidley either. Perhaps, Cora thought, she had been foolish not to allow herself to be fully happy. Perhaps it did not matter that she had not been his choice, that he did not love her. Perhaps love was not as important to men as it was to women.

Perhaps the same would happen with her marriage as had happened with Gabriel and Jennifer's. If Francis had not told her, she would never have guessed that their marriage had had an inauspicious beginning. They were very wellbred. They did not embarrass their guests with any show of public affection. But they did not need to do so. It was there for all to see in the faces and manner of both—the fact that there was a deep emotional attachment between them.

Perhaps . . .

But she would not hope for something that would probably never happen. She would merely learn to accept and appreciate what she had. What she had was not so very bad at all.

But what if it was not acceptable to Francis? What if time only made him less and less happy?

Ah, life was a hard business, she thought, full of ifs, ands, and buts to distract one just when one thought one had it all figured out.

And something else worried her. There was another large estate adjoining Chalcote. Highmoor Abbey was only a few miles away, the seat of the Marquess of Carew. The marchioness was Jennifer's cousin and the two families frequently visited. At the moment they were in Harrogate for a few days, but they were expected home.

"We will be able to offer you a little more company, Cora," Jennifer said with a smile. "You will like Sam, I believe. She is more like a sister than a cousin to me. We were brought up together after the death of my aunt and uncle, her parents. Can you imagine how delighted I was when she married Hartley just this year and came to live close to me?"

The prospect of meeting them made Cora feel slightly sick even though she told herself that by now she should be quite blasé about meeting members of the aristocracy. She was even one of them now, she reminded herself. She was Lady Francis Kneller, sister-in-law of the Duke of Fairhurst. She did not feel a great deal better.

She thought at first that she must have met the Marquess of Carew. The name sounded familiar. But think as she would, she could not put a face to the name or remember where she might have met him. And then she discovered that he and the marchioness had married early in June, when she was still in Bath, and had returned home soon after.

No, clearly she was mistaken.

*   *   *

At first he thought he had been saved from himself. They were in Harrogate. But not for long, it seemed. They were expected back every day.

"They cannot be separated from Highmoor for too long, those two," the earl told Lord Francis. "They are having a bridge built across the narrow end of the lake there and must supervise the laying of every stone. Carew is widely renowned as a landscape gardener, as you are probably aware, and Samantha has embraced his interest with enthusiasm. An unlikelier pair you never saw, Frank, but you can tell that for each of them the world only really contains the other."

"You mean they do not hide it as well as you and Jennifer?" Lord Francis asked dryly. But in reality his stomach was churning and his heart was thumping and he wished fervently that Cora had not persuaded him to come here. Which was being grossly unfair to his wife, of course.

They came on the fourth day, unexpectedly, quite early in the afternoon just as the earl and countess with their children and guests were about to begin a walk to the lake. Indeed, they would have been on the way if Cora had not discovered as they stepped out onto the terrace that she had forgotten her parasol. Lord Francis ran upstairs to fetch it for her. When he came back down, he found her standing in the middle of the hall looking round-eyed and white-faced—a familiar look. He half guessed even before she spoke.

"Francis," she said in a loud whisper as if she were afraid her voice would carry to the outside, "there is a carriage coming. Jennifer said it is the Marquess of Carew's."

If she had slammed her fist into his stomach he could not have felt more robbed of breath. He smiled at her. "Cora," he said, "you found the courage to meet and to speak with Prinny himself. This is a mere marquess. You will find him quite unthreatening, I promise you."

"Oh," she said, "you think I am foolish and you are quite right. But you do not understand, Francis. You were born to all this."

He set his hands on her shoulders and drew her against him despite the presence of a footman in the hall. He wished he could take her back to their room and close the door. He wanted this meeting as little as she did.

"Come," he said. "I will be there beside you, dear."

She looked up at him. "Francis," she said, "do not let me fall down the steps. There are four of them—or is it five? Oh, I cannot remember whether there are four steps or five. What if I think there are four and there turn out to be five?"

"Your eyes would see the fifth," he said, tucking her arm through his. "But there are only four."

He could hear her drawing a deep breath and releasing it slowly.

The carriage was already being drawn away in the direction of the stables. Carew was saying something to Gabe. Samantha was bent over Mary, listening and smiling at her.

God!

And then she looked up and spotted them coming down the steps. Her eyes lit up as only Samantha's could and she straightened up. There was no outer sign yet of her condition, he half noticed. She was dressed all in pale blue. Small and dainty and blond, she was all delicate beauty and light.

"Francis!" she said. "Oh, we knew you might come, but we did not know for sure. We did not know you had come. Hartley, look who is here."

"I see, my love," Carew said. "Good to see you, Kneller."

But Lord Francis only half noticed him. Samantha was hurrying toward him with eager light steps and a brightly smiling face, and both her hands were stretched toward him. He was saved from making an utter fool of himself only by the fact that though her hands came to rest in his, her smile was for Cora, who was still clinging to his arm.

"Cora, dear," he said and then wished he had not added the *dear*—it sounded affected. "Meet the Marchioness of Carew. And the marquess."

He had a chance to complete only half the introduction. Samantha dropped his hands and took Cora's.

"I have been so eager to meet you," she said. "Francis has been a dear friend for a long time. I take it unkindly that he married in such eager haste that Hartley and I could not even attend. He attended our wedding, you know."

"It was rather hasty," Cora said.

Carew had come limping up to them. He bowed to Cora and smiled. "Lady Francis," he said, "I am happy to make your acquaintance. We were delighted to learn of your nuptials from Bridgwater and Gabriel. Now tell me what you think of Yorkshire."

Samantha laughed. "Hartley swears that there is nowhere on earth to compete with it for beauty and the freshness of its air," she said. "You must be careful to give the correct answer, Lady Francis. Though you must not let him bully you. Francis, lemon yellow for the afternoon? You match your wife's dress almost exactly. I am delighted to discover that you have not become a *sober* married man."

They decided to join the walk to the lake. Carew's disability never stopped him from doing almost all that other men did, Lord Francis had discovered—even challenging far larger men to fisticuffs. Carew offered his arm to Cora, who appeared to have mastered her terror, perhaps at the sight of a very ordinary-looking marquess who was no taller than she and who could very easily pass for the landscape gardener he loved to be.

Gabe swung his daughter up onto his shoulder and took a hand of his son. Jennifer took the other.

Lord Francis offered his arm to Samantha.

She was very tiny. The top of her head reached barely to his chin. There was a familiar feel about her on his arm, a familiar fragrance. He marveled that for six years he had been part of her court. He had danced with her, walked with her, ridden with her, driven her, talked and flirted with her, even offered her marriage. And yet never had he felt the trembling awareness of her that he felt now. He did not like the feeling at all.

She talked to him about Highmoor, about the building of the bridge, which she had planned with Carew after she had first met him, when she had not even realized that he was

Carew but had mistaken him for the landscaper, she told
him now with a laugh. She told him about the little pavilion, the rain house as she called it, that they planned to
build next year at the far side of the bridge. She asked him
about Cora, and he found himself telling her about his
wife's fame as a heroine. He told her with some amusement
about her encounter with Lady Kellington's poodles and
about her chase after the Duke of Finchley's hat.

"Do you wonder that I was enchanted with her?" he
asked and was surprised to find that the words had come
without conscious thought. Cora *had* enchanted him. She
still did. He thought with some affection of her recent terror, when she had realized that the Marquess and Marchioness of Carew were approaching.

"No, I do not wonder at all, Francis," Samantha said.
"Oh dear, she is so wonderfully tall and elegant. I am mortally jealous. When I reached my twenty-first birthday, I do
believe I was still persuading myself that eventually I
would grow up. With the emphasis on the *up*, that is."

Cora did indeed look very fetching today. She was wearing the yellow dress with blue accessories that she had
worn in the park the first time he drove her there. Somehow
the clothes had not been permanently damaged as his own
had been. Someone had sewn the sleeve back into the
bodice. She was talking to Carew and laughing at the same
time. His usual sunny Cora.

"Hartley and I are going to have a child," Samantha said.
"Did you know? I am very proud of the fact that it does not
show yet, but Hartley cannot wait for it to do so. I am not
putting you to the blush, am I, Francis? I have never
thanked you, by the way, for what you did for him that
morning at Jackson's. Though I am still ready to do murder
over the fact that you allowed him to fight. You and the
Duke of Bridgwater both. Oh, his poor face. It took weeks
to heal."

She did not monopolize the conversation. She listened to
him and led him on to tell her more about himself and Cora
and their wedding. But when she did talk about other

things, he noticed, it was Carew who was at the center of everything. The focus of her life. The center of her universe.

It never ceased to surprise Lord Francis that of all the men who had courted her over the years—and they were legion—she had chosen Carew. Carew was, of course, the wealthiest man of his acquaintance. But he knew it was not that. Hers was a love match. The realization had never brought Lord Francis a great deal of comfort.

"If it is any consolation," he said, "I daresay Rushford's face is still healing and never will entirely heal, Samantha."

"That name." She shuddered. "Please do not mention it. Tell me how Lady Francis likes Sidley. Has she made any changes yet? Has she gone to war with your cook? You were always shamefully in awe of the woman."

"They are the best of friends," Lord Francis said. "They have exchanged recipes. Cora gets fed in the kitchen. I still do not dare set a foot inside it."

She laughed. "Lady Francis is a woman of character," she said. "I saw it in her face when I first looked into it and everything you have said about her confirms me in that impression. You are a very fortunate man. I am delighted for you. I have wished for your happiness more than for anyone else's I know." She squeezed his arm a little more tightly. "You need a woman of character, Francis, because you have so much of your own."

Yes, it was true, he thought, looking at his wife. She was still laughing gaily with Carew. She had a great deal of character. Delightful character. Even her weaknesses were utterly endearing. She was terrified of aristocracy but of almost nothing else that he had discovered. Yes, he was a fortunate man. He felt a sudden and totally unexpected rush of nostalgia for Sidley and the weeks he had spent there with Cora, getting to know her in every way a man can know his wife, learning to adjust his ways to hers, accepting the comfort she had brought into his life.

He longed to be back there. They would spend most of their time there, he thought, rather than moving restlessly between London and Brighton and other spas in search of entertainment. They would make a home of Sidley. They would bring their children up there and spend time with them, as Gabe and Jennifer did with theirs. She had told him once that she wanted half a dozen children. He hoped he could keep himself from burdening her with quite so many. But he had the feeling that Cora would never do anything by half measures. He smiled.

"Francis." Samantha squeezed his arm again. She was looking closely at him. "You are fond of her. Jennifer told us what happened and I was so afraid for you. Ask Hartley if I was not. But I was hopeful too. You had written to Gabriel that the first time you were caught together you were both laughing so hard that you had to cling to each other. And the other time you were rescuing her because she had been duped into going to the rescue of a child who was supposed to be stuck in a tree. She sounded so nice— what a lame word. I did not believe you could help being fond of such a woman. And you are. I can see it in your face. I am so glad."

He was exceedingly fond of her, he thought. Exceedingly. He could not quite imagine his life without her now. He tried to imagine being here alone, unmarried, unattached, free. He tried to imagine having taken his leave of Cora at the end of the Season if they had not been forced on each other. He tried to imagine her at home with her family in Bristol and himself here alone at Chalcote.

He would be missing her. He would be lonely without her. The laughter would have gone out of his life.

In fact, he thought, he doubted he would have stayed here. He would have seen, as he was seeing now, that his friends, though undoubtedly fond of him, had lives of their own, Gabe's entwined with Jennifer's, Samantha's with Carew's. As they should be. He would be the outsider, the one who did not quite belong despite the warm hospitality with which he would have been treated. He would have been lonely.

And he would have remembered Cora. He would have

missed her. Dreadfully. He would have gone after her. He was sure suddenly that he would have gone after her.

Why? Just because he would have been lonely? Just because she made him laugh?

"Yes," he said, "I am fond of her, Samantha."

"I am so relieved," she said. "I really feared that—that I had hurt you. I would have hated that more than anything in the world."

"I told you at the time," he said, covering her hand with his own for a moment, "that I had been teasing, Samantha, that I had been trying to punish you for deserting your court by so suddenly announcing your betrothal to a man we did not even realize you knew."

He had told her in a rash moment that he loved her and had then had to spend days retracting his words, convincing her that he had not spoken the truth.

Had he spoken the truth? Had he loved her? Did he love her? She was a beautiful woman who had been his friend for years. She was married to a man she loved. There was no place for him in her life. He was married to a woman of whom he was exceedingly fond, a woman he might well have married, he realized now, even if circumstances had not forced him into doing so. There was no room for Samantha in his life. Marriage, he realized now, was a very private business. A universe of two that would expand only with the birth of children.

Yes, perhaps he had spoken the truth. Certainly there had been enough pain. But that was the past. This was the present. His future was walking on the arm of Carew.

"Well, I am very glad, Francis," Samantha said, sounding as enormously relieved as he was feeling. "Now we can resume a friendship that I feared might be broken."

They were all inside the boat house looking at the boats. All except the children, who had grown tired of standing still, especially when Gabriel had told them that it was a little too windy today to take the boats out. They had gone outside to play. Cora wandered out too after a while. She had done nothing but chatter and laugh ever since they had begun this walk. She was tired of chattering and laughing.

Her heart was bleeding. She examined the words in her mind for theatricality. But she could not persuade herself that she was exaggerating her pain and her misery. Her heart *was* bleeding.

There had been that familiarity again when the Marquess of Carew's name had been spoken. But she knew as soon as she saw him that she had never met him before. Even if she had forgotten his face, she would not have forgotten his severe limp and his twisted right hand, which he tended to hold against his hip. And then the marchioness's name had been mentioned—Samantha. Jennifer had only ever referred to her as Sam. Samantha—the name had sounded so familiar, but Cora did not know this lady and she could not think of anyone else she knew with that name. They had been married quite recently, just a few months ago.

And then suddenly, out of nowhere, it seemed, as she had walked from the terrace on the arm of Lord Carew, it had hit her like a hammer over the head. She could almost hear Pamela Fletcher's voice. *Lord Francis was a part of Samantha Newman's court for years, you know . . . He was devoted to her . . . It was rumored that he was heartbroken when she married the Marquess of Carew earlier this Season . . . He is a cripple.*

Samantha, Lady Carew, was exquisitely beautiful. She was everything Cora would most like to be. She was small, dainty, blond, pretty. And she had walked to the lake on Francis's arm and had glowed at him while he had kept his head bent toward hers and the whole of his attention fixed on her. They had looked quite gorgeous together.

He was devoted to her . . . he was heartbroken.

Cora had walked all the way to the lake with Lord Carew, who was a kind and an unassuming gentleman, making gay conversation, laughing, having a merry time, and every step of the way she had been aware of Francis walking with the woman he loved. And yet he was stuck with her, Cora, for the rest of his life.

She walked along the bank beside the lake, not seeing anything, feeling about as miserable as it was possible to feel. How he must *hate* being married to her when he loved Samantha, who was the embodiment of female perfection. How could she have done this to him? How could she have allowed herself to be drawn into accepting his very gallant proposal? It was to Samantha, or someone beautiful like Samantha, that he should be married.

She wanted her papa. She wanted Edgar. But even the realization of how self-pitying and how childish she was being did not help.

"Papa," she whispered.

"Papa!" a voice shrieked and Michael hurtled headfirst into her.

"What is it?" She caught at his arms and looked down into a frightened little face.

"Mary," he said, gasping. "She is stuck up that tree." He made a sweeping gesture behind him with one arm. "She will not come down. She is going to fall. And I am for it. I called her a scaredy and she went up. Now Papa will spank me." He began to wail.

A child stuck up a tree. Cora winced for a moment, but this was no ruse. There were no thugs with stinking breath attached to this plea for help.

"Come along," she said, taking the little boy's hand. "We will rescue Mary together. I am a famous tree climber. I have a brother too, you know, and had to keep pace with him while we were growing up. Your papa will not even need to know. It will be our secret."

She marched along the bank, forgetting all about self-pity and misery. There was a child in difficulties, even perhaps in danger. An infant who was sitting on a branch of an old oak tree, clinging to it with both hands while her feet dangled over the water of the lake. An infant who was too terrified even to cry.

"Hold tight, Mary," Cora called cheerfully, pulling off her hat and tossing it to the grass, and hitching her dress above her ankles with one hand. "I am coming for you. You are going to be quite safe."

"Aunt Cora, do be careful," Michael said as she set off on her ascent.

Chapter 17

〜

H
e had noticed her leaving the boathouse but had not immediately followed her. Perhaps after all she was overwhelmed with the company, he thought, and would welcome a few minutes to herself. But after a while he left quietly and looked in both directions for her. The others followed him outside.

There was no sign of her. Only of young Michael, who was standing beneath a distant tree, hopping from one foot to the other, or so it seemed, until he spotted them. Then he raced toward them, waving his arms wildly.

"No. Go back," he could be heard to be yelling when he got a little closer. "Go back inside."

"Mischief," the Earl of Thornhill murmured in Lord Francis's ear. "They are up to something and do not want us to know. It doubtless involves getting their good clothes either wet or dirty or torn or all three." He raised his voice. "What is it, Michael?"

"Where is Mary?" the countess was asking.

Where was Cora?

Michael burst into tears. "It was all my fault, Papa," he said. "I am owning up, as you said I should always do."

"Where is Mary?" The countess asked a little more sharply.

"I called her a scaredy," Michael said with fresh wails. "And she went up the tree. She cannot get down. She is going to fall".

"The devil!" the earl muttered, striding toward the tree his son had indicated. "*What* have I told you about leading Mary into danger? She is little more than a baby."

Michael trotted along at his side. "But she will be quite all right, Papa," he said. "Aunt Cora has gone up to rescue her."

Lord Francis had not needed to hear it. When his eyes had gone to the tree Michael had pointed to, he had seen something alien among its branches. Something yellow with a blue sash. Something with very visibly bare ankles.

Of course Aunt Cora had gone to the rescue.

He would have grinned if he had not also been able to see Mary, a tiny infant perched out on a tree branch that overhung the lake. Jennifer, both hands over her mouth, had seen the child too and was making noises of acute distress. Samantha was setting an arm about her shoulders and making soothing noises.

Lord Francis and the Marquess of Carew hurried after the earl to the base of the tree.

"Stay very still, Mary," the earl said in a voice of dreadful calm, "and do not look down. Aunt Cora and Papa will get you down in no time at all."

It was plain to see that Gabe had not lost any boyhood skill at climbing trees, Lord Francis thought. Cora was already at the inside end of the branch on which Mary sat. She was chatting to the child as if they were both sitting on the nursery floor whiling away an idle hour. She was also showing a delicious expanse of leg—or not so delicious, perhaps, when he remembered that she was showing it to two other men as well as to him.

"Let me, Cora," the earl said when he had climbed up close to her. "You go on down. Be careful. Frank is down there to catch you."

But she was already seating herself on the branch and sliding very carefully along it toward Mary. It creaked and Jennifer, somewhere behind Lord Francis, stifled a moan with both hands.

"You would not be able to reach her from the trunk," Cora said, sounding very calm, "and this branch is not particularly strong. It will bear my weight, I believe, but not yours. I will hand her back to you."

The branch groaned again. So did Jennifer. Samantha gasped.

"You are over water," Lord Carew called up, all calm practicality. "It will be a soft landing at least if the branch does not hold. Can you swim, Lady Francis?"

"Of course she can swim," Lord Francis said. "She saved a child's life in the river in Bath earlier this year." He raised his voice. "Be careful, dear."

She was sitting beside Mary, smiling at her. Her dress was up almost to her knees. Gabe was leaning out from the trunk, stretching out a hand, which was at the end of an arm approximately three feet too short to pluck his daughter off her perch.

She really was a cool one, Lord Francis thought, staring appreciatively, wishing that Carew would have the decency to lower his eyes.

"Mary," she was saying conversationally, though her words carried quite distinctly to the ground, "I am going to pick you up. I want you to pretend that I am Mama or Nurse lifting you from your cot. You must not fight me. I am going to hand you to Papa, and Papa is going to carry you down to Mama. All right?"

Mary did not reply. But she played her part to perfection. Perhaps she was too petrified by terror even to fight when she was lifted away from the illusory safety of the branch, Lord Francis thought. Cora lifted her slowly across her own body and set her down again on the branch, where Gabe could reach her. He scooped her up with one hand and swung her in to safety, between his body and the trunk of the tree.

"There," Cora said briskly, smiling brightly. "That was not so difficult, was it? There really was no danger at all."

The tree branch disagreed. It creaked and groaned. And then with a crack that would have put a pistol shot to shame, it snapped free of the trunk and plunged into the water below, taking its shrieking occupant with it.

Jennifer was at the foot of the tree, arms reaching upward. But she turned her head and screamed. So did Samantha. Carew yelled. So did Gabe, who came down the tree with Mary with reckless speed. Michael whooped. Mary was crying loudly.

Lord Francis, having assured himself that the branch had not hit his wife on the way down, knelt on the bank and reached out an arm toward her. He was grinning. If everyone else only knew her better, they would all be doing likewise. Only Cora, he thought.

"Come on, Cora," he said, when she came up gasping and sputtering. "Grasp my hand."

Her scream was cut short by a watery glug. But her head shot up again almost immediately to reveal to him two panic-stricken eyes.

"I-CAN-NOT-SW—"

She was under again, but Lord Francis had not waited to hear even the half-completed final word. He had dived in to the accompaniment of more screams and bellows from the bank.

She fought him like a wild thing. He had to confine her arms with one of his own, turn her over onto her back, and clamp his free arm beneath her chin before he could swim the six feet to the reaching hands that extended from the bank. But he ignored them and hauled her out himself.

She acted as if she had swallowed half the lake. She knelt on all fours, coughing and heaving and wheezing, gripping the grass with clawed fingers. Her ruined dress clung to her like a second skin. Her hair, still partly caught up in its pins, hung about her face in an enviable imitation of rats' tails.

Lord Francis knelt beside her, leaning over her, thumping her on the back. "Don't fight it, Cora," he said. "The breath will come. Try to relax."

Finally she was only gasping. "Oh," she said, staring down at the grass, "I want to die."

"I think you have cheated death for this afternoon at least, dear," he said. He caught sight of the sleeve of his lemon coat and grimaced inwardly. He was beginning to feel the reality of the breeze that had kept Gabe from taking out the boats.

"I want to die," she repeated.

"Towels," Jennifer said. "There are towels and blankets in the boathouse."

"I will fetch them, Jenny," Samantha said and went racing off along the bank. Carew went after her.

Lord Francis patted his wife's back as reassuringly as he could. He had understood her wish to slip quietly out of this world. She did not want to straighten up and have to look anyone in the eye.

"Here, Cora." The earl knelt down at the other side of her and set his coat over her back and about her shoulders. "Sam and Hartley will have towels and blankets here in a few moments. My dear, how very brave you were. You must have known that branch would go as soon as you made the exertion of lifting Mary. I do not know how we will ever be able to thank you."

Mary was crying quietly in her mother's arms. Jennifer's voice was tearful too when she spoke. "To me you will always be the heroine who saved Mary's life, Cora," she said. "You risked your own doing it and very nearly lost it. How very wonderful you are. How very fortunate Francis was to find you."

"It was all my fault." Michael began to wail. "I nearly killed Mary and Aunt Cora. It will be quite all right if you spank me, Papa."

"That is extraordinarily magnanimous of you, son," his father said dryly. "My guess is that your punishment has been ghastly enough. But on the way back to the house you and I will have a little chat about the care we owe the ladies who have been placed under our protection. And although gentlemen are allowed to cry when there is good reason, as Mama and I have told you before, they are not well advised to wail in prolonged self-pity."

Michael was quiet again.

Samantha and Carew were back with an armful each of towels and blankets. Enough to dry and warm a whole pack of drowned rats.

"Wrap yourselves up, both of you," Carew said, "and

hurry back to the house. Samantha and I will go ahead as fast as we can, if we may, Jennifer, to order water to be heated. At least it is a warm day, though I do not imagine either of you can feel the truth of that at the moment."

But Cora was still on her hands and knees, observing the grass a few inches from her face. "I want to die," she muttered.

"I think it would be best if you all left us here," Lord Francis said, taking one of the blankets and draping it over his wife after first removing the earl's coat. "We can get out of our wet clothes. And Cora needs a little time to recover."

He could see at a glance about the group that they all understood. Cora was huddled under her blanket like a lopsided tent, her bottom elevated higher than her head.

"Come when you are ready, then," the earl said. "We will have hot drinks ready for both of you and enough water for two baths. Take my hand, Michael. We will stride on ahead. Is Mary too heavy for you, Jennifer?"

"I will help with her," Samantha said. But before she left with Jennifer and the child, she knelt down and set her hand lightly on Cora's head. "You were wonderfully brave, Lady Francis," she said. "How I admire your fearlessness."

"Bravo!" the marquess added quietly. "It is one thing to look up at a height and think it is nothing at all. It is another to be up there looking down and knowing that there is a very real danger of falling. My congratulations on your courage, ma'am."

"Oh, Francis," Samantha said, "your poor coat. And it was so splendid."

And finally they were gone.

She could hear that they were gone. She knew that he had not. She wished he had. She wanted to be alone. She wanted to be a million miles away. Preferably dead.

"Get out of your wet things, Cora," he said. His teeth were chattering. His voice came from somewhere above her and then she felt a dull thump close beside her. He had thrown down his coat. His poor ruined coat. It was the second coat of his she had caused to be ruined. Something else fell on top of it. He was undressing.

"There is no one here," he said, "and no one will come back here. You will feel better when you have taken off your wet things and dried yourself and wrapped yourself in a blanket. I will spread our clothes out in the sun. They will dry in no time at all."

What he said made sense. But there *was* someone there. He was there. She did not want him to see her. She was so very *ugly*. She wriggled out of her dress under the protective covering of the blanket and then, after a little hesitation, out of her chemise. She hauled off her silk stockings. One shoe had still been attached to her foot. The other was not. It was probably resting on the bottom of the lake. She teased the pins out of her hair and pulled at the matted mess. It was hopeless.

"Here," he said, "Take a towel."

"The blanket has dried me," she said. "Francis, I have never been so mortified in my life."

He was silent for all of two minutes. She suspected he had walked a little distance away to spread their wet clothes on the grass. Then he was sitting beside her, wrapped in another blanket she saw a few moments later. He somehow knocked her off balance and then caught hold of her and turned her so that she was sitting beside him. It was very deftly done. She clutched the blanket closer and tried to hide her head beneath it—without much success.

"There really is no need to feel embarrassment, dear," he said, freeing one bare arm and setting it about her shoulders. "What you did really was very brave. I do not know how Gabe would have got Mary down without you."

"Probably with great speed and dignity," she said.

"No." His fingers were combing through her hair, easing their way patiently through the matted knots. But his hand stilled suddenly and he fell silent. Cora could see it coming as if it were a mile away and galloping inexorably toward her. She hunched her shoulders and braced herself. "Cora, you *cannot swim?*"

"I never could learn the trick," she said. "Edgar tried to

convince me that water is heavier than I am, but I have never been able to believe it. I expect to sink like a stone when I lift my feet from the bottom, and I always do."

"Then how in thunder," he asked, "did you save Bridge's young nephew?"

It was too embarrassing for words. She had tried to *tell* everyone at the time, but no one had been willing to listen.

"I jumped in without thinking," she said. "And I caught hold of him and tried to save him. But I was only dragging him under with me. Fortunately we were right beside the bank and Edgar reached out and grabbed us both. He told me afterward that it was obvious little Henry *could* swim and that he was in the process of doing so when I dived in. Left to myself, I would have *drowned* him. Edgar said I was brainless—he is forever saying that—and I was. And so I became a great heroine while Edgar was censured for cowardice because he did not jump in. He said it was unnecessary because little Henry was so *close*."

It was a lengthy, horrible tale. And now Francis too would know just how great a fraud she was.

He threw back his head and shouted with laughter while her stomach contracted with humiliation.

"Cora," he said when he had finally brought his glee under control, "you are priceless. Only you! You truly are the delight of my life."

She finally succeeded in burrowing her head beneath the blanket. She set her forehead on her knees and clasped her arms tightly about them.

"I want to go home," she said.

His hand stilled again on the back of her neck. "No, dear," he said. "There is no need. Truly there is not. What was embarrassing to you was proof of your great courage to everyone who watched. They will be waiting for you at the house, Cora, to thank you again. Believe me, they were all overcome with admiration and gratitude for what you did."

The thought of going back to Chalcote was frankly terrifying. But she had not meant that. "I want to go *home*," she said.

His voice sounded sad. "We will go then, dear," he said.

"Tomorrow morning. I have been missing Sidley too. We will go home and spend what remains of the summer there."

"To Bristol, not to Sidley," she said. "I want to go home to Papa, Francis. Where I belong. You must stay here with your friends. You will be happier when I am gone. We will both be happier."

She was on her back on the grass then, the blanket stripped right away from her face. And he was looming over her, a frown on his face while his eyes searched hers.

"Cora," he said, "what is this? I have hurt you? But I did not laugh in derision. I laughed because I was amused by your peculiar form of intrepidity. You act first and think later when you perceive that someone is in danger, do you not? It is a delightful aspect of your character. But I ought not to have laughed. I am so sorry, dear. You needed comfort and I laughed at you. Please forgive me."

His face blurred before her vision. "I am so *ugly*," she said. Ugly inside and out. She was so abject and cringing and self-pitying. She had never been like this before *not* rescuing little Henry and before being taken off to London to meet the *ton*. Before meeting Francis and being *stupid* enough to fall in love with him. She had had some dignity once upon a time.

"Ugly." He repeated the word without expression. "Ugly, Cora? You?"

"I am as tall as a man," she said. "I have large feet and hands. And I am—I am a *lump*. I have a coarse face and a bramble bush for hair. I am *ugly* and you must *hate* me." There. How was that for groveling, sniveling self-flagellation? And she hated herself too at that moment. And hated herself for hating herself.

"Cora." There was amazement in his eyes. She blinked her own and saw it there. "I can remember your concern about the size of your feet though they have never looked noticeably large to me. I had no idea that you perceived yourself as ugly. I am amazed. Almost speechless again. How can you not have realized how very beautiful you are?"

"Ha!" She would have been proud of the world of scorn she threw into the single syllable if she had not been feeling quite so wretched.

"Cora." He wrestled with her for a moment, but he won—of course. Her blanket parted down the middle and she lay fully exposed to his view in bright, sunny daylight. And view her he did, moving his gaze slowly down the full length of her body to her toes. "You are quite out of the common way, dear. I think I would have to agree that your face is not pretty in any accepted way. It has far too much character for bland prettiness. Your hair is—glorious. I have been selfishly glad since our marriage that only I am permitted to see it at its most glorious, when it is down. Your body—well, perhaps I had better bring up the memory of my humiliation on our wedding night. I—ended it all far too fast because I had lost control. Because of your— beauty, Cora. You are truly—magnificent. You see how tongue-tied you always succeed in making me?"

Francis. Always so very gallant. She reached up an arm to touch his face but let it drop to the grass again.

"I wish I could be beautiful for you," she whispered, "as she is beautiful."

"She?" His eyes snapped to hers.

"She is so small and dainty and pretty and blond-haired," she said. "And so sweet too. I wish I could be those things for you, Francis. Or better still, I wish I had said no when you asked me. I meant to say no, but when I opened my mouth to say it, yes came out instead. She is as lovely as I have always longed to be."

"My God." He lowered his head to rest his forehead beneath her chin. "You are talking about Samantha. You know! Ah, Cora, I had no idea you knew."

She threaded her fingers through his hair. "It is all right," she said. "You said yourself I was not the woman of your choice. But you have always been good to me, Francis. I think I would like to go home, though. Home to Papa."

"Ah, Cora," he said, lifting his head and looking down into her eyes. "I would not have had you know for worlds, dear. If there were someone with whom you had been infat-

uated not long before our marriage—and indeed, perhaps
there is—I would not want to know. I would feel inferior,
insecure. I would know that you did not marry me for love
and I would imagine that you did love him—that you still
do. I wish you did not know about Samantha."

She smoothed her hands through his hair.

"I must admit," he said, "that despite the great contentment I have found with you in the month of our marriage, I
was a little apprehensive about seeing her again. I need not
have been. I walked to the lake with her earlier and all I
could see was you—your tall elegance as Samantha described it *with envy in her voice*. All I could think about
was you and how I wished we were at home alone together
in our own haven of domesticity. All I could think about
was being with you and talking with you and laughing with
you and loving you. Perhaps for me it is as well I came
here. I have discovered just how deep my feelings are for
you. But it has been a less pleasant experience for you.
Don't leave me. Please don't leave me. Give me a chance
to make you as happy as you can possibly be with me. To
make you love me as I have come to love you."

"Francis." She smoothed her fingers over his temples and
through his hair. "I really am brainless. I fell in love with
you even when I still thought—oh, *you know*." She could
feel herself flushing.

He smiled slowly at her.

"Besides," she said with a sigh, "I could not really go
back to Papa to stay, Francis. At least I do not think so. I
knew it all along but ignored it. I have to stay with you. I
think we are going to have a child. Nothing has happened
since our marriage and something should have happened
more than a week ago."

He lowered his head again to rest between her breasts.
He said nothing. But she could hear him drawing in slow,
deep breaths.

"Francis," she said wistfully after a while, looking up at
tree branches and fluffy little clouds and blue sky, "do you
really not mind that I am so large? Do you really think me a
little bit beautiful?"

He groaned.

"My breas— My bosom is not too large, Francis?" she asked him anxiously. "My hips are not too wide?"

He was grinning when he lifted his head. He was also flushed and there was a certain look in his eyes. "Shall I prove to you just how very beautiful and attractive you are to me, dear?" he asked.

"Here?" Her voice had gone up a few tones in pitch. "Now? But would it not be dreadfully improper, Francis?"

"Dreadfully, dreadfully so," he said. But one of his thumbs was already feathering over one of her nipples.

"Francis," she said, "you *never* behave improperly."

"Shall I stop, then?" he asked into her mouth without removing his own first.

"No," she said hastily. "No, I will never tell anyone. I promise. Oh, what are you doing now?"

But what he was doing was so very pleasurable that she gave no more thought to daylight or sunshine or impropriety. At least not for a long, long time.

They were lying side by side and hand in hand on the grass, gazing up at the sky. He thought he had probably been sleeping for a few minutes. He had never before made love in the outdoors. It was an experience well worth repeating and one he certainly would repeat since he appeared to have a very willing partner in impropriety. He squeezed her hand.

"They will be wondering back at the house where on earth we are," he said. "Perhaps we should begin to think of going back."

"I shall die," she said, but she sounded reasonably cheerful at the prospect of her own demise.

He could not resist. "They probably all know very well what we have been up to," he said. "They will greet us with rosy faces and shifty eyes." He had no doubt that it was the truth too.

"I shall die!" she said with considerably more conviction.

"And they will all be purple with envy," he said. "Doubtless none of them have ever had the courage to do what we have just done."

"Someone might have *come*, Francis," she said. "I would have died."

"Actually," he said, "while you were panting and mindless with passion, a dozen or so gardeners did emerge from the trees. They did not stay long, though. They were very discreet."

She shrieked and he threw his free hand over his eyes while he laughed.

"You are horrid," she said, having realized too late that he teased. "Francis, I am just *cringing* when I remember. I cannot stop remembering."

"Now to which of your most embarrassing moments are you referring, dear?" he asked.

"I sat on that branch," she said, "after handing Mary to Gabriel. I was a quivering jelly of terror because I have always been afraid of heights. Do not laugh, Francis. That is most unkind. But I could not merely *say* so, could I? I could not warn you to be on the alert because I could not swim. Oh no. I could not even just keep my mouth shut. I had to call out gaily and with *stupid* bravado. What did I say?"

" 'There. That was not so difficult, was it?' " Lord Francis said. " 'There really was no danger at all.' "

"Word perfect," she said with a groan. "But my question was rhetorical. *Don't laugh.*"

Lord Francis laughed.

"And the branch chose that very moment to break off," she said. "It would have been perfect if I had been acting out a farce. I must have looked so *inelegant*, Francis. All arms and legs and shrieking panic."

He laughed. "I can assure you," he said, "that we were not all lined up on the bank assessing the elegance of your fall, Cora." He could not stop laughing.

"It will head the list of topics for my nightmares for the next ten years," she said. She giggled.

"Oh, I hope not," he said. "No, no, dear, I have every confidence in you. You will find something else to replace that particular embarrassing memory before another month has passed."

She was laughing at the sky with open and loud merriment.

"How horrid you are," she said. "Do you mean what I think you mean, Francis?"

"I most certainly do." He paused for a hearty laugh. "You will continue to be the delight of my life, Cora, for the rest of my days. I feel it in my bones."

They both roared with hilarity.

"And I shall continue to ruin your most splendid coats for the rest of mine," she said. "I feel it in my bones."

They rolled onto their sides to face each other and clutched each other as they bellowed with mirth.

"P-p-prinny—" he managed to get out. But more words were impossible.

If they had been standing they would have had to hold each other up. Fortunately for both, they were not standing.